Prais
The Guest B

The Man in Cabin Number Five

"Masterfully written. An entertaining work that will keep the reader hooked until the end. Congratulations on an exceptional book." *Readers' Favorite*

"An engaging drama with a strong cast and a final surprise." *Kirkus Review*

The Girls in Cabin Number Three

"This book takes up where *The Man in Cabin Number Five* left off, with plenty of intrigue in the idyllic mountain locale." *Susan Denley, former Associate Features Editor, Los Angeles Times*

"With themes of love, family, friendship, new beginnings, and the complexity of life, readers will get hooked from the very beginning." *San Francisco Book Review*

The Starlet in Cabin Number Seven

"Braun continues to engage her readers with *The Starlet in Cabin Number Seven*. With memorable characters who have their own stories to tell, she successfully brings them all together." *Susan Denley, Former Associate Features Editor, Los Angeles Times*

"Chrysteen Braun does it again with *The Starlet in Cabin Number Seven*. We meet her childhood friend Sarah, and a new design client whose mother was the starlet who stayed in the cabins during the filming of her first picture. Braun's unique storytelling style successfully blends her character's personalities and their stories." *Kate Osborn, formerly with the Mountain News, Lake Arrowhead*

Books by Chrysteen Braun

The Guest Book Trilogy

The Man in Cabin Number Five
The Girls in Cabin Number Three
The Starlet in Cabin Number Seven

Coming Soon:

The Maidservant in Cabin Number One: A Prequel
Dear Noah: A Guest Book Novella
Family Portrait
The Storyteller
Table for Eight

THE GUEST BOOK TRILOGY  BOOK THREE

THE STARLET IN CABIN NUMBER SEVEN

A NOVEL

CHRYSTEEN BRAUN

Design and distribution by Bublish

ISBN: 978-1-647047-20-7 (paperback)
ISBN: 978-1-647047-21-4 (hardcover)
ISBN: 978-1-647047-19-1 (eBook)

chrysteenbraun.com

CELESTE

1980

I knew there was a purpose for standing here in my closet, but I had a splitting headache, and the reason was escaping me. When I saw the tall jewelry box, I went to it and stood there for a few moments, and then I remembered. From the top drawer, I took out my wedding rings; the first was from Joseph, and the second from Andrew. I hadn't worn either in years. I skipped the second drawer, which was filled with the costume jewelry I'd worn over the years of my career, although now I couldn't recall which pieces I'd worn in which movie. But it didn't really matter. It was the third drawer I was most interested in, and I found what I wanted. Under one of my mother's embroidered handkerchiefs, I found the gold necklace with the locket and the diamond watch my grandmother left me when she died.

I wrapped them in the handkerchief and put them in my purse. I carried my suitcase downstairs to the entry, and set it next to the small painting I'd chosen to take with me. I'd forgotten I needed to wrap it and pack it safely in between my clothing. I would do it after I called my travel agent to book my flight.

PROLOGUE
Annie
Today

I've fallen again; this time I was coming down our stairs. I've cracked three ribs and there's never anything they can do for you when that happens other than give you a brace and wait for the ribs to heal. I'm wearing it now and it's hard for me to breathe.

I'm staying in our downstairs guest bedroom and I'm actually sleeping better down there. I'm not awakened by my husband's breathing machine when the mask moves away from his nose, making the hissing air that wakes me. It's usually in the middle of the night and then I can't get back to sleep.

I must sound like the crotchety old woman I've become.

I'm growing tired, and I've thought about not finishing my third book, but I actually feel comfortable sitting at my desk when I wear my brace. I haven't told my husband, but I'm beginning to forget where I've left off, and I often have to reread what I wrote the day before. I've started keeping detailed notes so I can easily go back to edit.

My sweet neighbor just brought over a vase of flowers she'd cut from her beautiful garden, and I've set them on my desk where I can enjoy them.

A friend once told me I'd live to be eighty-six and I'm now eighty-two. If I fall again, it might be a hip that gets broken...or worse. I could hit my head and die from internal bleeding like my father did so many years ago.

This afternoon I had a phone call from my stepson, sweet William. He wanted to let me know he'd become a great grandfather. How on earth did that happen, I wondered? But then I count back the years, and if I'm eighty-two, that makes him seventy-two. Yes, that's hard to believe, but he was only ten years younger than me when I married his father, David.

"They've named him after Dad," he said, somewhat cautiously.

"Oh," I said.

"It was on his birthday."

"What was?"

"When David was born. Yesterday."

"Oh," I said again. I'd long ago forgotten dates that were at one time so important to me—especially those from so many years back.

"And his middle name is Andrew. I thought of it; after you, after Annie."

"Oh!"

"I hope you don't mind."

"Oh, of course not. I'm actually quite thrilled. Although I've never been called Andrew," I said, chuckling.

I told him about my fall and about the lovely flowers on my desk. He asked how I was doing otherwise, and when I thought about it, all the complaining I'd recently done was mostly because I didn't have anything else to do.

"Let's see," I said. "If your father was alive, he'd be..." I had to take a moment to calculate it. "Ninety six. Or ninety seven. Now *that's* old."

"I told you that before he died, actually many years before that, he wished he would have done things differently."

"I know, dear, we all would have. But it is what it is. Isn't it? And it was so many years ago..."

It is what it is. I hated that saying, but sometimes it just fit.

When we hung up, I told my husband that William called and that I should now be referred to as *Andrew*.

Not surprisingly, that night, I dreamed about David. Dreams are always so funny; sometimes they can make no sense at all, but they seem so real. This one was sharp as ever.

David actually came to me and wanted me back. We'd been divorced for almost forty years. I was seventy, and he was eighty-five. He didn't look it; he was still fit and distinguished looking. Except for his mustache, he'd never grayed.

He never apologized for seeing someone else while we were married, but he assumed enough time had passed that it really didn't make any difference now. I hated to admit that I was still fond of him; that I'd always saved a place for him in my heart. And in the dream, I remembered he'd come back to me on more than one occasion, and for some reason, I always let him come back home.

"You'll have to stay at home this time," I said, and he looked at me quizzically. "Oh, you can work in the garage, but you can't stay away whenever you feel like it."

I drew my eyebrows together in thought, and then said, "And we'll have to figure out our finances." I didn't feel it was fair that what was mine would now be his. And then I thought about sex; he wasn't the most romantic lover so many years ago, and I wondered if he still had it in him to even *have* sex.

"I'll try to lose a few pounds," I said.

I remembered he never liked it when I gained weight, and I was still plump.

Then it woke me. I never knew my decision, whether or not I took him back. And even though I knew it was just a dream, it stayed with me all that next day, like some dreams do.

I tried to recall if I'd had that dream before.

Even as I sat down to write, my attention drifted as little thoughts niggled into my consciousness. I tried to remember how hurt I'd felt so many years ago, but so much time had passed it was difficult to remember the details. When we divorced, I'd discovered my notion of being married forever was just an illusion. And I think that's what devastated me the most...the romantic fool that I was.

I thought back to when we split up; moving through the silence of our house as we made our lists of what we each wanted to keep. I refused to break down; I could have, I was so angry...but I was also sad that a portion of my life was coming to an end.

I must have dozed in my desk chair, which was not an easy feat, for I was suddenly aware of my surroundings.

Now, where was I?

Oh, yes.

I was in love. My life centered ground Noah and my business, and any notable changes come from both my newest client and someone from my past.

Where We Left Off...

CHAPTER ONE

1981

It was my second year up in the mountains, and I couldn't believe how quickly it'd become the end of February. I was hoping the new year and the rest of winter would bring us only a pocket full of challenges since the previous year had presented us with many. Just to tease me, a gust of ice cold wind blew my sweater open, and I pulled it tight around me. We'd just come off an unusually heavy snowfall, and all the roads were piled high with berms that would keep some people locked down until they could get a snowplow to dig them out.

This latest storm downed power lines in various communities, which left those of us without generators, with no power.

"I don't remember *this* from last year," I said to Sam.

I'd bought the cabins from him last year, and I was still learning about the B&B and mountain life. He'd lit the fireplace to warm up the office, and I set out food bowls for our camp cats, Jezebel and Socks, who gladly made their way inside.

"Well, it probably happened, but it didn't last long. It happens regularly," he said. "Sometimes we're down for twenty minutes, and sometimes a day. The good news is you can always store your refrigerated foods outdoors when it's so cold."

If we could make it through the rest of this winter without too many repairs, the next thing on my list was to get some pricing to install a generator large enough to run all the cabins if need be.

Thankfully, we were between guests, so it spared us having to creatively heat and light the cabins. That night, Noah and I bundled up and sat on the sofa in front of his fireplace; the glow of the fire lit his whiskered face and when I reached out to touch him, he took my hand and kissed my palm.

"If you're thinking what I think you're thinking, we're going to need a heavy blanket," I said, my body already aching for his.

"I already have one," Noah said, reaching for his thick plaid comforter. "A boy scout is always prepared."

We were still at that stage in our relationship where making love in awkward places just added to the intrigue. It seemed no matter when we made love, Noah's eagerness always created a longing within me, and my heart skipped a beat whenever he sometimes looked at me.

Afterward, we slept cuddled on the sofa, surrounded by the dogs, and I stirred when he got up to add more logs to the fire early that next morning.

Ginny stayed with Sam and the cats so he could remain on the property in case of an emergency.

The next morning, the sun was out, and it looked like it was the end of the storm. No matter what the weather was going to be, I knew it was going to be a great day. As I looked out to the tree just outside the French doors, I saw a squirrel sitting on one of the large, low branches. His coat was covered in snowflakes, his eyes were closed, and he was concentrating on eating whatever morsel his little paws held. I'd never seen anything so adorable, and the sight of him made my heart swell.

I quickly turned to call to Noah so he could witness this sight, and unfortunately, he wasn't as quiet as he could have been. I turned as the squirrel heard us break the silence, and he scampered off before Noah could see him.

"Darn it," I said.

"Sorry," Noah grimaced.

"Will you take the day off?" I asked.

"I only have a few things to do today, so if you want to grab lunch, we can do that. We can take two cars."

I loved driving the snowy mountain roads once they were cleared, marveling at the snow-covered trees and ground, and one of my favorite roads was the one going into Blue Jay where Ginny's Café was. It was a two-lane highway, most of it under trees that formed a canopy, arching so you felt like you were driving through a tall tunnel. Every now and then, a clump of snow would fall from a low-lying branch, hitting either the windshield or the roof of the car, and it would startle me. There were a couple of icy spots on the road, so even the most seasoned mountain drivers kept to the speed limit.

Older cabins lined the road, some with parked cars covered so deeply in snow, it would take forever to melt and clear. I noticed one couple standing with arms on their hips, no doubt wondering where to start the enormous task ahead of them, and I didn't envy them.

I'd called Sam and offered to bring him something to eat and just when our power was restored, he told me a large tree had fallen across the highway in front of the cabins, creating the worst jam-up he'd ever witnessed.

"It'll take a day before the highway maintenance men finish cutting the tree up and hauling it away," he said.

In the meantime, before they could get down the highway enough to redirect traffic, cars were pulling into our parking area to turn around. Sam and I alternated guiding people in and out, keeping them from damaging our trees by accidentally bumping into them. I wouldn't know until the snow melted just how badly our landscaping had fared, but I envisioned the worst.

"The only good news," Noah said once he could finally get through, "is that we now have power."

I'd bought the cabins from Sam Jackson, who'd been up here for years, and he'd stayed on and helped me run them. He'd lost his wife some time back, and we were kind of good for each other, as he'd told me; I

3

came into *his* life helping fill a void and he came into mine when I was starting my divorce.

I'd just discovered my husband had been seeing someone else, and had come up to the mountains for a change of scenery. Even though I eventually reconciled to the humiliation of it all, I found I still struggled with constant mental conversations in my head and inner conflict in my heart. I alternately blamed him and then me for the failure of our marriage. I'd hoped the emotional roller coaster would come to an end, if not slow down, and eventually it had. And having the opportunity to buy the cabins had given me the determination I needed to start over.

I now went into the office to warm up by the fire, and Jezebel and Socks greeted me, letting me know in no uncertain terms they missed me and were unhappy with all the noise. Jezebel circled my legs as I turned, and I accidentally kicked Socks.

"Sorry, girl," I said.

I missed them terribly too, but I knew if I took them to Noah's, they'd have to get used to the dogs and the new surroundings, and Sam would be without his two furry friends. Cats were so different from dogs; you could take a dog with you anywhere and they'd quickly feel at home. Cats, on the other hand, got stressed just looking at their carriers, and spent hours slinking around their new surroundings before they could relax.

I decided to make my time in the lobby worthwhile, so I dusted the counter, furniture and tables, and then rearranged the magazines and local maps. I took the last of our cabin brochures out of their box and set those out, too. If I needed them for gift basket donations, I'd know where they were, and I took a quick minute to see if there was anything I needed to update before I had more printed.

My dear friend Sarah had designed them for me, and I wondered how she was doing. If it was cold and snowy here, it had to be cold in Las Vegas. Was it my turn to call her? As I read through the brochure, I didn't see any changes, so I called our local printer and ordered another box along with more business cards.

4

Sarah must have sensed I'd been thinking about her, for the next day she called. We'd been very close throughout school, and she'd moved away the day we graduated. While we spoke regularly, I hadn't seen her in over three years. She'd become a graphic designer and had helped me with my marketing materials for the cabins.

"I'm going to stop and see my mom," she said. "I'd love to come up and see you and these cabins, and I need to rethink my life."

"It's a great place to do it," I said. "Just let me know when. If it's soon, dress warmly. We still have snow."

Something was going on, and I figured I'd find out, eventually.

"I was hoping it could be next week?" she said.

CHAPTER TWO

Sarah
1981

I looked up my mother's address in my map book and then found a place to stop for lunch at a small coffee shop on main street. It turned out to be on the original Route 66, and not too far from her place. She'd been living in Barstow for several years now, and even though it was only about two hours out of Las Vegas, it was the first time I'd driven out to see her.

When I pulled onto a badly paved road, misgivings about seeing her only got worse and then I ended up on a dirt road that stopped right in front of her house trailer. I waited a few seconds to let the dust settle around me before I got out of the car.

The moment she came to the door, I knew I'd made a mistake. She was dressed in an old housecoat and her bare feet were dirty. I was taken by surprise, and it threw me off balance.

"Well, you came to see me after all," she said, taking a drag off her cigarette.

Once inside, I could see the carpet looked like it hadn't been cleaned, ever, and the fabric on the recliner chairs and sofa had darkened where body oils had discolored the arms and backs. I could hardly bear to be in the house, much less sit when she motioned me to one of the dinette chairs.

I hadn't spoken with her in about a year, which she quickly brought up.

"I don't hear from anyone much anymore," she said.

I knew why. I wanted to say, 'have you ever thought about the way you treated us when we were growing up?' But I didn't. She looked old for her fifty-four years. She'd done nothing to disguise about two inches of her gray roots, and I noticed she had dandruff. Her eyes were puffy, and her skin was pale, which was unusual, especially since she lived in Barstow where the sun was so hot.

"When was the last time you heard from the girls?" I was referring to my sisters, Jess, Beth and Ruby. They all knew where I lived, and we'd kept in touch, but I was curious if my mother had heard anything from them recently.

"It's been a while, but I think they're all okay. I did my best, you know..." she said, and then asked if I wanted some ice water. She didn't wait for my answer, but brought out a water stained glass with cold water in it. It was cold and wet, which was appreciated.

"So...I got married..." she mumbled.

I thought I was going to choke on my water.

"You have?"

"Yes, and he's a very nice man. Name's Charlie...he lives here with me..." She fidgeted with her housecoat, trying to cover her knobby knees.

"Where'd you meet him?" I asked.

"Well...he works at the diner as a cook. I work there too. And we got to know each other and, well, here we are."

"How long?"

"About six months."

It was hard not to judge her or the house she lived in. I never felt she'd done the best she could have for us girls. But I also knew the life she'd chosen limited her, and I'd tried to forgive her for that.

"He's just out of prison."

She dropped that one on me like a bomb!

"What?"

"It wasn't his fault, really. There was a fight, and the man who started it ended up hitting his head. He died, so they found Charlie to be the blame."

She looked at me for some type of acceptance. I really didn't feel like I could give her much and I couldn't help it. I closed my eyes and took a deep breath.

"And I've been received back," she said, referring to her religion.

"I guess that's saying something, Mom," I said.

Then Charlie's car pulled onto the dirt driveway and came to a stop in front of the house.

"That's him now, Sarah. Please be nice," she pleaded with me.

"Hey, who's this?" Charlie said in a huge voice. He was a big man, and he filled the doorway to the trailer. He wore white chef pants and a white knit tank top that did little to cover his large hairy arms and chest.

"Charlie, this is my daughter, Sarah. She's out from Vegas."

"Well, how do you do?" he asked, taking my hand.

For a killer, he was pleasant and friendly.

"I'm hotter than hell, and it's February," he said, going into the kitchen. He came back out with a beer. I'd always thought people who'd been in jail weren't supposed to drink, but what did I know?

"Whew!" he said, plopping down in what was obviously his chair.

"I work the breakfast shift," my mother said. "And Charlie works breakfast, lunch, and early afternoon. That way, we have time together in the evenings. Don't we, Charlie?" My mother sounded happy enough about that, but I couldn't help see she'd come down a couple more notches from the sad life she'd lived with my father.

"Well," I said, "I hate to eat and run, but I want to make it into Long Beach before there's too much more traffic." I'd brought nothing in but my purse, so I grabbed it and headed for the door.

"Aren't you going to kiss your mom?" my mother asked.

I hadn't given it much thought. "Oh, I'm sorry." I gave her a quick kiss on the cheek and said, "I'm really glad for you."

"What are you going to California for?"

I hadn't told her I'd left Mark.

"I'm not sure yet. I'll see if any of the girls are around. Then I want to call Annie. I haven't seen her in quite a while either."

I said nothing else, but just turned around and got into my car. I sat there with the air running full blast for five minutes before I took off.

And that's when I called Annie.

I stopped at a gas station in Victorville to fill my tank and called my sister Jess to let her know I was on my way to Long Beach. When she didn't answer, I left a message on her machine.

"Hey, it's just me. I'm heading your way and wanted to let you know."

It seemed like I was striking out everywhere, for I'd already left messages for Beth and Ruby before I left Barstow.

Road trips meant munchies, so after I used the station restroom, I realized I was craving a Dr. Pepper and Cheetos. For good measure, I added a dark chocolate bar to my purchases.

I found a nice place to stay in Long Beach, and after a hot shower and nap, I called my sisters again. I finally got through to them and we made a brunch date for Sunday. I'd heard the hotel laid out a big spread, and I planned on gourmandizing.

Sunday morning, I waited in the lobby for them, and Jess showed up first. She'd cut her hair, and it looked really stylish. I could smell cigarette smoke on her as I hugged her, so she'd not made good on her last promise to quit smoking.

Beth had gained more weight since I'd last seen her, and she tugged at a snug sweater top as she came up to greet us. She'd done her full makeup, and she was still so pretty, just rounder.

Ruby still wore her beautiful blonde hair long, and she flipped it over her shoulder as she approached us. She was trim and had rings on almost every finger. We all hugged and got teary-eyed.

"Let's go," I said, leading the way to the main dining room. We were led to our table, and when we sat, our waitress placed our napkins on our laps.

"Orange juice?" she asked.

"Yes," we all said at once.

"Help yourself to the buffet when you're ready, ladies."

"I'm starving," I said. "Can we grab our food now, or do you all want to get caught up?"

"Let's go for the food," Jess said, and the other two agreed.

We made our way through the buffet line and filled our plates high, like we hadn't eaten in weeks. Once we sat again, we ate in silence for a few minutes.

"Well?" I asked. "Someone has to start."

"Well," Jess said. "I'm good."

Jess's childhood was almost as bad as mine, her being the second child. I was the lucky one; I got my clothes from thrift stores, but she got my hand-me-downs. She was the most mischievous of the three of us; sneaking out in the middle of the night, meeting friends from school that she was absolutely forbidden to see.

Jess had had a hard time keeping a relationship together for longer than a few years. She married once, but when she realized it had been a mistake, she got a divorce. She was the toughest of us all. I knew I could hold my own, but Jess had actually been in a few fights, proudly declaring herself the victor in all.

"I have a new boyfriend," Beth offered. Beth also got a lot of crap from our parents, but quietly accepted her fate of being kept a prisoner in our home. However, once she was out of school, she bolted like I did. She moved to Washington State, and once she settled down, she started community college. She ended up studying psychology and currently worked in a clinic back down here, helping children cope with their environments.

"I'm engaged," Ruby said, holding up her left hand. She was the baby, and she'd had it the worst. I could still picture her wearing dreadful clothing that had been passed down so many times. Our father was not her father, and he rubbed her nose in it every opportunity he could. He still wanted her to call him Dad, but he was the roughest on her, believing he was toughening her up for the real world.

Ruby also stuck it out as long as she could, then finally moved in with Beth until she graduated from high school. She stayed in Long Beach, attending community college first, then working full time and taking night classes at Cal State Long Beach. She also wanted to work with young people and became a court case coordinator. Her primary responsibilities were to prepare weekly court cases and coordinate judge's schedules. She originally wanted to work directly with the children, but found it too depressing, so she transferred into the administrative side.

"Anyone seen or talked to Mom lately?" Jess asked, looking around the table. Everyone but me shrugged.

"I just saw her," I said. "She's married."

Jess, Beth and Ruby turned to me.

"He just got out of prison."

"What?" Jess said.

"What for?" Ruby asked.

"Good god," Beth sighed audibly.

"Apparently, he got into a fight with someone and the other guy fell and hit his head. He died, and they charged Charlie with his death."

"Good god," Beth said again.

"He seems nice enough. They both work at the local diner. He's a cook. They stay at Mom's, and I didn't get any bad vibes from him."

"Well, that's a relief," Jess said sarcastically.

"Mom looked like crap," I said. "She wore an old housecoat and her feet were dirty. She wanted me to stay, but the house was a mess and reeked of smoke. She says she's happy."

The table went silent as we ate. Finally, Beth said, "I hope she figures out how to find happiness."

"Okay then, let's talk about something else," I said.

We all chatted. It was warm for February, so we talked about the weather. We shared the mundane things going on in our lives.

"I've left Mark," I finally said.

"Wow," Ruby said. "That's a bummer."

"And Annie's up in Lake Arrowhead. She's gotten a divorce. I've called her."

When brunch was over, we kissed and hugged and said, "We should do this again but not wait so long," but I think we all knew we had almost nothing in common at this stage in our lives. Certainly not much that was positive. And that realization was depressing.

I was racking up quite a bill at the hotel, but I just couldn't find the energy to move. I spent the next two days eating and sleeping. I couldn't think straight and I craved the solitude. On the third day, the skies turned gray, echoing my mood and soul, both of which had become heavy. There was a slight rain outside, just a drizzle; perfect to walk in, to get the surface of your clothes wet, but not soaked.

I was getting hungry again, so I foraged through the two trays of room service from yesterday that were on the small dining table in the corner of my room. There was nothing there worth eating, so I broke down and ordered a hamburger and fries.

I figured I had enough time to take a hot shower before my meal arrived. I let the water soothe my stiff neck muscles, and I tried to focus on the sound of the water, allowing it to wash my thoughts away.

As I wound a towel around my wet hair, I heard a knock on the door.

"Room Service."

"I'm coming," I said. I was famished.

After eating, I felt alive again. I knew staying there wasn't going to do me any good, so I called Annie.

"Please come up. There's plenty of room for you," she said when I told her I was in Long Beach.

"I'm dying to see you," I said.

"It's raining up here, and there might be fog, so please be careful coming up the hill."

"I will."

Hopefully, seeing her would be more rewarding than brunch with my sisters had been.

CHAPTER THREE

When Sarah pulled into our parking area, she did the same thing I'd done when I first came up; she stretched her arms high above her head, took in a deep breath and said, "It's so peaceful here."

"It is. That's why I stayed. Let me help you with your things," I said, and then looked into the back seat of her car. It was filled with boxes and tied up trash bags.

She saw the look on my face and said, "Most of my things are staying in Las Vegas. This is all I kept. My suitcases are in the trunk."

"Let's get you settled. I have you in Cedar Lodge Cabin."

When I opened the door to cabin number three, Sarah held her breath and said, "Wow." I'd added pinecones to the grate before I lit the fire and the air smelled like warm pine.

"So far, two of the cabins have histories we've learned about," I told her. "A woman, Elizabeth, and her husband Thomas stayed in this cabin for three months in the early 1930s while they were finishing their lake house cabin up here. Actually, it's a huge, wonderful old home, and not a cabin at all. People up here call their homes cabins.

"After she died, I worked with her granddaughter, Carrie, to bring their house up to date. Both the house and Carrie were a dream to work with. It turns out her grandmother knew Bugsy Siegel. In fact, I've had professional photos taken of the finished project, and I'd love to have you add them to my portfolio."

I realized I'd been doing all the talking while Sarah looked around the cabin, taking in all the details; the painting over the fireplace, the updated bathroom and kitchenette.

"Sorry, I've hogged the conversation," I said.

"No, Annie, I could tell by the photos you've sent you've done a wonderful job. I knew you were good, and you should be really proud of your work," she said, unlocking her suitcase.

"Can I get you anything?" I asked. "Water, cookies? Do you need some time to rest after your drive?"

"I'd love all the above," Sarah said, putting her folded clothing in a dresser drawer. "Let me just have a few minutes, and I'll come get you. Are you hungry?"

"Always. I think it's the altitude. Oh, and you'll need to drink plenty of water up here. It can make you light-headed. Do you want me to leave the fire on?"

"No, it's so beautiful out, and I'm not the least bit cold."

"Okay, you might be when we get back. I'm in cabin one, so come get me when you're ready."

We went to our old standby, Ginny's.

"Wow, you're famous," Sarah said as I greeted the locals.

"It doesn't take long to get to know most of the people up here," I said, leading her to an empty booth.

"So, how's your mom?" I asked, splitting our sandwich when it came.

"Nothing's changed. Once I got to her place, I could hardly wait to leave."

"I'm sorry," I said, and I genuinely was. Time apparently hadn't helped their relationship. She didn't elaborate, and I was okay with that. I knew eventually I'd hear everything she wanted to share with me.

"I've been seeing someone since we talked, last," I said, peeking over the menu.

She put hers down and asked. "Is it serious?"

"I think so. We spend a lot of time at his cabin."

We talked about the mountains, what it was like living in a small town, the seasons, and almost everything else. Sarah didn't seem to want to share about her and Mark, and I decided against telling her about my recklessness with my design client, Grayson Underwood; more than wondering what she'd think of me after just telling her about how happy I was, I felt it was disrespectful to Noah. And if I was honest with myself, just thinking about it made me shiver.

"Are you all right?" she asked.

"I'm fine," I lied.

It was cooling down, so when we got back to the cabins, we brought blankets out and sat in the Adirondack chairs in the garden. The cats seized the opportunity for warm laps and snuggled under the blankets. I knew Sarah was exhausted, and I quickly realized I could use a nap too, and within moments, we were both out. I awoke before Sarah did, and I watched my friend sleep. I wanted to reach out and touch her hand, to let her know I was there for her, but I didn't want to wake her.

Seeing her now took me back to elementary school. She was standing near a group of kids, observing as a boy entertained his friends by calling me names. But the first time I actually *met* Sarah was when the boy did it again, and she flattened him. When the young man cried, his friends were no longer interested in me, but started laughing at him instead.

"Crybaby," they called as they turned to leave him.

"Well, that should be the end of that," Sarah said, wiping her hands in triumph.

And it was.

We were five.

My mother was born and raised in California, and my father in Taiwan. He came here as a student and stayed when he married her. I looked more like her, with her German heritage, but there was always something about me, something that made people look at me, as if baffled. While I never felt that way, my husband, David, called me exotic looking.

I told no one but Sarah about being teased before, but I knew my older sister Loni had had the same problem. I'd also told her that I hated it when someone met my mother, and she was introduced as Mrs. Chang.

She looked like the rest of the other moms, but our surname didn't match us; it set us apart.

So Sarah started calling her 'Mrs. C,' and soon that's how my mother started introducing herself.

"Show me around," Sarah said when she woke.

"We do still have some daylight left...are you sure you don't want to put your things away?"

"I can do that when we're done."

"Okay then. We'll start with my cabin first."

"The photos make me feel like I'd love to stay here, but they don't do the place justice," she said. "Each cabin is perfect. I love the names you've given them, and I love the mix of old and new. I can't think of anything more original to say than I love them all." She gave me a big hug.

"I wanted to save the most dramatic for last," I said, opening the door to cabin number five, the Pinecone Cabin.

I told her how Alyce Murphy came up to see where her father hung himself after he killed his business partner and his family. It happened years before Sam bought the cabins, and other than speculation in the newspaper, there was no definitive answer as to why he'd done it.

"They'd used the cabin as storage for over twenty years, and Alyce came up while we were clearing it out for restoration. Unfortunately, there wasn't anything in there to give us any insight about what happened.

"About three weeks after she left, I found a note tucked away in an old clock Sam wanted to clean up and use on the counter in the office. It said something like, 'I'm a monster and I'm sorry for destroying my family.' I wasn't sure the note would add anything but more disappointment for her because it didn't unearth the real reason for her father killing his partner. I was tempted to keep the note to myself and just put it in our trinket box where we keep mementos our guests have left behind. Both Sam and Noah thought I should send the note, and in the end, I sent it with a letter telling her I hoped she was doing okay. She'd never know why he did what he did, and by hiding the note in the clock, it's a wonder it ever got found."

"I told Mark I was unhappy," she then said. "He wanted to know how I could feel that way, and I knew for a long time I never should have married him."

Her mouth twisted slightly.

"He wanted to know if I wanted to have a baby. I wanted to say, 'you don't get it' but I didn't, because he always thought everything was all right. And that's when I knew I couldn't stay."

Her blue eyes teared, and my heart went out to her.

"Sweet, uncomplicated, oblivious Mark. I never loved him. I started seeing someone."

Without thinking, I raised my eyebrows in surprise.

"What?" she asked.

"When you said that, I couldn't help but think about David seeing someone."

"I'm sorry Annie. I never thought about that. But he loved you in the beginning, I'm sure." She managed a weak smile. "Oops. I've just made it worse."

"I hope so," I said wryly. "I'm fine. Go on."

"I feel like a shit," Sarah said, reaching for me. "For saying that to you, and for leaving Mark a note when I left. I keep picturing him sitting there reading it. And then when I stopped to see my mother, I saw what my life could have turned out like if I didn't do something about it. She could never figure out she had options, and now she's in Barstow. With Charlie; a cook at the diner and a murderer."

That night, we had dinner with Noah and his friend Josh at the Cowboy Bar. We got there first, so we ordered our wine, and talked about sharing my favorite, the rib eye and fries since we were both still a little full from lunch. When Noah and Josh got there, they ordered their beers from the bar and then joined us.

I saw a glimmer of a smile when she saw Josh coming towards us. His eyebrows lifted slightly as he sat down.

"Sarah, this is Josh," I said.

"Hey there," he said.

Noah and I exchanged glances.

CHAPTER FOUR

Noah stayed with me in my cabin that night, and the next morning, after he left to go home and change for work, Sarah and I had breakfast at Ginny's.

"I kind of like him," she said about Josh.

I liked Josh, and didn't want to discourage Sarah, so I said, "He's not had the best of partners, which I think makes a lot of difference. Can you tell if he likes you?"

"I can," she said simply.

"Did he tell you about Bunny? They've been working on a huge remodeling project." I hated to bring her up, but she'd been a big part of Josh's life these last few months and could present complications.

"I hate to say she's just sex to him, but I'm gathering that's all she is. I certainly wouldn't want to be there when he tells her he's not going to see her for a few days."

"So you've already talked about it?"

At that, Sarah scrunched her mouth and said, "Yeah. We talked about it last night."

I said, "Just take it slow."

"Look who's calling the kettle black," she answered quickly, then smiled.

"Don't go getting your heart broken." Then I changed the subject. Sarah was a big girl and could make her own decisions. "What do you feel like doing today?"

"I don't want to interrupt your work, but I'd love to have a tour..."

"Actually, my schedule is pretty clear. I work part time at the flooring store in town to help them and to find new clients, but I don't go in again until tomorrow. Do you want to drive around after breakfast or go back to the cabin first?"

"I'm good to go, if you are."

I took her on the same tour Noah took me on when I first got up here. I showed her my favorite store, Timberline, and she went crazy as I'd expected. We drove up to Wildhaven Ranch, and while I knew we couldn't get in, I wanted her to see there was an active animal preserve up here. We drove around the lake and she commented on the houses along the highway; how some looked occupied and others didn't. We ended up at the Village so she could see the lake and feed the ducks.

During the week, no one set up a table outside to sell duck food, so I went into the fast-food store there to buy a loaf of bread. When I told the store owner it was to feed the ducks, he said, "No, you don't. I have food for them. Bread might get stuck in their throat. Most of the junk people feed them isn't good for them."

When I told Sarah how stupid I felt, she said, "Go back in there and tell him to make a sign that says he has duck food. What a jerk. How are people supposed to know something like that?"

"Well, people who know anything about animals would have known that."

"I'll go tell him," she said and went into the store.

I hoped she'd learned some diplomacy over the years, and when she came back out, she wiped her hands together, like she had when she defended me so many years ago and said, "Well, that takes care of that."

I looked at her and we both burst in to laughter.

"What did he say?"

"He actually thanked me for the good idea. He said he was going to work on a sign today, then have something permanent made up."

"You're too much."

When we got back to the cabins, Sam had taken a message from my mother, so I called her when I got Sarah settled.

"Hey there," I said.

"Hi, honey. I wanted to let you know Loni is coming to see us. I think she and Jerome are getting a divorce."

"That's too bad," I said. "When's she going to be there?"

"In about a week. She's taking a bus."

"A bus? Doesn't she have a car?"

"Well, I hate to talk about it over the phone, but I think she lost her license."

"Aha."

I was hoping my mother wasn't going to ask me to come out while she was there, but if she did, I'd have to come up with a logical reason why I wouldn't be able to.

"I know you two haven't been real close these last few years. I guess I was hoping you could try to at least talk to her while she's here."

"I don't know if I can take the time off to come visit..."

I closed my eyes and sighed.

"I know. I just wanted you to know."

The line was silent.

"I'll call you when she gets here, okay?"

"Sounds good, Mom. Love you and Dad."

"Love you too, honey."

The next morning, a few minutes after I arrived at the flooring store, Liz, the owner, said she wanted to talk to me about something. Typically, when someone said something like that, it was bad news, and my stomach sank. We went into her office and she closed the door. *That* made me feel even *worse.*

"I wanted to let you know I'm thinking about retiring," she said.

My stomach sank even deeper.

"You are?"

Just when I was feeling like I knew what I was doing, I was going to have to look for somewhere else to drum up clients.

"And I've given this a lot of thought...since it would be a shame to close the store, I'm looking for someone to sell it to."

I let this sink in. I thought to myself first, 'I'd love to have a place to work out of.' And then I said aloud, "This could be perfect for me."

Two heartbeats later, I caught myself and wanted to make sure she was actually asking me if I wanted to buy her business.

"Are you asking me if I'm interested?"

"Yes, I am. I can make it manageable for you to do it, and I don't really need a large down payment. We can work on a payment schedule, and you already know what you're doing." She raised her eyebrows in anticipation and smiled. She waited patiently for me to say something.

Of course, I immediately started thinking about everything I could do with a store. I'd bring in a collection of fabrics, and I'd add catalogs for some of the furniture I'd been ordering...

"Is your mind racing?" she asked.

"Boy, is it."

"I wanted you to have the first opportunity. I really hate to put it out there for just anyone; I think I'd close it before I did that."

"Well, don't do that," I said eagerly. "I'll do it."

My mind went into overload, and my heart raced as I thought of all the possibilities just waiting for me.

"It's a deal. When do you want to work out the details?" I asked.

"What I thought was that if you had any money to put down, we'd write up a contract. I was thinking ten thousand for the business and all the samples, and you could make monthly payments."

"I have five thousand dollars saved...but I'd like to have a little cushion. Please don't think I'm trying to take advantage, but could I put three thousand down, and then pay three hundred a month?" I could hardly stand the thought of not going through with this!

"I think that's perfect," Liz said. "Let's start with that."

"Have you told any of the girls? What will we tell them?"

"I'll tell them. I know they'll be pleased to see you take over. And I know you'll do an outstanding job, Annie."

Tears came to my eyes as I said, "Thanks, Liz. That means a lot to me."

"No crying," she chided.

"Thanks, Liz," I repeated. "I won't let you down."

"I know that, Annie, and that's why I wanted to give you first dibs. I've seen you blossom since you've been here, and it reminds me of myself at your age. Nothing could hold me back. It makes me feel good."

"I'm so excited, I can hardly stand it. I know that's not the most professional thing to say, but it's how I feel."

"Never lose your spontaneity. It's one of your best features. And of course, so is your talent. You've always done your best with our customers."

I left her office, then sat at one of the tables on the floor and surveyed the store, but from a fresh perspective. It had everything I'd need; maybe I'd eliminate a couple of sample racks so I could hang fabrics. I'd have Sarah work on a brochure and show some examples of my recent design jobs...

I forced myself to settle down and focus on working, although it was difficult to keep my mind from wandering. We only had a few customers that day, which was fine with me. It gave me the opportunity to sketch some things out and just daydream. I came down a few notches when I thought about telling Noah. I knew he'd think I was crazy, and maybe I was.

"Oh, my god," I said to myself. "I can't believe this is happening."

Then reality set in and I sat, stunned. There went my impulsive behavior again! I instantly had a lump in my stomach. How was I going to manage my design business, the cabins, and now a store?

I knew how!

I was just going to do it.

"Oh, my god," I said one more time.

Then I thought about Noah, and reality set in. I'd made myself a silent promise to include him in any future decisions, and to ask his opinion, even if I knew what I was ultimately going to do. How was I going to tell him I was jumping into another business venture?

It was an opportunity I couldn't resist. I knew this would throw him over the top, but I couldn't pass up an offer like this. It was like it was being handed to me on a silver platter. Noah was so slow and steady, and that's what I loved about him. And I was just the opposite. I knew I sometimes frightened him with my ideas, and I wanted him to be there for me as my support.

When I got back to the cabins, I told Sarah about the opportunity and she was almost as excited as I was. I asked if she'd be okay on her own for the night, so I could talk to Noah.

"Actually, I have a date with Josh," she said. "We were going to include you two, but this is okay, too. I can get to know him a little better," she said coyly.

It was a perfect night, with a bright, full moon. I commented on it as we pulled up in front of Ginny's. I shivered when I got out of Noah's Jeep, more from the adrenaline than the cool evening air.

"I have an incredible opportunity," I started once we ordered. "I know you're going to think I'm crazy, but Liz at the store is retiring and has asked me if I'd like to buy her business." I waited only a second for his response before I went on. "It would be a great way to build my design business and promote your construction business."

Noah leaned back in the booth, and I could see frustration cross his face. He sighed deeply and I could see the wheels turning. He was gathering his thoughts.

"Well," he started, "My first thought was you already have enough on your plate, and I wonder about you taking on another responsibility." He shook his head. "I don't know, Annie."

I tried to keep him from dampening my enthusiasm, so instead of just blurting out that I'd already said yes, I took one of his hands. "I really want to do this, Noah. I also want us to work on our relationship, and I know I have a tendency to jump into things. But that's how I am, and I usually land on my feet. This is a great chance for me to expand my business, and I have all the people in place. I want you to be a part of this, and I want you to be happy for me."

He looked at me suspiciously. "Happy for you as in you've already decided?" His jaw tightened then.

"I cannot lie. I've told Liz I'm really interested." I hated to withhold the details, but I also would not let him keep me from doing something I really wanted to do.

He sighed again and then scratched his head with both his hands.

I knew I'd pushed him again.

Our dinner came, and I said, "Well, let's eat and we can talk about it later."

I couldn't help thinking out loud and said, "I'd add fabric samples, and if you felt like going to San Francisco again, I could look at furniture vendors who wouldn't require me to have large opening orders. Liz doesn't have an area rug rack, so I could look into that..."

Noah looked at me and shook his head again, but this time, even though his grin was tight, I knew he was going to support me.

"I don't know what to do with you, Annie," he finally said.

"Just love me for who I am," I said back, blowing him a kiss.

When we came outside, the beautiful moon and all the stars were hidden behind new clouds, and the sky had darkened. All I could see was gray, and I should have seen this as a forewarning of what was to come.

Three days later, my mother called again. I expected her to tell me Loni was there and settled, but that wasn't to be the case. Before the bus she was on reached Prescott, it struck a semi-truck parked on the side of the road. The bus landed on its side, and Loni was one of three people critically injured.

"I don't know if she's going to make it."

My mother struggled to keep her voice calm. She caught her breath.

"I don't think she's going to be all right. She has problems with her liver, and it's losing its function."

"Mother," I said, "she's going to be okay. She'll be fine."

I said it, but even then, I knew I was lying. I didn't know any of the details of the accident, or how bad Loni's injuries were; it was just my first thought, my gut reaction. I didn't believe my own words. If Loni had continued drinking all these years, I assumed she'd caused a lot of damage to not only her liver, but to her other organs as well.

"She has internal bleeding," my mother said quietly.

"Do you want me to come out?"

"No. She's in and out of consciousness, and I don't think she'd want anyone to see her. I don't know if she even knows where she is."

Suddenly, I felt awful for trying to think of ways I couldn't, *or wouldn't,* come out to see her.

"I can come if you want me to."

"No, you can come later," my mother said before she hung up.

I couldn't help it, but I blamed my sister for getting herself into this mess. Granted, she hadn't caused the bus accident, but she had put herself at risk. For years she'd abused her body, causing who knew what deterioration that would now most likely kill her.

Clearly, I knew I was being too harsh on her, but that didn't seem to stop the anger I felt inside. Images of her lying in a hospital bed hooked up to tubes and equipment, with my parents by her side, made it even worse. Even though she was most likely dying, as my mother suspected, such hard feelings and frustration startled me. I was resentful she was needlessly putting our parents through this.

First, it was making them worry about her divorce—but hadn't I done the same thing? For some reason, that was different. I didn't come crawling home. I didn't expect them to take care of me. She'd obligated them. And now, she was making them deal with her death.

My mother contacted Jerome, who had a meltdown and had to hang up. His mother called back later, and the two women made plans for them to come out.

"You know, they were talking about divorce," his mother said.

"We'd like to bury her here," my mother answered.

"Had she been drinking?"

Then my mother hung up.

Jerome and his parents stayed in a nearby hotel, and as Loni's husband, he should have been responsible for making her funeral arrangements.

I went with my mother to meet them at the mortuary, and I alternated between pity and contempt for both Jerome and his mother. He couldn't stop crying as his mother pulled him along like a small child to look at the caskets.

"Choose this one," she finally said, pointing to one. "This will work."

I laid my hand on a nicer one, and said, "I like this one better."

The mortician glanced at his watch, and my mother finally said, "Yes, let's take this one. We'll pay for it."

I knew it went against everything my mother thought was proper to avoid Jerome's family, but avoid them, she did. We didn't see them again until the service, as the small group of us entered the chapel.

"I think she's wearing that awful dress she wore to the wedding!" I whispered loudly.

"Annie, please," was all my mother said.

During the service, my mother kept a tissue to her closed eyes, and quietly sobbed. My father rested his forehead on his open hand and covered his eyes. From time to time, a tear escaped and ran down his cheek.

I always cried at weddings and funerals, and this was no exception, although I know my tears were more for my parents than for my sister. My anger towards her had somewhat subsided, and for that I was grateful, but I felt resentment take its place. There is resentment; and there is jealousy. I obviously wasn't jealous of Loni lying there in that coffin, but these mixed feelings still disturbed me.

I'd felt the same anger when I discovered David's infidelity, and it had almost driven me mad. And while these events weren't at all related, the feelings were the same. Eventually, all those emotional ups and downs faded away as time passed. I knew the bitterness towards my sister would fade as well.

I stayed a few extra days, and I did everything I was expected to do with the best of intentions; I went through all the motions and especially supported my parents throughout the ordeal. After all, Loni was gone; her struggle with alcohol was finally over. *At peace now*, as everyone liked to say, as their way of expressing their condolences.

CHAPTER FIVE

We had an unusually hot and humid week for the beginning of March, and while it cooled considerably in the late afternoons, I hated the constant need to wipe perspiration from my face. It was a waste of time to put make-up on, but I started each day hoping it would get better. The cabins didn't have ceiling fans, so when Noah went down the hill to get some other supplies, he bought ten of them for me; one for each cabin, and three for the office and Sam's bedroom. I wasn't aware Sam had asthma, and it acted up with the humidity, so he spent most days at Ginny's in the restaurant. He left a message on the answering machine telling any callers we had openings and he'd call them back as soon as he was back in the office.

I spent as much time as I could at the flooring store in air conditioning, drawing up floor plans and figuring out where I'd put new fabric racks when they came in. I was eager to start organizing my new office and Liz didn't mind helping me pack up the files I could put into storage. I ventured out and found a bookcase I could use for my business catalogs now that I could move them out of my cabin.

I ordered an addition to the store sign; I kept the original name but added Interior Design Services. Sarah created a new store brochure, adding construction services, and her name, as the graphic designer.

Since she had an artistic side, I asked her if she wanted to work part time in the store until she figured out what she wanted to do. At first she was a little hesitant, thinking she wouldn't be able to help people with product choices until I pointed out that's what she did all the time with her graphic design business. She had plenty of talent and once she was familiar with the products, I reassured her she'd grow to feel comfortable making suggestions.

It was a momentous day when I turned the utilities on in my name. I now had a physical design studio! And more bills.

As I'd expected, Sarah was good with customers and colors and she encouraged them to use our design services, which was great for me. I was still the only designer we had on staff, and I was able to take on any new projects that came in.

It was then she told me she and Josh were going to try spending more time together and wanted to make sure it was okay if he stayed with her in her cabin.

"That gives you and Noah a chance to be by yourselves too," she said, and then added, "Are you okay with Josh's dog staying there with us?"

Shep, Josh's German Shepherd, was a handsome, well-behaved dog, but having him in the cabin all day wasn't ideal.

"Wouldn't he be better off staying at Noah's? At least there's a large fenced in pen, and he wouldn't be cooped up in the cabin all day. I don't think he'd be happy, and honestly, I don't think I want to worry about accidents."

Sarah scrunched her mouth in thought.

"I hadn't thought about that."

"Let me talk to Noah," I said. "I'm sure one more mouth to feed will be okay. Josh can always come take him for the day."

That night when I mentioned Shep, he agreed about the dog staying at his cabin.

"There's plenty of room here, and you don't need the worry of additional liability."

Dear Noah, always the logical one.

He continued. "Speaking of Josh, I'm glad we only have a few touchups at Bunny's house," he said. "Since Josh told her he wasn't going to see her anymore, she's been a nightmare," he finally said.

"Oh, dear. I can only imagine her reaction to being the one who got dumped."

Noah looked at me funny.

"I didn't mean it that way," I quickly added, but secretly I *did* mean it. Then I wondered how she would treat Noah going forward. "I hope she doesn't take it out on *you*."

"I'm hoping as well. Everything we have left to do doesn't involve Josh, so she should be okay. We'll see."

When we had lunch the next day with Josh, we heard all about it. Bunny hadn't taken the news well at all.

"She threw stuff at me and called me a loser," Josh said, trying to make a joke out of it. We could both tell her comment hurt him.

"If she thought you were such a loser, then why did she want to have a relationship with you?" I asked. "You know the type of woman she is, Josh. And she's the loser, not you." I touched his hand and pouted for him.

"You had a good ride," Noah said, "no pun intended."

"Noah! That's awful," I said. We all laughed. Then I added, "Look at it on the bright side. You got to get all that wildness out of your system so you could try to have a good relationship with Sarah. You both deserve to have someone in your lives that cares about you. I'm sure it'll be hard, but try to put the cougar out of your mind and focus on Sarah. She's a much better catch, anyway."

"I agree," Noah said.

"I do too," Josh agreed.

The next day, I was reorganizing the storeroom at the store when I heard the front door slam.

"Sorry," Sarah called out.

She threw her things onto her desk and then planted herself in the doorway.

"You'll never believe what just happened," she said, tears filling her eyes.

Even after I wiped the damp hair from my forehead with my arm, I felt sweat trickle down my face.

"Josh and I were having a quick breakfast at Ginny's and in walks that bitch Bunny. She marched right up to our table and said, 'Here... you forgot your toothbrush.' She slammed it down and then gave Josh the nastiest look I've ever seen.

"My first instinct was to kick her ass, but as I got up from the booth, Josh got this look on his face that stopped me cold. I wondered if he was going to push me down or grab Bunny. Instead, he took a deep breath, and then took the toothbrush *and* Bunny, and walked her outside."

"Dear god," I said.

"They were out there about ten minutes, but it seemed like an hour. I felt like everyone was looking at me and waiting to see what was going to happen." She leaned forward and lowered her voice. "It was awful."

"'Show's over,' Josh said, as he came back through the door. 'Sometimes a guy's just got to put his foot down and turn a woman back in the right direction.' Some of the men laughed, but I thought I was going to die. I sat there, though; no one was going to make me run."

"And I wouldn't expect you to. Remember that one kid you hit because he was teasing me?" I couldn't help but smile, thinking about it.

"Yeah, and he had it coming."

"Are you okay?"

"I will be. I'm not sure what he said to her, but if she comes back again, she'll have me to deal with."

"Let's go outside and get some fresh air," I suggested.

There was a wooden bench in front of the candle and honey store next door, and we sat there in silence for a few minutes.

"Take a deep breath," I suggested, doing the same. We mindlessly watched cars drive by, some pulling into the grocery store parking lot across the street. A young mother wrestled with a stroller, and we both giggled.

"It's one of those perfect mountain mornings," I said, taking in another breath. "The kind that makes me want to just sit and breathe."

"If I wasn't so upset, I'd agree," Sarah said.

"I never told you what Bunny did to me."

When Sarah turned to look at me, there were tears in her eyes again.

"The first time I met Bunny, Noah and I were eating lunch, and I could smell her perfume before I even saw her walk in to the restaurant." I went on to tell her about how she took over the conversation, and how angry I was that I allowed her to make me feel so insignificant.

"Her job was perfect for Noah, and it's kept him busy for months. But it's had its drawbacks. The second time I met her, she insisted she join us for Noah's birthday dinner, by showing up at the restaurant just when we'd ordered wine. She knew we were celebrating, and she'd even brought him a gift. She monopolized the evening, and when the evening was finally over, I could smell her perfume in Noah's clothing. It just about ruined everything."

She brightened.

"Did you give him his birthday present?"

"Only after I made him take a shower!"

We sat for a while longer, then Sarah said, "Ready to go tackle that storeroom?"

One afternoon in mid-March, I met Hudson and Constance Fisher when they came into the store. They were originally from L.A. and had moved to the mountain a year earlier. They both worked from home and they were considering moving from their existing mountain home to a larger one. So far, they'd looked at several houses, but all of them needed updating and they wanted to see who was available locally to do any work they might want to do.

"My mother stayed up here in the late twenties while filming a movie," Hudson offered.

I was intrigued.

"Do you know where?"

"Not really." Hudson said. "The studio built some cabins, and she stayed there. That's about all I know."

My brain clicked in and I said, "I have a series of cabins built for the studios in the late twenties. I wonder if they were the ones."

Hudson shrugged and nodded. "Could be."

"What is your mother's name?" I asked, knowing I could look her up later.

"Celeste Williams," he said, flipping through flooring samples.

I couldn't say I was familiar with the name, for that was definitely before my time. I also wasn't an old movie buff, but I was definitely going to look her up when I got back to the cabins.

Hudson pointed to a hardwood sample. "I like this one, Constance," he then said to his wife.

"Me too," she replied.

Constance was very attractive, and they made a very handsome couple. She was tall and slender, with her blonde hair pulled back in a ponytail. On her left finger she wore an enormous diamond ring, and on her left wrist were a Rolex watch and a gold and diamond bracelet. Her nails were done in a French manicure, which suddenly made me want to hide my hands. I'd just trimmed my nails short, and I still had a terrible habit of picking at my cuticles.

I think Hudson also wore a Rolex, so by all appearances, they could afford to remodel any home they decided on. I always felt a little guilty stereotyping people, but usually my instincts were good.

"Well, I'd love to work with you in any way you'd like," I said. "I can do a little or a lot. We have contractors we can refer if you end up finding something you'd like to remodel or update. Are you looking for an older home or something newer?"

"We're open to either," Hudson said. "We know we don't want a total cabin look, though, and we'd need two offices."

"Well, I've worked with both a contemporary mountain look, and with homes where my clients want to update, but keep the original character and old charm and flavor. What do you do?" I asked.

"I'm an attorney, and Constance is a court recorder."

I nodded.

"How do you feel about driving up and down the mountain? Some people don't care for it."

"I actually like it," Hudson said.

"I do too," said Constance. "Hudson goes down when he has court, and my work is by assignment."

"Well, I'll let you look more if you'd like to. But let me know if you have any questions. I'm here to help." I left them then to browse on their own.

From my office I could see them take everything in, even pulling some furniture catalogs I'd moved out into the store. They seemed easy going and my first thought was they'd be pleasant to work with. My ex-husband was an attorney, and while I'd never worked with one as a client, I was aware firsthand how some of them could be domineering and condescending. I didn't sense those characteristics in Hudson.

Before they left, he peeked into my office and said, "We'll be back in touch. We like a lot of the things you have."

"Thanks so much," I said, getting up to hand them a card. "I look forward to working with you."

For a moment, I wondered what type of home they would eventually end up with and then went back to my paperwork. Before I forgot, I made myself a note to look at the old guest register books in the office. The cabins weren't rentals when they were built, and I was hopeful there were at least some records of who stayed there for the studio.

It was a fairly busy day, so it wasn't until late afternoon, just before we closed, that I had time to talk to Sarah. She hung a few fabric samples and came to sit beside me.

"Listen to this," I said to her. "A couple came in today and are thinking about buying another place up here. His mother was an actress from the thirties, and he said she stayed up here while making a movie. I hope we have those records."

As we locked up, I noticed the temperature had dropped, and I went back in to get my sweater. I loved it when the weather turned crisp, as it was then. I wanted to stop by the cabin office before heading to my cabin, and was looking forward to seeing Sam and the cats. Sarah had an errand to run, so I got there before she did, and as I pulled in, I saw Sam watering some of our flowers. I always tried to keep seasonal colors around the grounds; not only for our guests, but for us, too. They made me happy.

I went inside and Jezebel was sitting on the counter cleaning herself. I stood there quietly, watching her before she noticed I was there.

"Hi, girl," I called in a little voice. She looked up at me and meowed.

I went into our storage cabinet and pulled out the books from the time I thought Celeste Williams might have stayed here. I'd forgotten the studio guest books were more like ledgers that shop keepers kept their accounts in, and were for studio use only. They listed the different movies that were filmed, along with dates, cabin numbers, actors' names, and some autographs. Within a few minutes, I found what I'd been looking for.

It was the end of 1929, and Celeste Williams first stayed in cabin one, along with another unfamiliar actress. And several weeks later, her name was added to cabin number seven, where a John Robert Scott was staying. I quickly scanned the pages to see if there was anyone else I recognized and was disappointed to only see a few; Cecil B. Demille, and Gloria Swanson being two of them. Did Celeste Williams and John Robert Scott have an affair? I let my mind wander...I was now really hoping Hudson and Constance would be back so I could share my findings with them.

Then I thought about it; I wasn't sure I should share the romance possibility.

Sarah and I then went through our lost and found 'trinket box' to see if there was anything that looked like a glamorous movie star would have accidentally left behind. We'd kept everything we found that looked interesting, but aside from a single earring, there was nothing interesting. And that could have belonged to anyone.

CHAPTER SIX

Hudson Fisher
1941–1981

"Huddie?" my mother called out to me in annoyance. "Where are you? We need to go." I heard her gather her car keys, but she hung back a few more moments to see if I would appear.

I was hiding in the entry hall closet, which I often did just to drive her crazy. I was only three, but I'd learned early on which buttons to push when I felt like it, and I delighted in peeking out the closet door to see her frantically gathering her things so we could get going. It didn't seem to make any difference where we went; I rarely wanted to go. Of course, I'd have to admit that if we were going for ice cream, I was always ready and willing.

"Damn it, Huddie. Now!"

In her words, I was always precocious.

I wouldn't have siblings until Mother remarried. First came Robert, and then Andrew Jr. joined us. Until then, I had Nanny to myself. She was never adventuresome, and I was easily bored; once I learned to read, I wasn't the least bit interested in having her continue to read to me. I wanted to do everything myself, and I made up my own stories to share with anyone who would listen.

Nanny wasn't as easy to rile as Mother though, so I constantly tried to find new ways to make her think she'd forgotten or misplaced something.

When she grew tired of my little games, she'd stop paying attention to me, or say, "Oh well." When I heard her sigh, I knew I'd won.

My mother provided a car for her to run errands and do the grocery shopping, and of course, that included taking me with her. Not being content to sit, I had to stand up on the front seat to see where we were going. If I felt I'd missed something, I'd quickly climb over the seat and stand and look out the back window.

My name is Hudson Fisher. My last name really should have been Keller, but I took on the name of my stepfather, since, as my mother always reminded me, he *was the one who raised me while she was off being a movie star. Because my brothers called him Dad, I did too, but I also referred to him as 'The General.' It never seemed to bother him, since that's what he was when he retired from the Army after the end of WWII.*

The General always loved to tell the story about me and the icebox. When I was a baby we lived in Pearl Harbor (with my real father, whose presence was always omitted) and when the Japanese attacked, my mother put me in a cardboard box then placed me in the icebox to protect me in case the bombing continued. Of course, I was only a few months old, so I had no recollection of the event, so I could only retell the story my mother always told me. The General would laugh and say, "What if your mother'd forgotten you and the next day remembered where she put you?" When he first said that, I stopped to think about that possibility, and was horrified; but then realized she never would have done that. So I quickly learned to laugh along with him.

When my brothers were old enough to hear the story, I always felt special, even to the point of feeling fair-haired and best loved. Of course, as my brothers (and others) grew bored with the tale, The General told it less often. It wouldn't be until years later, when reminiscing about childhood with friends, that I'd recall that story.

Mother hated it when I went outside and played fort in the dirt flower beds. I loved building roads with mounds of dirt that could hide my military soldiers. For buildings, I cut windows and doors out of cardboard boxes. I could spend hours by myself driving my tanks and blowing up the enemy. Sometimes, one of the neighborhood boys around my age would see me outside and come see if he could play. He didn't have his own soldiers, so I had to let him use some of mine, and while I never told him this, I would have been more than happy just playing by myself.

Knowing my eventual fate when Nanny called me to come in, I never made it easy for her to get me to do so; the moment I heard the front door open, I'd run around the corner and hide behind a large hedge of bushes. I could only hold her off just so long though, for she knew where I was hiding, and she'd unwind the hose from the wall mounted hose reel and turn the water on me full blast. By then, of course, I was a muddy mess, and I had to take an extra long bath to get all the dirt off. She'd clean the leftover soil from under my fingernails so that when my mother returned home from the studio, she would see me clean and ready for bed.

I also loved to collect postage stamps. Most of them came from the five and dime store, where I'd buy everything they had in stock. Once I'd get home, I'd spend hours putting them in my books, and when I'd run out of stamps, I could hardly wait to go back the next week and get more. Some of the magazines The General read had ads for stamps in them, and even though the instructions said, 'do not mail cash', he'd give me the money to send away for a large bag. I had a voracious appetite for everything that interested me, and I still do, often to the consternation of my wife.

She says I can be annoying.

Once I turned around eight, with Nanny's help, I subscribed to stamp magazines and constantly asked her to send away for books and stamps themselves. As I grew to learn more about stamp collecting, I had an entire shelf in my bookcase filled with books on collecting and my partially filled stamp albums. I learned that stamps were first introduced in the United Kingdom in 1840 and in the United States in 1847. Before 1861, private companies could buy old printing plates to print and sell their own stamps, actually competing with the U.S. Post Office. I also learned that most collectors ended up narrowing down their collections to specific countries or time periods. I, myself, have stuck with U.S. stamps.

I recall when my brother Robert was born in 1946. I was five, and very inquisitive. It amazed me how he could turn from a normal pink color to *bright red when he cried, which was, to me, often. I'd watch as Nanny would change him, and one day I realized someone had also changed* my *diapers when I was a baby! I was mortified that someone else had seen my private parts.*

I also recall him being uncovered one morning and while waiting for his new diaper, Robert peed a tall stream of liquid into the air, hitting Nanny in the face as she leaned over him. Rightfully so, she screamed with surprise, then quickly covered him before she ran into the bathroom to clean herself up.

I stepped up to his changing table, and on my tiptoes, asked him, "Did you do that on purpose?"

When Andrew Jr., or JR as we often called him, was a baby, Nanny always made sure he was well covered before she left him for even a moment. It was the poopy stuff, as I called it then, that I couldn't fathom, and even when I had my own children, I didn't do well with dirty diapers. In those days, disposable diapers hadn't been available, so diapers were rinsed and put into containers that the diaper service would pick up. "New" sterilized diapers would be dropped off and the cycle would begin again. To this day, I hate the smell of sitting diapers.

My mother was away for long periods of time, either filming a movie or spending a summer in Europe. The General would go with her on her European forays, and she would send us postcards from where they stayed. She always brought something back for us, usually some worthless trinket, but the three of us had our own wooden boxes where we kept our "treasures." I figured she had to have thought of us at some time while she was away, or she wouldn't have remembered to buy us something. Many years later, during one of The General's many binge drinking, soul-cleansing sessions, he would tell whoever was there that he was the one who made sure they brought something back for us. And sad to say, I believed him.

Although I was sure she loved us, on a day-to-day basis, my mother was not demonstrative about her love and affection; with us or The General. Later in life, I would wonder how she could be a successful actress, but not successfully act the part of a good mother.

Nanny did everything for us; meals, getting us ready and taking us to school, sometimes even meeting with a school official or going to an open house if Mother and The General weren't in town. I should add here that our nanny had a name: Elena. But we weren't to address her by her given name, and calling her Miss Elena didn't fit. So we just called her Nanny.

Mother went through a musical period where she thought we should all take some type of lessons. She bought a piano, and for a while, we all tried that. We took lessons from a woman who came in once a week, and that sad attempt to add music to our education lasted for a year. I was the only one who picked it up, but only slightly.

Next came guitars, and after that, drums, and even I couldn't bear listening to the three of us practicing. Nanny finally convinced my mother we boys were not musically inclined, and Mother donated everything to the local Boys and Girls Club.

We were each allowed to have a small pet in our room. I decided on a turtle and named it Louise, although we never knew if it was a male or female. I made weekly trips to the pet store to buy crickets and cockroaches to keep Louise fed, until one day Nanny realized the roaches could get out of the cage and said, "Your mother will have a fit if she sees cockroaches in this house. I've just killed two in your bathroom!"

I agreed that if by some chance any of the creepy-crawlies got out of the Louise's habitat, I'd probably freak out too, so I agreed to change her diet. Plus, they'd kept me awake at night with their stridulating. (I looked it up, and it's what crickets do.) And I hated the sight and sound of them crunching in the turtle's mouth. The earthworms and lettuce I ended up with were much quieter and easier for us all to live with.

Robert chose a hamster, so JR decided on that too. Their two-story cages were everything a hamster could ever want in life; a food bin, a water bottle, and two wheels for them to get 'nowhere fast' on.

With a turtle, I couldn't have a two-story set up, so I originally felt I came out on the short end of the stick. But then I realized my turtle didn't smell up my room, either.

In the end, all we did was add more to Nanny's already busy day, but she took it all in stride.

Nanny was probably forty, slightly overweight, and wore comfortable shoes with heavy nylons; most likely to help tired legs that had her running after us all day long. As I grew older, I was curious about her life, since all I knew about her was that she lived with us. She had her own bedroom and bathroom, albeit it was on the other side of the house. She wasn't allowed to do much decorating, but she had a Jesus on a cross hanging on her wall, and a small picture of the Virgin Mary on her dresser.

One day, while she was sitting at the kitchen table cutting up vegetables, I thought I'd join her and find out more about her.

I've never been one to beat around the bush, so I sat and watched her work for a few minutes. She gave me an odd look, but kept cutting.

"So," I started. "Where are you from?" I thought that was innocuous enough.

She looked at me for a minute and then went back to her work. She smiled. "I'm from Mexico."

"I know. But where?"

"Mexico City."

"You were born there, right?"

"Yes. But I've lived here in America for a long time."

Over the years, I hadn't given her a lot of thought, which I now realize was very selfish on my part, and it was during this conversation with her I realized she didn't have a heavy accent.

"Do you have family there?"

"I do. My parents are there and they live with my sister and her husband." She didn't go on, so I did.

"Are you married?" Good one.

She looked at me again and smiled. "I almost was. He was very handsome," she sighed wistfully. "But a few months before we were to be married, he was killed." She stopped and thought for a minute. "He was a police officer, and it was while doing work under the covers during a drug bust."

"Wow..." I said, astounded. I never knew anyone who'd died. I picked up a carrot and munched.

"I came here to find a good job and to find a new life."

"You think this is a good job?" There had to be hundreds of other things she could be doing.

"Of course. I have a roof over my head, plenty to eat, and three children to look after. Four if you count The General," she said, smiling again.

I couldn't believe she called him that!

"Don't you ever get lonely?"

"I do. But my life here is so full; I know I could never have all this back home."

I thought about this, and about all we had, and wondered what it would be like if we had to go live somewhere where we had nothing.

"Do you see your family? You're always here."

"Your mother periodically gives me time to go. She's always filming, and because the other boys are so young, I don't feel right leaving you." She looked like she was going to say something more, but didn't. "You boys are my family now."

That was sad, because I'd never really thought of her that way. As being my family. Robert and JR needed her more than I did now, so that's probably what she was talking about.

"Well, I'm glad you're here. If it weren't for you, there'd never be enough of anything to eat in the cupboards or refrigerator. Cooking is not one of my mother's strong points."

It was inevitable I'd grow bored with my turtle; it wasn't really very entertaining. So one day I asked if I could have an ant farm. They were really popular and when I saw an ad for one in our science magazines, I thought it would be a perfect addition to my pet collection. When it came time to make my argument for the ants, I pointed out a few other creatures that were also interesting to me; snakes, or a tarantula...I got the ant farm.

No one ever confessed, but it only took a week before one of my brothers came into my room and picked up the ant farm, already with its very interesting labyrinths, and dropped it, spilling everything onto the floor.

41

I quickly called Nanny to the rescue, and she vacuumed what she could see, but I swore for weeks I could feel ants crawling all over me as I slept at night! Even though I really wanted to replace it, I never did.

Next on my list was seahorses! I saw these also in my science magazines, and they were really cool. I couldn't imagine them actually being alive! So I ordered some and could hardly wait until my package came in the mail. As soon as it did, I set up the container that came in the box and I made the saltwater.

They were incredible! I fed them the recommended shrimp brine, and all was well for a couple of weeks, then they started dying! I couldn't figure out what I'd done wrong. Without the boys hearing, The General told me that the seahorses could never thrive in the man-made environment people put them in. I had to realize it was not my fault, but a gimmick, and the people who sold them were to blame. To give them a fighting chance of surviving, they'd need a full saltwater aquarium set up, which very few people had.

I appreciated his explanation and understood. Nonetheless, for weeks, I felt terrible about participating in killing something so harmless. As an adult, I saw one in a saltwater aquarium once and learned they mate for life and it is the male who gives birth to their babies.

I wasn't really sure what The General did during the day besides golf. Nanny drove us to all our activities. As children, we're so absorbed in our own worlds, we only thought of grownups when we needed something, or when we didn't get what we wanted.

I was so preoccupied with myself, I didn't realize until I was a teenager that The General was a drinker. His face had always been red and splotchy, but I'd attributed it to being in the service and out on the golf course every day. I'd never been around anyone who drank, so I wasn't quick to put it all together. I asked Nanny about him once and all she would say was, "The General has his demons, I think."

"From what?" I asked.

"From the war, maybe."

Most of the time he went into my parents' room to take a nap, but sometimes I'd see him dozing in one of the family room chairs while he sat in front of the television set. He'd have a glass of scotch in his hand and the bottle on the end table. Sometimes the newspaper would be open, but most times it would be on the floor.

I knew I could never ask my mother about it, for while I never heard her speak of it, on more than one occasion, I'd seen her give him looks of disapproval. She'd say nothing to him in front of us.

One time, I came home before the boys to find him passed out on the sofa in just a tee shirt, his boxers and his socks. His fly was open and his family jewels were hanging out. Thankfully, Nanny wasn't around and I quickly pulled a blanket out of the hall closet and covered him with it.

I think Mother would have killed him if she'd seen him like that.

CHAPTER SEVEN

In April, we had the grand opening for the flooring and design store. I'd hung my fabric sample books on metal hooks, and Noah built me a decorative furniture catalog cabinet out of rustic pine and branches and I moved the old bookcase into my office. I added a small area rug sample rack of natural materials that would suit most houses up here. I found a candle line wrapped in birch and filled a cabinet with accessories customers could buy when they were in the store.

I invited local realtors, past clients of mine from both up and down the hill, and about a hundred former customers of the store itself. Sarah did all the artwork for me for the invitations, the new brochure, the ad in the newspaper, and for posters and the banner we hung outside.

I couldn't have asked for better weather; it was a cloudless spring day, and we had a good turnout. Liz was there, which was super, and she introduced me to all the store's past customers. Everyone was sad to see her retire, but happy for her *and* me. Sarah and the staff mingled, and when I could, I introduced Sarah as a member of our staff and the graphic designer who'd done all our artwork.

Even Noah, always handsome in his tight jeans, rolled-up shirt-sleeves and disarming smile, was genuinely happy for me. Once he'd thought the idea through, he jumped in to help me get everything ready. Sarah made up some posters showcasing his work, and people showed a lot of interest. He had people lined up to talk to him all afternoon.

Sarah made up another poster showing examples of invitations and business brochures she'd made. I noticed some realtors from the office across the street were interested in her services and she gave out several cards. She thanked me later for making her step outside her comfort zone to promote herself.

Ginny's was just a couple doors down, and she provided cheese and crackers, an incredible feta cheese and spinach dip, and some artichoke parmesan bites. We set platters up on tables with soda and wine outside under the store sign where we'd hung our new Interior Design Services sign. Sarah had designed new takeout menus for Ginny, and we put them in a branch stand Noah made.

Josh had done quite a bit to help me in the store when he wasn't working on a new project Noah started. He helped me rearrange some display fixtures; he planted some new pine trees along the side of the building, and he hauled all the debris to the dump when he did the final cleanup. He volunteered to work as our server, and he surprised me by wearing a white shirt and black vest, along with his jeans and boots. It impressed me how easily he mingled with people, and I could tell he took his job seriously.

A few times, I caught glimpses of him with Sarah, either bringing her something to drink, or just giving her a light hug and kiss on the cheek. He seemed quite fond of her, and I could tell the feeling was mutual.

If I had to rate our success for the day on a scale of one to ten, it was an eleven.

A week later, I agreed to work with the Chamber of Commerce on a Memorial Weekend Festival. It was something they'd wanted to do for several years, and had decided at the last minute to sponsor it. We were getting a late start, but Sarah and I thought we could come up with a plan to pull it off.

As we got into it and saw how much work it was going to take, I hated to admit to Noah that working on the festival was biting off more than I should have. But I thought it was important, and being a new business in town, I wanted everyone to know I cared about our community.

"Go ahead," I said, when I complained how tired I was. "Tell me I've managed to get myself knee deep into another project."

Thankfully, he never said, "I told you so," but instead asked if he could do anything to help.

Sarah again donated the artwork for banners, fliers and posters. I worked on advertising and coordinating with local artisan vendors to set up booths on both sides of our street. We had a meeting with the local businesses and came up with a reasonable amount for everyone to chip in to cover some of the expenses. All but one of them was fine with it. The only opponent was the souvenir shop across the street, who felt they didn't need to pay anything. They never came out and said it, it was apparent they felt it was their right to ride along on the shirttails of the event and reap the rewards of all the potential customers we were attracting. I wanted to make an issue of it, but the Chamber felt we couldn't come out and tell the public who didn't take part or donate. So instead, we only acknowledged those who paid their share in the advertising.

I suggested we print up entry forms with all the sponsors on it, and as customers went to each store, they could get a hole punched in it. When they filled up their card, they could drop it in a basket to win a grand prize of items we all donated.

When I gave an entry form to one woman, she looked at the list and asked why the souvenir shop wasn't on it. I kindly explained they weren't a sponsor.

"These businesses listed actually helped cover expenses," I said.

I loved it when later, the shop owner came into our store to actually ask why they weren't included in the raffle, and I had to bite my tongue to not say, "Because you're stupid."

I didn't want any problems with any of my new neighbors, so instead I said, "At our planning meeting, we thought you said you weren't chipping in. I'm sorry. You should have let me know you changed your mind."

Noah and Josh volunteered to be traffic guards on the day of the event, making sure we had no issues in the street. The local fire truck came and firemen passed out plastic helmets and decals to the children who got to sit in the truck and sound the alarm; it was a great success.

We had all kinds of vendors; a face painter, lots of jewelry makers, a snow cone vendor, a hot dog cart, artists, quilters, a sign maker and a candlemaker. Sarah had suggested finding a band, but hiring one was beyond our small budget. Instead, she contacted a young singer from down the hill to see if she would do a benefit concert for us. She was eager to promote her new recording, and if we could set up the sound system and some type of stage, she agreed to perform for us at no charge. Sarah contacted the high school, and they donated everything we needed.

I'd learned the weather could be fickle and unpredictable in the mountains, and I recalled the last Memorial Day it had turned cold and foggy. But this year there was only a small breeze which cooled off the warm afternoon. All the hard work paid off, and attendance was outstanding. A lot of new people, permanent residents, part-timers, and tourists came into the store and looked around. Some commented they'd never been in before, and that was music to my ears. After all, that was one of the primary purposes for doing all that work!

At the end of the day, my feet were killing me, and we were all exhausted by the time we finished cleaning up. We went directly from the store to the Cowboy Bar for steaks and drinks. I paid for the four of us and our staff, including Liz, to thank them all for all their help.

"Cheers," I toasted. "It was a perfect day, and we couldn't have done it without you all."

That night, after a long soak in the tub, I headed for bed. Noah massaged my feet, and as I watched him, it seemed my love for him just continued to deepen.

"It was a great day," he said, working his way up my legs.

"That feels wonderful. Don't stop."

"As in, don't stop? Or don't stop there?"

"Don't stop there," I said.

His kisses were surprisingly gentle at first, and then he whispered, "I love you, Annie Parker."

In the past, Noah had to borrow a friend's boat when he wanted to go out on the lake. In June, he and Josh decided to go in partners to buy their own boat and trailer so they could go out any time the weather was good. With Sarah and me as witnesses, they agreed to split everything fifty/fifty and promised to never get into any arguments about being partners.

They knew the boat needed a little work when they bought it, but as is often the case, once they started working on it, there was more to do than they originally planned on. But it gave them a project, and they were determined to get it up and running before summer. Because renting a boat dock was not in their budget, they stored the boat and trailer in one of the garages at Noah's. It took some effort to get it in and out of the property, but they eventually came up with a workable routine.

Once it was ready, we could go out almost every weekend. We'd pack cheese and crackers, some beer and sodas, and kept blankets and towels on board. We never seemed to tire of driving around the lake, even if Noah constantly sped around making sure we all got wet. Sarah and I learned to drive the boat and to water ski. Sometimes we'd pull in to the docks at the Village and have either a late breakfast or early lunch at the Belgian Waffle Works restaurant, where no matter what time it was, we always had waffles.

The name of the boat was 'Money Pit', which, after the initial overhaul, thankfully didn't live up to its name. The guys didn't want to tempt superstition by renaming it, but they referred to her as 'Our Girl' after me and Sarah.

On warm afternoons when they were finished with work, they'd come by the house, quickly change into their shorts and get out on to the water. Most of the time, they'd be back before either Sarah or I were home from work. If they got a late start or wanted to stay out longer, Noah would call me at the store and they'd dock the boat at the village and we'd meet them for dinner at Papagayo's, our favorite Mexican restaurant.

At the end of summer, there was news of another child abduction, the second in two years. Lake Arrowhead was a town with no history of crime, other than a few miscellaneous petty thefts. Like the first abduction, we heard about it on the news while having breakfast at Ginny's.

Flashbacks of last year's grim discovery were all over the news.

"The first child, Sophia Rodriguez, was discovered floating in the water last summer and the person or persons who molested and killed her were never found," the newscaster said.

Pictures of the campground where the Rodriguez family stayed were on the screen, the yellow caution tape surrounding it, as well as the footage from when the child's body was retrieved from the lake.

The reporter at the new campsite continued. "Today we're reporting about another little girl who's missing, and an alert is going out to everyone on the mountain to volunteer in a search. Her name is Jasmine Benson, and she's five years old. So far, there's been no body discovered, which is an encouraging sign, but since she could be out there anywhere, time is of the essence. If you can be part of a search, or if you've seen anything suspicious, please contact the Sheriff's department at the number on the screen. Back to you in the studio."

Noah wrote down the number, and he made a call. He and Josh worked on a team with about fifty others to search the most likely areas where a child could be hiding. Safety Patrol Officers patrolled the lake continually, and they inspected all boats on and off the water in the immediate area.

They found nothing in the most popular campsites, so the teams started spreading out. It took two nerve-wracking days, but the little girl was eventually found alive. She was sitting next to a tree, naked and sobbing. One searcher immediately wrapped her in a blanket and called out to the rest of the team.

"I ran away from him," the little girl cried.

She was filthy from being in the forest for two days and her tears had run tracks down her dirty face. The news showed images of her hysterical parents and of the ambulance arriving at the hospital.

"Thank God they found her," I said to no one.

The Sheriff asked another team to begin a search beyond where the child was found, and again, Noah and Josh volunteered.

He told them, "I need you all to know we're looking for something in particular, but for now, we're not letting the public know. That means not even talking about this with your friends and family. Last year, we found what we think was the site where our perpetrator actually camped, and he left behind a coffee can filled with cigarette butts. So we're looking for another camp-out or something that can point us to the same guy."

Noah and Josh kept their word, and didn't tell me or Sarah anything until another team found a site complete with the can of butts.

The recovery of the little girl was all over the news. I could tell Noah and Josh were disappointed they hadn't been there first-hand to either discover the child or the evidence, but they were really glad to have been part of the search effort. And Sarah and I were proud that they didn't hesitate to volunteer.

"If we don't catch him, I can't help but think something like this is going to happen again," I said, voicing what I was sure we'd all been thinking.

"I hope the mountain can relax again," Sarah added.

Josh and Noah just looked at each other.

CHAPTER EIGHT

Sarah

The first images I recall of my father are those of him sitting on his side of the sofa with his feet up on an ottoman. He usually had a sleeveless t-shirt on, and he always had a beer in one hand and a cigarette in the other. Empty cans scattered the floor where he dropped them. He would sometimes call me over to sit with him, but I didn't like the smell of beer on his breath or the dried sweat from under his arms. When I tried to climb down, he would pull me back up and make me sit until I cried. Then he'd get angry with me and push me off his lap.

When that happened, my mom would rush into the room to see what was going on, and the minute she'd see me on the floor, she'd scoop me up in her arms and hold me until I stopped crying.

"Damn it, Lou!" she'd yell. "One of these days you're going to hurt her!"

And sure as she predicted, one day, my face hit the beer cans just right, and I got a cut under my eye, which made me cry even louder.

He puckered up his mouth in a sour scowl. "Well, she don't want to sit with her dad!"

"I don't blame her. You stink!" Then she walked away before he could get up and go after her.

"I need to take her to the doctor. I think she might need stitches."

"You don't need no doctor," he said. "She'll be all right. Just clean her up."

From then on, whenever he called me, I'd pretend I didn't hear him or I'd run the other way.

When my sister Jess was born, my mother returned to her childhood religion. She'd gotten caught up in all the drinking and drugs, and the only way she knew to straighten herself out was to repent and go back to meetings.

My father was a drunk and an atheist, and my mother was an on again, off again religious fanatic. They made quite a pair, but they somehow managed to stay together for almost sixteen miserable years.

I was the eldest of four children, and actually fathered by another man (whom I've never met). Two of my sisters were by who I referred to as my father, the man who raised me, and the youngest one was by his best friend. But I'm getting ahead of myself...

My name is Sarah Jones, and I've known Annie just about my entire life. We grew up together in Long Beach, California, and until I left home, she was my only friend. Compared to me, with thick reddish blonde hair that wouldn't take a brush, Annie, with her silky dark hair and large brown eyes, looked like a princess.

I'd seen her on the playground when a boy from another class pushed her, and by the time I'd figured out what he was doing, she'd run away. The second time I saw him, he called her names, and I knew I needed to kick his ass. And that's what I did. If I learned anything from my dad, it was to not be afraid of anyone.

I was still too young then to remember what all the house rules were; what we could and couldn't do, so I was always being reprimanded. But the one thing that stood out for me early on was while neighbor kids were celebrating their birthdays with parties, I could never go to one. And I could never celebrate with a party of my own, even within the family.

After my next sister Beth was born, my mom was back into drinking with my dad, and it was a good thing she never breast fed us; we would have all turned out to be alcoholics.

My parents had some pretty wild parties. As usual, we always had to stay in our room, but I remember one time having to go to the bathroom so bad I thought I was going to wet myself. I knew I'd get in more trouble for that than if they caught me sneaking out, so I took a deep breath and made a beeline for the toilet. I rushed to do my business, but on my way back to our bedroom, I got caught up in the music and stood in the hallway looking into our smoke filled living room. My eyes burned, and at first, I thought I saw a man who wasn't my father kissing my mother. She had a drink and a cigarette in one hand, and was trying to keep her balance while she swayed to the music.

I then heard my father's voice coming from the kitchen, and I thought for sure he'd seen me and my heart pounded in my chest. I quickly realized he hadn't been talking to me, but to a woman who was saying, "C'mon. Dance with me."

"There's something else I'd like to do with you," he said, and then I ran back to our room as fast as I could.

There were no kids my age on our street, so I walked by myself to school and back. If I didn't dawdle, it would take me about twenty-five minutes, and it became the only quiet time I had for myself. Only two blocks away, the neighborhood changed; just slightly, but for the better. I quickly learned if I left the house early, I could sometimes pretend to tie my shoelaces and quietly observe other people as a husband left for work, or a mother rounded children up to drop off at school. I noticed their manicured lawns, their clothes, their newer cars, and the fact they had two of them. Some even had dogs that got to go with them.

I wondered what they thought of us just around the corner, some houses, like ours, with overgrown weeds and bicycles on the front lawn. We had one car, and when my dad was home, his motorcycle was parked up near the front porch. After school, other than at our house, kids ran wild, playing baseball or jumping rope. I could hear fathers whistle or mothers call loudly for their children to come in to eat.

I wondered what they ate for breakfast, especially when there wasn't enough cereal for all of us on any given morning. Even if I was starving, I'd say I wasn't really hungry, so my sisters could eat. Then I'd hope there would be something left to eat at school before I had to start my morning.

One morning, Annie's mother pulled her car up to the curb and Annie called out, "Hey Sarah! Wanna ride to school?"

In my heart, I knew my mother would kill me if I took a ride with a stranger, but this was Annie, and I only thought about it for a minute before I jumped into the car. When she introduced me to her mother, I couldn't believe how pretty she was, with her hair done, and lipstick on. I didn't know much about Annie's family then, and it surprised me how she looked different from her mom. I'd always thought Annie was prettier than I was, with her beautiful shiny black hair and dark eyes.

I was distracted as Annie ate a piece of something that looked and smelled delicious, and my mouth watered.

When we got to school, Annie's mother said, "Give me a kiss," pulling Annie back in before she could jump out of the car.

I climbed out of the back seat and shut my door.

"Thanks for the ride." I said, leaning into the passenger window.

"You're welcome, honey," her mother said. She waited for us to get up the school steps before she drove away.

"Wow, your mom's really cool," I said. "What were you eating?"

"My mom warms up an apple fritter for breakfast. They're my favorite thing in the world."

"It looked delicious," I said. "I'm starving."

After school, I waited with Annie near where her mother dropped us off, and when she got into the car, I started off on my way home.

"Get in the car," Annie said.

"Nah, my mom will kill me."

"Don't be silly," her mother said. "Get in the car and I'll drive you home."

"Okay," I said, but when we got close to my house, I said, "You can let me off here."

"You sure?" Annie asked.

"Yeah."

"Okay, see you tomorrow."

The next day, I made sure I left the house a little early so I could get to the same spot where they picked me up the day before. I pretended to still be walking so I could look surprised when the car pulled up.

As soon as I got in, Annie handed me a warm apple fritter, and I thought I'd died and gone to heaven.

During recess, I wanted to ask Annie about her mom, and what it was that made them look so different. I hadn't developed diplomacy yet, so I just came out and asked her.

"I'm half Chinese," she said matter-of-factly. "My father is from Taiwan."

I digested that for a moment, and then said, "Nothing like that ever happened to me. In fact, I don't know who my real dad is. And sometimes my mom is a on a religious kick." Like that explained everything.

Doing laundry was a never-ending job in our family. Our washing machine was in the garage, and there was an area in our yard where we could hang our clothes to dry. I was not allowed to use the wringer on the washer, but I was responsible for taking all the clothes down when I got home from school. When my mother only used a few clips, I could sometimes just pull the clothes down, but when I did that once and broke a couple of clothespins, I nearly got the belt. After that, I used a wobbly old stool I found in the garage to climb up and undo our clothes the right way. I'd wear my mother's apron with the pockets on it to put all the pins in. One time, I stepped on one of the apron strings and lost my balance and fell off the stool. I braced my fall with my arm, but I bit my lip and no one but Annie's mother noticed my mouth was swollen for two days.

One time, when our washing machine finally broke down, we didn't have the money to fix it, and we hadn't done laundry in days. I had to rummage through my cramped closet to find something to wear to school. Balled up in the mess on the bottom of the closet, was a dress I'd torn while playing on the playground. I had no choice but to wear it, and as I put it on, I felt a gnawing in my stomach, for I was sure someone would notice the wrinkles, and I'd die of embarrassment. When my mother wasn't looking, I took a long sweater out of her closet and rushed outside to put it on before she saw me.

When Annie and Mrs. C picked me up, I climbed into the back seat and I lowered my head in shame. I wanted to disappear into the upholstery. When I didn't respond to Annie's offer of the apple fritter, she looked back at me, then at her mom, and said, "I've forgotten something. Can we go back home?"

"What?" her mom answered.

"It'll only take a minute."

"All right. But make it quick. I don't want you two to be late."

We pulled back in front of their house and in no time, Annie was back out with a plastic bag. She tossed it in the back seat, and inside was one of her dresses.

"Put it on," she said.

With renewed humiliation, I set the bag back on the seat.

"Put it on. You can do it before we get to school."

Her mom winked at me in the rearview mirror, and I carefully pulled out a red and yellow plaid dress. I'd seen Annie wear it before and had always admired it. In no time, I changed into it, and even though there was no mirror to look into, I suddenly felt a powerful relief. I hated that something as simple as a pretty dress could make such a difference in my opinion of myself.

"Here," Annie said. "Don't get fritter on it. Keep the other dress in the car, and you can change back into it on the way home."

From that point on, every day, Annie brought something for me to wear and I became a quick-change artist. Only once, when we had to walk home, did I forget to change back into my old clothes and when I came in the door, one of my younger sisters said, "Wow. That's a pretty dress. Where'd you get it?"

"I got it the last time we went shopping," I quickly lied. "You were busy with your own stuff." I took the dress off and put it in a paper bag and hid it under my bed. I quickly changed into some blue jeans and a T-shirt, and went into the kitchen to study.

One basic house rule we all remembered was that unless we were eating or doing homework at the kitchen table, we had to stay out of the way and in our room. The three of us shared that room, and they put me in charge of keeping everyone in there. Because I was the oldest, I had my own bed, and Jess and Beth shared a bed until my mom talked my dad into getting them bunk beds.

When my dad was home, under no circumstances were we to play in the living room where we could disturb him, and that suited us fine except when *the summer heat was so stifling it made us dizzy. I pleaded with my mother to get us a fan so we could at least circulate the air, and one especially hot summer, when we all came out with red blotchy faces and our hair plastered to our foreheads from sweating, she relented.*

At supper time, my dad would sit at the table with a large wooden spoon to the right of his plate. If we didn't mind our manners, he'd whack our hands. Sometimes, for effect, he'd play with it, tapping it on the table, then slapping it down. One time, when it broke, and we all laughed, his face turned beet red, and I thought for sure he was going to pull his chair out and beat us all. But, he suddenly saw the humor in what he'd done, and he burst out laughing. Suddenly silent, we looked at each other to make sure he wasn't trying to trick us, and then we laughed harder.

I think that was the only time I ever saw him laugh out loud.

I was hoping he 'saw the light' as my mother would say, but when we came to the table the next night, there was a new, larger spoon sitting by his plate.

After dinner, he'd take turns tackling us, pinning us down on the floor, saying, "Get up if you can!" supposedly training us to be tough enough to take care of ourselves when we grew up. Once Jess threw up from being tossed around, and my dad said, "Jesus Christ," as he pushed her away from him.

"Lou," my mom said. "Serves you right for doin' that right after dinner."

Once, when my mother was back in her religion and sober, my dad was drunk and stoned, and they had a terrible argument. He grabbed her and then threw her down on the floor. She threatened to leave him if he didn't stop drinking.

"Then do it. You can leave anytime!" he shouted.

So she did. She packed us up and drove our one car to Billy's house, down the street and around the corner. Billy was my dad's best friend, and I thought it was odd that he'd just take us in like that. But he did.

The next day, my dad came and got the car.

My mom moved us all back home two weeks later.

And nine months after that, Ruby was born.

While some people shopped at thrift stores to find treasures, they were our only source for dresses, pants, T-shirts and shoes. I was considered the lucky one, for out of all us girls, I got to wear the best clothes first, and when I outgrew something, it would pass down to my younger sisters.

We'd go on Saturdays, when everything was on sale, and one day I recognized a girl working behind the counter and realized she lived on our street. I was mortified. I turned to leave, telling my mom I'd wait for her outside, but she pulled me back into the store and said, "Knock it off, Sarah." She'd seen her too.

"But I see someone."

"Too bad. There's nothing wrong with you getting some nice clothes. And the little girls need things too."

I tried everything I could to stay hidden behind the clothing racks, but eventually the girl came to say hi.

"I thought I recognized you," she said lightly.

"Yeah, me too," I answered lamely.

"I volunteer here on Saturdays. It helps with my senior credits."

I was eight. What did I know about credits?

"Are you looking for yourself?"

"Ah, no. For my sisters."

"Oh," she said. "I think some really cute things came in and I think you'd like them."

"Really?"

"Yeah. Let me go in back."

In a few minutes, she came back with a couple of dresses, and the minute I saw them, I turned to my mom with a wide grin.

"Now you're going to need to be extra careful you don't ruin them," she said, as we got in the car.

From then on, on Saturdays, I looked forward to seeing what our neighbor set aside for me. That was, until my worst nightmare came true.

"Nice dress," a girl said, actually touching my sleeve.

"Thanks," I said proudly.

"It used to be mine, dork," she said, turning to her friends.

She pointed me out, and I realized she was making fun of me. I froze. I couldn't turn away from them. I tried to put on an air of indifference as I held my head high and turned back towards the classroom, where I stayed for the rest of the day. I tried to focus on my lessons, but I could only think of was how I was going to leave school without her seeing me again.

"What are you doing?" Annie asked when she found me still in my classroom after the last bell.

I burst into tears and told her about the dress.

"I hate her, and I hate myself for crying. I should just kick her ass."

Annie dragged me out of the room and outside, where her mother was waiting for us.

"Don't kick her ass, but we should definitely think of something mean to do to her," Annie said.

When I got home from school that day, I told my mother what had happened, and asked if the next time we shopped, we could go to another town so no one would recognize their cast offs.

"Don't agonize over what other people have to say to you in life. When they do that, they are being the sinful one. You're better than they are. And never forget that."

Of course, that really didn't make me feel any better. Before I let her see new tears, I went to my room and flopped down on my bed. From then on, even in the hottest of weather, if Annie didn't bring me something to wear, I wore sweaters to cover my clothing.

It wasn't that my mom didn't offer to make school lunches for us, but they were always awful; bananas and mayonnaise, bacon and peanut butter, and even leftover spaghetti made into a sandwich. The only things edible were the chips and cookies, if we had any.

Mrs. C. worked in the lunch program throughout elementary school, and it took me a long time to figure out how she always knew I was hungry. If she didn't pack a lunch for me and Annie, we'd go through the food line and we never failed to get an extra dollop of something on our plates. Sometimes I'd go back up and tell her I dropped my cookie so I'd get another one. She'd give me one and say, "That's a shame, honey. Here you go."

I remember once Annie gave me a transistor radio, and I hid it in my room. At no time were we allowed to listen to music or sing. If no one was home, I'd sometimes play it, and once, when my sister Jess found me out, she threatened to tell on me unless she could listen to it too. And then Beth found out, and the three of us ended up not only listening to it, but dancing whenever we thought no one would hear. Once, when Beth tried to do the twist, she looked so silly, we started giggling and my dad yelled, "Knock it off!"

One thing I always dreamed of was going to the movies, but in my mother's opinion, they all glorified violence and illicit sex. Even animated movies were off limits. I especially wanted to see "Swiss Family Robinson" when it came out, but no matter how hard I tried to point out the wholesomeness of the movie, my mother never relented. When Annie saw it, I made her sit with me, and while I closed my eyes, she shared with me every little detail. From then on, when a movie I wanted to see came out, Annie would go see it and she became my movie critic.

Aside from my dad's parent's house, Annie's house was the only other one I'd ever been in. I couldn't believe there were no beer cans strewn about, no ashtrays filled with cigarette butts, and, of course, no motorcycles sitting on the living room carpet. Going to a friend's house to play was forbidden. Heck, even having a friend was prohibited. My mother always wanted to know where we were and what we were doing, and she felt if we were in our room, quietly reading books she provided for us, then we were behaving. Annie had given me some of her old Nancy Drew books and I wrapped them in old Bible story book covers and hid them under my mattress. When my younger sisters were asleep, or engrossed in their own books, I'd pull one out, and read it.

My mom's parents didn't live in California, so we never saw them, but we did go to my father's parents for Christmas. We could sit at the kids' table and have dinner, but we were not to receive any gifts. We'd sit and watch our cousins open presents we could only dream of getting, and pretend we were happy for them.

"Wow," I said once when one year my cousin Julia got a new Hardy Boys book I would have loved to read. I stewed all afternoon about taking it and hiding it under my shirt when we left; she had so many books I thought she'd never miss it. But then I figured she'd know it was me since she saw my reaction when she opened it. And I knew she saw my mother give me a look that could have killed when I did it.

"I'm sorry you don't have gifts to open," my cousin said later.

"Oh, it's fine. We're used to it," I lied. "Besides, all our gifts are at home."

"I have some books you can have," she said.

"Oh, my mother would kill me. I think she'd think I stole them."

I wasn't sure why I'd added that last comment.

I told Annie what I'd said, and right after that, Mrs. C took the two of us to the main library. I was astounded by how many books there were. Along the way to the children's section, I touched their spines, and when asked if I wanted to check one out, I said, "Oh, no. I'm fine. I have so many books at home I haven't read yet. My mother would kill me if I brought another one home."

I finally understood why libraries were off limits to us: we'd have been exposed to so many books that could have taught us about the outside world, and raise possible questions about my mother's extreme beliefs.

What's crazy was our rules were in the name of religion. But my sisters and I were not raised in my mother's faith. In fact, we were raised with no faith, and we were never baptized. My father absolutely forbade it, reminding my mother she wasn't the best example of a genuine believer of anything. If she was, then she wouldn't keep falling off the wagon.

Plus, since he didn't even believe in God, he said we would be in contempt and mocking both sides. He also said we should be able to determine what religion we wanted to be when we were grown up and on our own. What he also made very clear was that we were only 'grown up' when we moved out of his house.

Only Annie broke the barrier of anyone from the outside visiting us. And it was only under the pretense she'd come to help me with my social studies. The first time she came to the house, both my parents had been drinking, and my mother staggered to the front door.

She thought about Annie's request to help for what seemed like forever, and then my dad, who was sitting on the sofa with his beer, chimed in, "Hell, Cindy, let the kids study."

By then I'd come into the living room, and my mom looked at him, then at me and then at Annie. "Well, I guess that would be okay."

And that's how Annie started winning my parents over.

CHAPTER NINE
Sarah

It wasn't until my youngest sister Ruby was five that I learned she had a different father than my sisters Jess and Beth.

My parents had been drinking all day and were sitting in the kitchen arguing. The four of us girls had been listening to the transistor radio, trying to drown out the fracas, and when my dad threw a full can of beer at my mom, it exploded and sounded like a gun went off.

"Stay here," I ordered, but my sisters got up and followed me out the door.

"Get the hell back in there," my dad yelled. By this time, he was in the living room.

I saw my mother standing there with a dishcloth in her hand, and she was wiping at her face. Beer had gone everywhere, and I went to reach for more towels.

"I said get the hell back in your room," my dad said, and as he turned to face us, he stepped on one of his empty beer cans and lost his balance. I watched in slow motion as he fell and hit his shoulder on the coffee table, breaking it into pieces. His motorcycle was parked along the wall, and he narrowly missed hitting it. Now he was raging.

"Go on," my mother hissed at us girls. To my father she said, "I'm leavin' and I'm goin' back to Billy's. He'll take us in."

"Go, and take that bastard kid with you," he said, opening a new can of beer and taking a swig.

My mom pulled all our clothes out of the closet and dresser drawers and packed us up again. We were like a mama bear, and her four cubs, marching our way down the street and around the corner to Billy's. She hadn't warned him; just assumed he'd welcome us with open arms.

"What the hell?" he said as we stood in his front door.

"I can't live with that man any longer," my mom said, barging in.

"Shit," Billy said, watching us follow her.

About a week later, my dad called Billy's and all I could hear was one side of the conversation; it was Billy, saying, "Hell, no!"

So we packed everything up again and walked back home, lugging all our belongings in trash bags and pillowcases. I felt like the entire neighborhood could tell by looking at us what was going on.

When we piled back into the house, my dad said, "Well, you bitches, you're back where you belong." Then he popped open a beer, and I took our dirty clothes out to the garage, while my sisters went to our room to unpack the rest of our things.

When I was in high school, my dad finally moved out of the house and in with another woman. That was truly a blessing. Now it was just my mother and the four of us girls. She'd found religion again, but at least we were free of my dad's drinking and roughness. He never touched us in any other way than to 'teach us to be tough', as he called it, but the way we lived left us all with scars.

My mother got a job working nights at the grocery store and between her paycheck, our welfare check and what my dad sent us, we could pay our rent and put food on the table. On weekends, I started cleaning houses and doing small chores for our neighbors to make my own money. I opened a savings account, and every week I'd walk in to the lobby of the bank like I owned the place, and carefully count my money as I filled out a deposit slip. I'd then find an open teller and proudly hand her my money. Although it didn't start out as much, it began adding up, and I watched with pride as my bank balance grew.

I'd long ago given up worrying about what my mother thought about Annie being an outside friend, and I would have gone to her house more, but I didn't want to leave my sisters alone while my mother was at work. Most nights, Mrs. C would send Annie over with dinner, and then we'd sit with the girls while they did their homework. After that, we'd watch the forbidden television until bedtime.

I knew that the minute I graduated from high school, I was out of there, so I tried to spend the next couple of years teaching my sisters how to survive. We each had our distinct personalities, and I knew we would all make do once we were grown up, but I worried most about Ruby. Even though we all had the same last name, she grew up knowing she didn't have the same dad as the other two sisters, and it troubled her for most of her life.

Billy ended up moving away and gave my mother some money before he left, but he was of no moral support and once he was gone, we never heard from him again. He was just as bad as our dad.

My father's first lady-friend didn't work out for him, and neither did the second or third. Three times, he rode his motorcycle up onto our lawn and casually arranged his riding gear, giving the appearance of belonging and of being cool. And then he asked if he could live with us again. Each time, thankfully, my mother told him to hit the road.

CHAPTER TEN
Hudson

My parents never acted like what I thought a married couple should act like. At least, not like what I saw on TV or in the movies. There was no public affection; no hugs, or even conversation. If The General asked, "How was your day?" Mother would always answer, "Good." And if she asked him the same, his answer was simply, "It was good."

Some mornings, I'd observe them coming out of separate bedrooms. Once though, when I looked at Mother, even before I asked, she said, "He snores."

I remember shrugging my shoulders. I just thought that was the way it was.

During the summer, Nanny took us to the beach almost every day, but only after we made our beds and cleaned our rooms. She also took us horseback riding, which I didn't really care for. I wasn't afraid of the horses, but I'd heard they could sense if you were uncomfortable around them, and I wasn't sure how to stop emitting any aura I might be letting off when I was around them. Robert and JR loved the horses though, so I went along, but most times I didn't ride.

When I was fourteen, I discovered my passion for swimming. I'd always thought our own pool was boring; it was for playing games like Marco Polo, or seeing who could collect the most ping-pong balls. If The General was outside having a cocktail, he would sometimes toss a handful of coins into the water and we'd see who could amass the most by diving to the bottom of the pool.

When I went to an Olympic sized pool for the first time, I only had to inhale the chlorine and feel it permeate my lungs to know I was hooked. The pool was about a mile from our house, so if Nanny wasn't available to drop me off, I'd walk early every morning, not only during the summer, but when school started again. I signed up for the swim team in high school, and by the time I graduated, I'd won an individual title at the CIF state meet, and my underwater streamline technique had set records.

My mother was rarely around to watch my competitions, but The General and the boys made it as often as they could. If he wasn't there, usually Nanny was, and that was around the time I'd quit calling her that. I was too grown up for that word. In the outside world, I referred to her as Elena.

By then, Robert was playing basketball, and JR was into baseball, so sometimes it was hard for us to support each other unless we were at home when we could revel in our wins, or whine about our losses.

A lot of girls hung out around the swim team, and I could have had my pick of any of them, the way they flaunted themselves. Not that I wasn't ready to have sex; after all, I was almost seventeen, but I had three things going against me. One, I didn't have a car like some of the other jocks; two, I was really focused on my swimming, and three, I'd met no one I was interested in.

That was, until I met Emma. I'd seen her a couple of times with her cousin, John, one of my teammates, and she'd blush when she shyly smiled at me. I think I must have turned ten shades of red myself, so we seemed to have a common affliction. She started coming by frequently, feigning interest in John, but I could tell it was me she wanted to see.

One afternoon, when she finally came up to me, I thought I was going to die! I'd been watching her from a distance, and as she looked me straight in the eyes, I could feel myself get aroused, and there was no way I could disguise it wearing my Speedos! I immediately grabbed my towel and hung *it in front of me. I pretended to be drying off my upper body, but I could tell she'd seen it!*

"See you after the meet?" I squeaked out.

"I'll be here," she said, turning and walking back to John.

I was turning seventeen in a few weeks, and I'd asked Mother for a car for almost a year. I'd used that time immemorial tactic of saying, "But all the guys have one," and since I was only sixteen, she'd reply, "That's nice. You're not 'all the guys'. See me when you're seventeen."

So I started hinting to her—I'd already done it with The General—and I was totally hoping she'd keep her word and let me have a car. Now that I had a girlfriend, I needed it.

For once, she didn't let me down. On my seventeenth birthday, I awoke to a 1954 Corvette with Polo White exterior, Sportsman Red interior, and a beige convertible top cover. It was hot! And it had 'speeding ticket' written all over it!

I could hardly contain myself, and I felt like a child, almost jumping up and down, waiting for her to hand me the keys. I think it was the first time I ever remember my mother smiling at me, and I swore I glimpsed what I took to be a glimmer of love in her eyes. Her smile remained, but the light soon faded.

Unfortunately, I don't remember ever seeing that look in her eyes again, even when she had grandchildren.

Like an impetuous teenager, I gave her a quick kiss on the cheek and said, "Thanks!" as I ran out the door.

I hadn't taken into consideration that the Corvette was a stick shift, and I had only driven with The General a few times in his sports car with its automatic transmission. He followed me outside, anticipating my dilemma, and he said, "Just take your time, Son, and you'll do fine. Take it slow. Want me to go with you for a spin?"

Of course, I didn't want to be caught dead with an adult in my new car, so I traversed the neighborhood, trying to never come to a complete stop. Then, once I felt more comfortable not gunning the engine while I released the clutch, I drove that car everywhere. I went to the store, crammed Robert

68

and JR into the front seat, and did any errands that needed to be done
without complaint. That car gave me my freedom. It was also where I lost
my virginity. It wasn't the most comfortable place to have sex, but when is
sex in a car ever ideal?

Throughout our lives, my mother and The General encouraged us to plan
for our future. They would have paid for my college education, but I wanted
to figure it out on my own. I knew I wanted to do something, but I wasn't
sure what. When an opportunity came up for me to apply for a full ride
scholarship to Oregon State in swimming, I jumped on it. I was accepted
and figured I'd come up with a major at some point.

Emma and I broke up in the middle of our senior year. She was going
back east to U. Mass, and we decided our relationship had run its course.
Her cousin asked her to go to Senior Prom with him, since he didn't have a
girlfriend, so I decided not to go.

The night we graduated high school, instead of us going to the all night
dance—where they locked you up so you couldn't go anywhere and get into
trouble—a group of us went to a buddy's house and someone brought girls.
His parents were out of town, and we all stayed in the detached rumpus
room out in the backyard. I was with a girl I hadn't met until that night,
and it was my first experience having sex in public. All of us were making
out, and no one seemed to care what anyone else was doing. We drank
until a couple of us got sick all over the backyard and passed out. When
we finally came to, we took turns hosing down the mess and clearing all
the trash.

When I came home that next morning, I went directly into my room,
hoping no one had paid attention to me, although I was as green as I could
get. I threw up once more before I fell into bed.

I vowed I'd never drink that much again, and I never did.

My mother wanted to have a going away party for me, but I convinced her it
I wanted it to be us and a few friends. We opted to go out to a nice restaurant
instead. Robert and JR brought dates, and I'd been spending some time with
a girl named Becky, so I brought her.

Becky and I were just friends, and we ended up spending a lot of time together over the summer. We went to the beach, to parties, to the movies. It was great having someone around to share your time with, but who wasn't possessive or needy. Her parents were pretty well off, and she was going to go to USC and stay on campus.

Mid-summer my mother had a break in filming, so the five of us made a trip up to the college so I could get the lay of the land.

While Mother and the three of us boys ventured into some of the wildlife preserves, (or I should say my mother sat and waited outside in the shade while we ventured out) The General was perfectly content to golf in the morning and spend the afternoon at the hotel bar. We met up for dinner, and I think it was the first time I realized we were stuck there as a family and we had nothing to talk about. Robert, Jr and I just looked at each other and tried to think of interesting things to say about our day.

I could tell Mother was merely tolerating the dullness of our weekend, with her sighing and feeble smiles, and yet The General didn't seem to be the least bit affected. He was in his own world, watching what people were doing, and having another drink. It was just like being at home.

"Yum," I said when our meal was finally served.

We agreed we'd seen what we came for, but we could only find four seats on an earlier flight back. The General agreed to take the later flight and assured us he'd be okay flying separately. He would no doubt fill the time drinking at the bar at the airport. Mother just sighed loudly and left him there.

I didn't want everyone to tag along when I left for school the first of September, so we said our goodbyes before I left for the airport. Nanny actually drove me, and I was grateful for her company. She'd been the only constant in our lives, and while I wanted to say something to her, I had a hard time thinking of what to say. I wrote her a letter once I got settled in; writing it down seemed a lot less daunting for me.

She dropped me off at the terminal and I saw she'd tried to surreptitiously dry the tears that had formed in her eyes.

"I'll be back," was all I could think to say as I got out.

Before I closed the car door, I bent to look inside, and she smiled. "I'll miss you, Mr. Hudson. You have your whole life ahead of you. Do something with it." Then she touched her fingers to her lips.

Since freshmen had to stay on campus in the dorms, I left my Corvette at home. I hated the thought of leaving it because I worried someone would drive it while I was away. I tried to talk my mother into letting me keep the keys with me, but she insisted she keep them, reminding me they might need to move it, and it would need to be started periodically so the battery wouldn't die. I told the boys, including The General, I would kill anyone who touched it. I prayed they took me seriously.

The first thing I did after moving my things into my dorm room was to buy a bike so I could get across campus and around town. I shared a room with a young man from Ohio, and he turned out to be quite the partier. I was up for a good time, but he'd bring girls into our room at all hours of the night. Of course, that was against the rules, but that didn't keep him from doing it. I tried everything, including buying ear plugs, so I wouldn't have to listen to him having sex all night long.

He too was on a scholarship and I reminded him that while he *might* not be interested in getting an education, I *was*, and that if he didn't stop bringing girls in to our room, I'd ask for a transfer and tell the hall director why. I guess I didn't scare him enough, for that same night, a new girl visited him around midnight.

The next day, I found the director and shared my story with him. He said he'd see what he could do and sure enough, two days later, I moved into another room. This roommate was perfect. Instead of bringing girls in, he spent most of his nights out. At least I could concentrate and get a good night's sleep.

I met Hayley in my Natural Science class. She was gorgeous. A quintessential California girl; blond, blue eyes, and a great figure. She wasn't sure what she wanted to major in, which I discovered was not uncommon among freshmen and even sophomores. I knew I wanted to study sciences, but I didn't have a clear direction either.

Hayley's father worked for the Forest Service, and one evening, when we went down to visit him, he asked if I might be interested in working part time up in Oregon. Getting a job scooping ice cream or working in a fast-food restaurant wasn't exactly my cup of tea, but having a part-time job with the Forest Service would not only be an exceptional experience, but it would help fill my coffers. Having a steady girlfriend was expensive.

I loved the work, and in fact, during summer break, I worked full time. The Forest Service was established in 1905 "to sustain healthy, diverse, and productive forests and grasslands for present and future generations." That's what it said on our monument sign, and I took those words seriously.

I had opportunities to go out with rangers and wardens who actually enforced the laws to protect the land, but I preferred working inside, where I could learn about engineering. Little did I know I would end up working for the Forest Service for twenty-eight years as a mechanical engineer (along with becoming an attorney).

I jump ahead in my story here by recounting this part of my life. However, along with protecting the land, there was also an issue of the significance of safety and noise in our forest system. I established measures of "pollution" caused by trail bikes and their use by rangers. Because I'd also developed a passion for racing motorcycles, I was totally in my element. Out in the field, their standard hard hats were made with tin, which proved to be very dangerous, and I helped them change to using motorcycle helmets.

By the time I retired, I figured I'd written over fifty percent of the reports we generated, which was frightening when you consider I was just one person in a full department.

Because we used airplanes and fire trucks to fight fires, I helped reduce the noise level of the fire line generators we used, while increasing the horsepower of the truck engines.

Also, I loved to fly, so I was the program leader for aviation. We had the first female pilot during my time with the service. But I lost seven friends because of the planes we were using at the time.

This all sounds so technical, but that first job enabled me to make significant differences, albeit most that the public has never been aware of.

The summer before my junior year, Hayley moved back down to California, and I pledged for a fraternity. If you ask anyone who knew me then, they'd most likely tell you I was pretty much full of myself. I was. I excelled in my swimming and won almost all meets I entered. I devoured technical knowledge, and even today, I'd be considered a geek. I have the mental capacity to remember an enormous amount of details, (sometimes even those not worthy of my brain power), and to write and memorize my own poetry, and that of others.

Because I was a jock, they recruited me to join Delta Upsilon, which still exists today. Back in the day, young men of the Jewish persuasion had not been admitted into the fraternity. But one man, whom I won't name, was deemed very cool, and made it in.

Some things that went on during pledging were deplorable and horrific. When my friend's brother also wanted to join, we invited him to pledge. One thing they did was start a fire in the fireplace. They made us take our clothes off, and once we were naked, we had to mount the stairs to the second floor, going backwards. Once up there, we had to fill our mouths with toilet water and run back down the stairs and spit into the fire to put it out.

My friend's brother wasn't very athletic, and after a few trips up and down the stairs, he lost his footing and fell into the fire. He wasn't badly burned, but I held him and shouted for someone to get ice. Then I turned to one upperclassman and shouted, "This shit has to stop!"

He paused for only a few seconds, comprehension dawning on him before he grabbed my arm and said, "What did you say to me?"

I could see the fury in his eyes, but I repeated myself. "I said, this shit has to stop."

He was seething and called to one underclassman near us. "Go get my paddle," he ordered, enunciating every syllable. He tried to grab me by the arm again. "You can't talk to me like that."

I snapped. I pulled away from him and in a voice bordering on mockery said, "You want to bet..." and before I could finish my sentence, he grabbed me again.

That's when I hauled off and slugged him in the face, knocking his two front teeth out.

73

That was the moment of reckoning for me. I decided fraternity life and all the bullshit that went with it was not for me and, after making sure my friend was okay to leave, we walked out the front door.

In my senior year, I knew I'd put off my toughest class, Differential Equations. I had to have it to get my degree, but most importantly, I had to understand it. My professor, Mr. Bartak (who spoke with a very strong Czechoslovakian accent), knew I was having trouble, so one day he asked me to stay after class. I thought for sure he was going to give me my final warning; that I was going to fail.

Instead, he said, "You're an excellent swimmer, yes?"

I was surprised. "Yes, I am."

"Well, I make you a good deal, Mr. Hudson Fisher. I am a terrible swimmer. In fact, I'm afraid of the water—of drowning."

This startled me.

"Yes, it is true. But if you teach me to swim, I'll make sure you understand the equations. And you'll have no problems passing your test."

I couldn't believe his offer. I didn't even have to think twice about my answer.

"Of course I'll teach you," I said. "This is great!"

"Good," he said, shaking my hand. "We both have a lot of hard work ahead of us, but we can do it."

That semester, Mr. Bartak learned to swim, and I learned Differential Equations, which is something I've used throughout my career.

CHAPTER SEVEN

In September, the Chamber of Commerce hosted their Annual Home Tour, which was their largest fundraiser for the year, and people came from all over to see inside some of the most expensive and interesting homes on the mountain. They asked if we'd put a poster in the store window and have fliers inside with information about how customers could purchase tickets.

My heart raced when I saw that my family's old Pinecone Lake House was listed as one of the homes on the tour! I could barely control my excitement. I wanted to rush to tell someone, but at the moment, I was the only one in the store. Images of our old bedroom with the bunk beds flooded my mind, and I pictured my collection of pinecones sitting on our dresser. I could almost smell their fragrance.

I contacted the Chamber and offered to sell tickets in the store, and they said they'd have someone drop them off. The moment they came in, I set tickets aside for the four of us to go.

"How do you feel about seeing your old house?" Sarah asked.

"If you want to know the truth, I can hardly wait. Of course, I'm dying to see if they've made any changes, and part of me wants it to be just as we left it. Or, I should say, how I remember it. You know, I was only ten when my parents bought it."

The week before the tour, strong winds loosened fall leaves and gray clouds threatened rain, and we kept our fingers crossed that the day of the tour would be a clear one.

That night before, I felt ridiculous telling Noah I couldn't sleep because I was too excited to see the house.

"You're silly," he said, but kissed me.

There was a map on the ticket showing all the homes on the tour, and I'd insisted we see our Lake House first, knowing I'd be a nervous wreck if we waited until the end of the tour.

When we got off the shuttle the next morning, I resisted rushing us up the driveway.

"I'm so excited," I said.

"We couldn't tell," Sarah said, locking her arm in mine.

"There must be over a hundred trees on the grounds," Noah said in awe. "Someone had a heck of a job clearing the land of all the pine needles. What a job to clear the property every year."

"If you don't," Josh told Sarah, "when the county sends an inspector by, if you haven't complied with the fire regulations, they fine you and charge you to do the cleanup."

"I love that the deciduous trees have started changing, but still have most of their leaves," I said, surprised with all the wind, the trees were still mostly full. "This is my favorite time of fall."

I'd driven by the house since I'd been up here and was a little disappointed the exterior needed some work. But in preparation for the tour, the owners had restained the wood siding, and they filled the property with fall flowers. I led everyone down to the lake and showed them the dock where our boat had moored, and where we'd sit dangling our feet in the water. I told them about my mother's first experience driving the boat; how she'd started out so hesitantly, then realized the power within, and drove like a madwoman!

I found the spot where my father had hung a swing from the largest tree branch; even back then, we were really too old for it, but when I started to say something to my mother, she put her finger to her lips to silence me. After it was up, I changed my mind, for even as a ten-year-old, I felt so free as I swung as high as I could, trying to imagine reaching the top of the trees.

"I used to run through the woods, sometimes ankle deep in snow. Remember when you came up, Sarah? We'd throw snowballs at each other and one of us would always get snow pushed down their back, especially if Loni came up with a girlfriend." I didn't give her a chance to answer. "And I remember seeing my first deer. I stood still as she lifted her head to see what I was going to do. She sensed I meant her no harm, and she slowly turned and walked away."

I held my breath just for an instant, and said, "Well, we might as well go inside. I'm dying to see what they've done to the place."

"This is incredible," Sarah said, following behind me. "It's just like I remember it. What a trip."

In a way, it was like stepping into a time capsule. All the wood walls had been cleaned and oiled, antique rugs were on the floors in the living room and dining room. Taxidermied deer and elk heads hung above the massive fireplace, just as we'd left them.

The kitchen had been redone in rustic wood cabinets. I stood at the kitchen sink for a moment and looked out at the lake, and I could almost smell the chocolate chip cookies we used to bake. I turned and while the kitchen table had obviously changed, I recalled the Sunday breakfasts we'd have; pancakes, bacon, eggs...when everyone was still young, and the mountains were still so mystical.

"Oh my gosh, Annie," Sarah cried out. "It's for sale!"

I turned as she held up a flier, and I could almost feel the blood drain from my face.

"Wow," Sarah sighed.

I took the flier and read it. I thought I was going to cry, and Sarah was instantly at my side.

"Our house." My voice broke. "My heart is breaking."

By this time, Noah and Josh were there, and Noah said, "What's going on?"

"Our house is for sale!" And now I could feel the tears. "I know it doesn't make sense after all these years, but I'm devastated."

I set the flier back down and stood again at the kitchen sink. "I just need a minute," I said to the three of them. "I'll get over it."

"Do you want to leave?" Noah asked.

"No, I need to get a grip and not ruin it for all of you."

"We're fine, Annie," Sarah said. "Why don't we just keep going?"

I sighed heavily as I looked in the old linen closet and expected to see the mismatched beach towels we kept on hand. It was where we kept the picnic baskets, rafts and volley balls. The pantry was filled with every type of food imaginable, just like it was when we'd come up, when nothing was off limits at the grocery store.

I'd calmed down as we climbed the stairs, yet the minute I went to our Bunk House bedroom, I felt the tears again. There were the old bunk beds, with new mountain bedspreads and pillows, and my old dresser was still there, with a bowl of pinecones sitting on top.

Images of my sister Loni came flooding back, and my shoulders tensed. I was once again a child. I thought about how she used to annoy me by moving my things around and feigning innocence; how she put some acorns in my bed once and swore a squirrel must have come in and done it.

My shoulders relaxed and I could feel my face soften. I hadn't thought about her for months, and I suddenly realized I was so self-absorbed in my own life, I had pushed my anger and any thoughts of her to the back of my mind and I felt guilty.

I sat on one of the bunk beds and tried to recall when we were very young; when we posed for pictures in our Easter dresses, and when she'd helped me up after I'd fallen from my bike.

"Are you okay?" Sarah asked.

"Yeah, just thinking about Loni. Trying to remember the good times, and I also remember being envious of her for being so pretty. It was so easy for her to make friends, and then she threatened to bury me in the backyard."

I peeked in each of the other bedrooms, which now also had hardwood flooring and area rugs, but they weren't as full of memories as our bedroom was. I went back again and stood in the doorway, remembering how Loni got drunk and threw up all over our board game on my birthday.

"Loni was a drunk even then," I said, then quickly regretted having said it.

"She *did* ruin your birthday," Sarah said.

"I wonder now if I should have said something to my mother. I don't know if it would have changed anything. Do you think they could have helped her back then?"

"It's hard to say, Annie. You can always go back. Could of. Should of. Would of. But maybe telling your mother would have just made Loni more angry. It might have made things worse."

I signed heavily. I couldn't help but think how they were never aware of Loni's travels down that deep dark hole of alcoholism until it was too late.

"I didn't realize how much I missed this house. I wonder how my parents would feel seeing it again," I said as we walked outside. "I'd never be able to buy anything like it today."

"Well, if it makes you feel any better," Sarah laughed. "Neither would we. Did I say wow? Are you okay?" She turned and gave me a hug.

"I'll be fine," I said, although I wasn't sure I believed it.

In the middle of September, we adopted a store cat. The woman who owned the candle and honey store next door passed away unexpectedly, and suddenly there was this beautiful girl inside the flooring store, crying because she was hungry. Of course, we had to feed her, and when I asked the landlord if any relatives had asked about the cat, he said no one had mentioned her. She was sleek and black, and we named her the Black Dahlia, after the famous unsolved murder in Hollywood. We called her Dahlia for short.

About a week later, I stood in the doorway to the store next door and watched as the landlord packed up the store's contents.

"What will you do with it all?"

"Probably just donate it," he said.

"Hmm."

A crazy idea burst out of my mouth before I could stop it.

"What is the rent on the store?" I asked.

"Two fifty a month. Three, if I have to clear all this stuff out and paint and carpet."

"Hmm," I said again.

"Interested?"

"Well, I know someone who would kill me, but I might be. So, if we do everything, it'll be two hundred fifty a month? Can I cut an opening into our store?"

My reaction seemed to amuse him. "Yup. Don't see why not, as long as you plug it back up if you leave."

"I'll take it. Can I have a month to get it cleaned up? I'll do the painting and flooring."

The owner took his hat off and scratched his head. At that instant, he reminded me of Sam.

"You've got yourself a deal," he laughed. "You young people."

I told Sarah first about the store, and she thought it was a great idea.

"We can put antiques in there, artwork, accessories, gifts..." she said.

"You're as bad as I am," I said. "I can't believe I'm doing this. Will you help me?"

"Of course."

I bit the inside of my cheek. "Now all I have to do is tell Noah," I said.

"So," I said to Noah when I saw him.

He suspected something was going on, I was so excited.

"I'm afraid to ask," he said.

"You know the lady next door with the candles and honey? Well, I can get her store for almost nothing. I told the landlord I'd do the painting and flooring...and we can make an opening into our store." I didn't let him comment before I went on. "If you'll help me, I have time to get the store open for the Scarecrows and Christmas. Or at least for the holidays."

I stopped to take a breath.

"I have the keys, and we can start tomorrow," I said.

He looked at me like I'd lost my mind.

"I give up, Annie."

The next day, Sarah and I sorted through the store merchandise to see if there was anything we could use, and it surprised me how much there was. Josh and Noah started making the opening into the flooring store, and then once all the boxes were out, they took out the old carpet.

"Can we find some pine for flooring? I'd love to have that rather than carpet."

"You can have anything you can pay for," Noah said, shaking his head at me.

We installed pine flooring, painted the walls, added wide pine trim around the doors and windows, and then Noah built me some pine shelves. I found long tree branches, and we hung those as drapery rods for some plaid drapery panels I found. We also hung a small tree on the wall to use for ornaments and wind chimes.

We hung a "Coming Soon" banner in the window while we hunted for antiques at yard sales, and I found a supplier who could quickly ship slender artificial pine trees. We could keep them up year round, and they did a wonderful job filling in spaces that were sparse. I ended up ordering seven more to use in the cabins.

We named the store "At The Cabin" and Sarah drew up our logo, which was a line drawing of the exterior of Noah's cabin. I rushed an order of printed brown shopping bags and found tissue with pine branches to use for gift wrapping.

If everything went well, we'd be open for the town's annual scarecrow competition. I'd missed it last year, so this October, since I had both the stores in town, Sarah and I came up with the largest display we could think of. We brought in bales of straw that could later be donated to Wildhaven Ranch, and added cornstalks, pumpkins, and a western scarecrow couple. We dressed the male as the town sheriff, complete with badge, boots and cowboy hat, and we dressed the female as a saloon girl with a tall feather in her hairpiece. We found a large old wood wagon and lined it up near the side of the building and filled it with more bales of straw and artificial fall flowers.

In a way, I felt guilty being a newcomer and all, when we won first place. We received a blue ribbon, a frameable award certificate which I proudly hung, a write up and photo in the paper, which Sarah framed, and dinner for four at the Grill at the Antler's Inn, in neighboring Twin Peaks.

Chrysteen Braun

Originally built as a dance pavilion in the early 1920s, it was a wonderful restaurant, and we hadn't been there. It would be a perfect place to take Noah, Josh and Sarah, for they were the reason we won the award.

The write up in the newspaper gave the stores great recognition, and I made sure it mentioned the restoration of the Cabins.

In November, with no notice to the mountain community, a drug rehab facility moved into a vacant office building on the highway. They also rented an old vacant lodge across the street, which was put to use as housing. Technically zoning didn't disallow it, and while we all agreed and recognized the need to get people the help they needed to get back into society, no one wanted that type of transient atmosphere in their neighborhoods. The people whose residences backed up to the buildings were most concerned, worrying that the patients would leave the premises and wander about unsupervised.

The newspaper wrote articles, residents complained to the county, and surrounding communities and property owners met and expressed their concerns that their property values would go do down if this new facility was widely publicized. In the meantime, we learned this wasn't the first and only rehab center up in the mountains, but it was the only one with a sign on the building; the rest were private homes in smaller neighborhoods.

During our meetings, we learned there were rules the patients had to abide by; there could be no drugs, alcohol, TV, music or movies. Romantic relationships among residents were not permitted. Attendance at meetings was mandatory. There were restrictions where the clients could go, and their schedules were highly structured.

Smoking was allowed, so what it created was clusters of people standing outside between sessions, smoking and leaning up against the buildings.

"It looks like the line at the unemployment office when you drive by," someone commented.

The homeowners on the hill above the facility regularly complained to the director that smoke filled the air around their properties and they couldn't leave their windows open.

Noah's house was up and over a street, but back far enough that he never really had any issues with them, except they were a negative element in the town. We all agreed it wasn't fair to stereotype people who needed recovery, but everyone also agreed they didn't want to see it in their backyard.

Just when we thought it couldn't get worse, one of the 'clients' went missing. There was a light dusting of snow that night, and even with the drop in temperature, the facility didn't bother alerting the Sheriff. When they realized he was gone, they figured he'd return on his own, but when two more days passed, they finally contacted the parents, who assumed he was still in the facility. There was such bad press from the local newspapers it triggered a chain of inspections from the county and they wrote the facility up on anything and everything.

They'd done an initial cursory search for the young man, but when several more weeks passed and they still hadn't found him, they formed another search, but this time they combed the side of the mountain just below the lodge. And that's where they found him, still partially buried from the newest snowfall. An autopsy confirmed he'd fallen almost three hundred feet, hitting his head countless times on rocks and fallen tree trunks.

Tragically, they determined he hadn't died immediately. He'd lain there, freezing from the falling temperatures. His parents filed a lawsuit and within two weeks, both facilities were closed and all remnants of anyone living there were gone.

No one but the family mourned the young man, and sadly, the town breathed a sigh of relief.

We weren't planning on visiting my parents in Prescott for Thanksgiving that year, so instead, we invited them to join us in the mountains. We were busy with the cabins, and I wanted to work in both stores. They took me up on the offer, since they hadn't been up since they sold our Lake House almost twenty years earlier.

I'd never been on the Lake Arrowhead Queen lake tour, so even though it was cold out, we bundled up in our blankets and we took the guided tour around the lake.

"All the colors of the trees against the backdrop of the gray sky is majestic," my mother said. "I always thought it was, this time of year."

"For those of you young enough," our guide said, "Doris Day and June Lockhart lived over here. And we'll pass Liberace's house in a few minutes. The lake averages a hundred feet deep, although some parts are deeper. And where you see that tower sticking out from the water?" our guide continued, "It stands about forty-three feet above the lake and goes down about a hundred and forty-five feet. They originally built it to release water from the lake for irrigation into San Bernardino, but that plan was scrapped. There's still an elevator that goes down there, but it's not open to the public."

"Thank goodness," my mother said.

Even Noah didn't know the Van Nuys family, (the namesake of the city), was the second owner of the lake; they changed its name from Little Bear to Lake Arrowhead.

"Well, you learn something new every day," he said.

We stopped for a quick lunch and a much needed pit stop at the Cedar Glen Inn, and I shared a turkey sandwich with fries and a Diet Coke with my mother.

Noah chipped in for our meal then said, "I need to pick up some supplies next door at the Trading Post, so I'll meet you outside?"

That afternoon, we made it to the last tour of Wildhaven Ranch wild animal refuge before it closed for the holiday. We watched as the bears got fed, and the raccoons were so cute as they opened jars of food the handlers had given them.

"It makes you think you could reach out and pet them," the Director said, "but always remember they're wild, and not always friendly. They're familiar with us, but that's because we're with them every day."

We watched several bobcats and coyotes catch the food as the handlers tossed them fish and turkey. And a mama deer was nursing her baby.

Nature always amazed me, and I never grew tired of seeing wildlife. I was grateful there was a safe environment where these animals could live, since they'd never be able to be released back into the wild.

After a long day, we dropped my parents off at their cabin for a nap before dinner.

On Thanksgiving Day, Ginny made a turkey dinner with mashed potatoes and dressing. My mother brought the cranberry sauce, pumpkin pie, and a green bean casserole from the grocery store. Sarah brought cut up veggies and dip, and I brought canned corn, dinner rolls, Brussels sprouts and cauliflower casseroles also ordered from the market.

We set the largest table in the coffee shop with a tablecloth, cloth napkins, wine glasses, water glasses and all different sizes of plates. We moved the chairs away from the counter and set everything up buffet style.

I told my parents about seeing the Lake House on the home tour and how the newest store came about. My mother was delighted to see Sarah after so many years, and Sarah talked about being a graphic designer, and how much she enjoyed being creative.

"I'm kind of at an impasse at the moment," Sarah shared. "Mark and I are still technically married, but..." then she paused and sighed. "I'm obviously going to have to figure out what I want to do. In the meantime, I absolutely love it up here. I've been helping Annie at the stores, and I've actually had a few small graphics jobs."

"And you have a new friend?"

My mother had a way of gently extracting information from someone when she wanted to know something.

"Yess, I do," she replied sheepishly.

Sarah looked over at Josh, who was talking with Noah and my father.

"Not only is he handsome, but he's thoughtful and warm-hearted. And very down to earth. Like Noah," she added.

"Sounds perfect, doesn't he?" I interjected as I came to sit with them.

"Oh, shush," Sarah said, blushing.

"Well, let's eat," Sam said. "I'm hungry."

My parents loved Sam and Ginny and the cabins. It had been different having my parents here in my world, in my 'home', and not at all uncomfortable. It made me feel I'd grown up a little, settling into my new life. And they'd accepted it all. They connected with everyone, and my father, who was normally on the reserved side, had no problems getting caught up in all the conversations. I could tell he felt a sense of relief that I was secure up here with my friends.

I knew I was an adult, but I didn't feel comfortable staying with Noah. We only had two guests, so Sarah and I stayed in our cabins and my parents settled into their own. Friday, I showed them the flooring store and At The Cabin, and then we toured the lake. I took them to Timberline in Cedar Glen and that night, we had dinner again at Ginny's. On Saturday, we went out in Noah's boat and he offered my mother the wheel, but she declined. I told her I'd told him about her and our boat, and her face flushed. I'd never noticed it in her before, but now I knew where I inherited that dreadful trait.

On Sunday, they headed back to Prescott. Before they left, I asked about the little neighbor next door.

"Oh," my mother said, "not too long ago his dog died, and he was so depressed he rarely left his motor home. His daughter insisted he move back near her in Tucson, which they all agreed made sense; so she came out, packed him up, sold the motor home, and he moved."

My mother said it when they were saying their goodbyes. "You've made a place here, Annie, and we're really proud of you."

"Thanks, Mom." I said as I kissed her goodbye.

"It seems Sarah's going to find her way again, too," she said, giving me a hug.

"I hope she does."

CHAPTER TWELVE
Hudson

I met my first wife, Deborah, in Oregon, a few years after I graduated. We were at a birthday party for a mutual friend, and she introduced herself. She was bright, attractive, and had an exceptional personality. We seemed to be an ideal match, so within six months, we married. We stayed in Oregon, and I continued working full time for the Forest Service. I added to my college education compliments of the U.S. Government by attending law school and working towards my Doctor of Engineering.

Although I knew I wanted children eventually, I hoped to postpone having them for a while. My life was full. I was so busy with work and with school, I often joked that I couldn't figure out how I'd had time to father our two boys when they finally came. Deborah would assure whoever I told that to, that indeed I was their real father. She never thought it was as witty as I did.

It surprised me she actually listened to my choices for their names; if the children were boys, I liked Hamilton and Coleman. I had thought little about girl's names so I told her she could choose whatever she liked and I'd be happy no matter what she came up with.

Life was crazy. Deborah was a teacher and went back to work after each of the boys was born. She kept busy with them and their schoolwork, and she was an exemplary mother. She was involved with the PTA and always made sure the boys had nourishing school lunches and snacks. Even if I wasn't home to eat dinner with them, she'd set a place at the table for me and then keep my plate in the oven. She was a den mother when the boys went through the Boy Scouts stage. I was always too busy to go on their camping trips, so she went with them and the other parents.

She went to all the parent-teacher conferences; she taught them how to bake cookies for the school bake sale, and she was on the school carnival committee. I, on the other hand, got to hear all about the experiences they shared, and tried to make it a point to focus on what they were saying. I gave kudos and hugs and said, "I wish I could have been there."

I'm not sure exactly when I realized I'd inherited the absent parenting role so similar to my mother's. There, but not really there. That's something I've thought about for years. Although they seemed to have grown up in spite of me, I've often wondered how much harm I'd done to my boys.

I wanted them to have a nanny, like I did, but Deborah was never keen on the idea. We did have a babysitter, but no one who was with the boys full time. I think she was right in not giving in to me about that; children need their parents, or at least one of them who can be active in their upbringing.

Because I was around the pilots in the Forest Service, I grew more and more interested in flying, so I convinced Deborah I wouldn't kill myself in a plane crash if I bought my own plane. She wasn't very pleased, but the boys were old enough to think it was awesome. I've always been the type of person who, once I have an idea, I figure out how to bring it to fruition.

It was a 1939 single engine two-seat Aeronca Chief, and of course this meant I spent the balance of any free time I might have, at the hangar, restoring it. I encouraged the boys to help me on the weekends, and at first they loved it; it wasn't long, however, before the novelty of having to actually work, wore off. Cleaning airplane parts isn't particularly interesting, unless, of course, you have a passion for them like I did.

This was about this same time I met my real father, Joseph Keller.

My mother never talked about him while I was growing up; once I'd asked about him and her answer was "He just disappeared." I accepted that and hadn't been curious enough to find out more about him. I assumed he'd died, and I was happy enough with The General.

One Sunday afternoon, though, it took me totally by surprise when a man who looked like an older version of me showed up on my doorstep. Although it was a warm day, he wore a plaid flannel shirt, black pants and a worn leather belt.

"Hudson Keller?" he asked somewhat hesitantly.

No one had ever addressed me with that last name, so I was a little puzzled.

"Hudson Fisher, but yes, Hudson Keller," I said.

"I'm your father," he then blurted out. He held his hand out to shake mine, but when I didn't instantly take it, he pulled it back.

"Oh," was all I could think to say.

"Who is it?" Deborah called from somewhere upstairs.

"I've got it," I said.

Then, to my father, I said, "I didn't even know you were alive."

He gave me an apologetic smile. "I was away for a while, and then I needed to start my life over."

He had me hooked. I invited him in. I motioned him to my office, where we wouldn't be interrupted.

"Something to drink?" I asked.

"Water is good."

"I'll be right back."

Deborah was in the kitchen by then and I whispered hoarsely, "My father is here!"

"What?"

"My real father." I got ice out of the freezer and made two glasses of water for us.

Deborah was speechless. "I'll wait here," she said.

When I went back in to the office, my father was standing by the framed photographs on the mantel, studying them.

"It looks like you've done well," he said, taking the glass of water.

"Well, I've certainly tried. I've had my ups and downs."

"It looks like you have a wonderful family."

I wanted to ask, 'Why are you here? Now?' but I didn't. He sat in one of my chairs and began to talk.

"You were just a baby when I was taken away. We were in Pearl Harbor when it was attacked, and I was out scouting a movie location. I was a movie producer then—and you were at home in our little rented cottage with your mother. She put you in the icebox to protect you."

He paused and I could tell he was thinking about how he would continue his story.

"You see," he started. "I was so worried about you both and had a hard time getting back there. Because the attack had just happened, no one could get in or out. But when I did finally make it, your mother and you were there, and I was so relieved. A couple of days later, the State Department pounded on our door, and they arrested me for being a Nazi sympathizer." He waited a moment for me to digest this. "It was a misunderstanding, of course."

"Wait. Are you saying you've been in prison all this time?"

"No. I was eventually released, but my life, as I'd known it, was over. Ruined. I was a movie producer and I couldn't go back to Hollywood. There was a time when Germany wanted to keep America from producing films that might depict them unfavorably. Unfortunately, it's a long story, and I was mistaken for a Nazi sympathizer."

I wasn't sure what to say.

"So, what have you been doing all this time? Did you try to find my mother?"

"I obviously knew where she was since her career had taken off, but no, I didn't try to see her. I felt it was best for her, and for you, if I stayed away."

This was crazy.

"So, where have you been?"

"Your mother and I were eventually divorced, so I moved to central California, where I ended up meeting a woman, and I started a new family there. I know that must sound cowardly, but I knew I could never have a life with your mother and you again."

"What the hell?" *I said aloud.* "So I have brothers or sisters?"

"Yes, a brother and a sister. And I'm happily married, and yet there isn't a day that goes by that I don't think about you. So, I had to find you and see for myself." He sounded almost proud of himself.

"Do your other children know about me?"

"No."

"Does your wife?"

"Yes."

I didn't know whether to kick him out or punch him. I decided on neither and just sat there trying to digest this news.

"How did you make a living?" I finally asked.

"Well, I'm a bit of an inventor, it seems, so I've patented several things, and have done quite well, actually."

"Jesus," I said, sighing.

My father stood then and prepared to leave. "Well, I just wanted to let you know I was still alive, and if you ever want to reach me, here's where I am." He gave me a piece of paper with his address and phone number on it. "I'll be going now," he said, making his way to the front door.

Foolishly, I just stood there on the porch and watched him leave.

I looked at this man who turned to wave at me, and I could think of nothing to do but wave back at him. There was no doubt he was my father; he was more slender than I was and had thinning gray hair. But we had the same eyes.

Until this time, I'd always been so sure of myself, but this was one of the few times in my life I didn't really know what to do. So I closed the door behind me and let him walk away. Dazed, I just stood there with my back against the door.

When Deborah finally came into the entry, she raised her eyebrows in anticipation of an explanation.

I felt foolish, but all I could think of to say was, "It was my father. He wanted me to know he was still around."

I had shared nothing about my real father with her since I knew nothing about him myself. I'd told her the Pearl Harbor story, but the rest of my childhood had been living with The General. I'd just accepted my life as it had been presented to me.

Of course, I called my mother, who was clearly surprised by Joseph's visit. But once she had a minute to digest what I shared with her, she simply said, "Oh, he wouldn't have been the best role model for you, anyway. We did much better with Andrew." Then she went on to tell me about her current movie project.

Looking back over the years I knew Joseph, I never felt a deep connection with him. Because he'd never been in my life, I couldn't picture him anywhere in it. I saw him a few more times before he died, and each time I did, I'd ask him questions that had stayed with me;

"Were you a Nazi?"

"No. But I knew some men who were sympathizers. I was guilty by association. And the funny thing was, like so many men in Hollywood, I'm Jewish."

"Why didn't you find me?"

"Your mother was insistent I didn't. She's quite a force to be reckoned with, which I'm sure you know. And her career was at stake. And—I did find you once, but I didn't have the courage to meet you, and then it was too late."

I met his new family, but we had nothing in common; no childhood memories, no similar interests. Nothing. His children had just found out about me before he died, and his funeral was awkward for all of us, to say the least. My father was older beyond his years, and I could only imagine what he'd gone through being incarcerated. I cared about him as a person, but I didn't mourn him as my father when he was gone. I've felt like there was something wrong with me for having this lack of sentimentality, but when I shared my concerns with Deborah, she said, "It's kind of like adopting someone else's pet. You never really love them the way you would if they'd been yours since they were a baby."

I thought that was an odd analogy, but in a way, it made sense.

CHAPTER THIRTEEN

Sam planned a get together with some of his old WWII buddies, and the first week in December they all flew in. He'd stayed in touch with ten of them over the years, and they'd been wanting to have a mini reunion for some time. I'd agreed when he asked about doing it up in the mountains, and we definitely had enough room for them to stay. If they all made it up, we'd bring in some roll away beds and put two in a cabin. It was the least I could do to thank him for everything he'd done for me. Sarah and I could stay at Noah's.

Sam was all fidgety and nervous during that week. He checked the weather every day and the cabins at least twice that I knew of to make sure everything was perfect, including having plenty of firewood and snacks in each. I'd wanted to reline the fire pit, so Noah brought in some large stones, and he and Sam laid them in a large circle.

His friends coordinated their incoming flights, so they all flew in on Friday morning within an hour of each other. Noah and Josh offered to be drivers for the weekend and went down with Sam to meet them all at the airport. I had bottles of water and baskets of fruits and nuts waiting for them in the cabins and was getting a little anxious myself, but looking forward to meeting them all.

They drew straws to see who would sleep where, and then got settled in. It was just before lunch, and they decided to grab a bite at Ginny's, so they headed into town and took over the back tables at her restaurant.

Everyone wanted to see the lake, so they piled back into the two Jeeps and Noah and Sam took them on a tour.

When they returned, we moved the Adirondack chairs into a circle and built a fire in the pit. Most of the guys wanted to take a quick nap, but a couple of them sat around and talked. Sam lit the fire with wood he'd been gathering all week. Most of the guys smoked, and we set out large soup cans Ginny gave us, and filled them with dirt. We always worried about campfires in the mountains, but Sam knew what to look out for and kept a close eye on how big the fire got.

Everyone wanted a light dinner, so we ordered sandwiches, fries and chips and I picked them up. Ginny packed up a couple dozen cookies for dessert. We set up a cooler with sodas, beer, and water.

One of the guys had lost a leg, and walked with crutches, and one pinned up his shirt sleeve where he'd lost an arm. They all complained about their aches, pains and injuries, and I worried they'd be unstable on the somewhat uneven grounds, but they assured me they'd be okay.

"Now don't go worryin' about us," Sam said, and they all laughed.

Everyone wanted to hit the sack early, so Sam extinguished the fire. They agreed to get up at dawn, go have a big breakfast, then see if they could all fit in Noah's boat. We packed lunches and drinks, and they promised to be careful and not drink too much.

I spent the next day in the store, and we were busy. I met a few new people who were interested in working on their homes, and we set up appointments for the next week. Sarah had accompanied me on consultations, so she could learn about the design process, and if she helped me with selections, it freed me up to work up pricing.

That night, Noah and I joined the guys at the Cowboy Bar. They were still talking about their war stories, some of them laughing at the stupid things they'd done, and how it was amazing they hadn't gotten themselves killed. Noah and I danced, and as usual, when he held me in his arms, he hummed along with the music.

When we got back to the cabins, the men settled around the campfire again, and as we watched the fire crackle, Jezebel came out and made friends with everyone.

"It looks like you have a piece of heaven up here, Sam," one of the guys said.

"I like to think I do. Of course, when my wife was alive, it was darned near perfect. I can laugh about it now, but I remember our first winter up here and, to put it mildly, we weren't prepared. The previous owner left us with shovels, but had always paid someone to clear the property when it snowed. I, on the other hand, wanted to live the life, so I went to Sears and bought me a snow blower. I took the salesman's word when he said it would be perfect for clearing the parking area and the walkways to the cabins.

"But a snow blower couldn't keep up with all the winter storms that year, and I finally had to break down and hire someone like everyone else did. Trucks with those snowplows attached to the fronts were up and down the highway several times a day. They did a great job of clearing the snow so people could drive on the roads, but they also created huge mounds that blocked some people, including us, from getting in and out of their property."

"Where I live in Colorado, we have the same problem," one of the men said. "I'm out there sometimes every few hours, but I love the outdoors."

"And what about you, Noah?" someone asked. "You and Sam seem pretty tight."

"Sam and I go way back," he said. "I was still in high school when we got to know each other. I'd help Sam clearing leaves and trimming bushes. Then when I lost my parents, I hung out with Sam here. He and I would build campfires and just sit and talk. Once, I brought home a dog thinking we could use the company. He was a chocolate Lab, and I called him Bear, and Sam said, 'Hell, no. We don't need no dog.' And I said, let's just give it a day or so and see what happens. Otherwise, I'll have to take him to the pound."

"Of course I had to let him stay." Sam interjected. "One night we *did* have a scare, though. Bear ran off chasing a squirrel into the woods, and he didn't come home that night. If you love your animals, you don't leave them outside once it gets dark. Not that we'd seen any bear around lately, but you never know when one will wander in. I couldn't keep images of that dog getting mauled out of my mind. It like to made me crazy all night."

"He did come home the next morning," Noah said, "Hungry. And we scolded him. He lowered his head for a minute, but he had no idea what he'd done wrong. So to make up to us, he came over and licked us both."

Everyone laughed.

"I have two dogs now. Rufus, who I found roaming around up here, and then Coco. She used to belong to my next-door neighbor, Jane. Well, one night, Coco barked her head off just about all night. At about four in the morning, when I couldn't stand it any longer, I got dressed and went next door to see what was going on. Turns out, Jane had fallen down her stairs and hit her head. I knew she wasn't alive, but I called the Sheriff and an ambulance. When they got there, they confirmed her death.

"I kept Coco for a couple of days until they could reach a relative; they found a niece in Michigan, I think. She flew out to take care of Jane's affairs, but she didn't have any use for a dog, so I told her I'd keep her. She and Rufus got along well, so what was one more mouth to feed?"

"We had a bird dog when I was growing up in North Carolina," one of the other men said. He stubbed his cigarette out in the tin can nearest him. "Purty was her name. One morning when me and my brother went out to play, we couldn't find her. We kept calling and calling and then we went out to the old woodpile where we liked to hide. There was Purty, and every time we got near her, she'd growl at us. Now, she'd never done that before, and when we went back and got our mother, she came out to see what was going on. Sure enough, when she got near that wood pile, there was Purty, growling at her too."

He took a swig from his beer bottle and then sat it down.

"Well, J.D., what the heck happened?" one of the other men asked.

"Don't rush me now. I was just takin' a breather. Well, we never could figure out what the heck was goin' on with that dog, so when my dad finally got home, we told him all about it, and he told us to wait in the house while he took his shotgun and went out there to see for himself. Well, lo and behold, when he came close to that woodpile,

Purty growled at him too. My dad scratched his head, and then walked around to the other side where Purty was standing, and she took up her pointin' position. Right there was a large copperhead snake just mindin' his own business."

"Well, what'd your dad do?" Another of the men asked.

"Why, he kilt it."

We decided to call it a day, and as we got up to leave, Noah reminded the guys he and Josh would be back around noon to get them back down to the airport so they could catch their flights.

"We'll let you guys get back to your war stories," I said. "Good night."

"Thanks for your hospitality, Annie."

"Good to meet you all."

"Thanks, Noah."

"See ya tomorrow."

"Thanks," Sam said as he got up to give me a hug. "This couldn't have worked out any better."

"You're welcome. I've enjoyed meeting the guys and listening to you all talk. Get a good night."

That night in bed, Noah and I joked about how we'd started acting like an old married couple, talking about things that'd happened during the day. It was our quiet time when I could tell him about how the store did, and he could talk about his jobs.

As much as I loved Noah's dogs, they were a lot bigger than sleeping with my cats, so we'd made a rule they could sleep with us in our room, but in their own new beds. But most nights, just when we got comfortable, first Rufus would jump up, then Coco, and once they got comfortable, we didn't have the heart to make them get down.

"I think they wait until they think we're asleep," I said.

"I think you're right."

That night, we talked about how much Sam enjoyed seeing his buddies, and I wanted to remember to tell him to invite them back next year if he wanted to.

"That's a great idea," Noah said. "I'll mention it too."

"I enjoyed hearing about you and him when you were younger. He loves you, you know."

"I know. The feeling's mutual. He's been there for me, and now it's my turn to make sure he's doing okay." Then he chuckled. "I'll never forget the time he tried to talk to me about the birds and bees, though. He was so uncomfortable. My parents were gone by then. I was dating a girl and one day, Sam called me over to sit with him.

'I don't know how to talk to you about this,' he said.

'Just talk to me, like you always do.' I said.

'You and that gal friend are getting pretty serious, heh?'

'Yeah, I think so.'

'Well, are you bein' careful?'

I know I turned beet red, getting the gist of what he was referring to. I finally answered, 'Yes, Sam. We're being careful.'

'Good,' he sighed. 'Not that I don't want any grandchildren…'

'Ok, Gramps.' I said. 'You don't have to worry. You won't be a grandpa just yet.'

"The girl and I broke up a little after that."

Noah crawled over Coco and landed on top of me. "I would like to give him grandkids one day, though."

He kissed me.

"Are you sure you want to do this in front of the kids?" I joked.

The next day, while the guys were at the airport, Sarah and I stayed with Sam at the cabins and started cleaning everything up. We moved all the Adirondack chairs back in front of the cabins, then cleared the fire pit and used the rocks to re-line the flowerbed in front of the office. We stripped the bedding, and I figured I'd be doing laundry forever. I thought about taking it all to the laundromat instead of doing so many loads, but I didn't want to spend the time and money. Plus, I felt our own washer and dryer were more sanitary, so I put the first load in and went back to cleaning.

Sam started cleaning the bathrooms and kitchenettes, and when Noah and Josh got back from the airport, they vacuumed each cabin. Sarah and I made all the beds and replaced the towels.

We set all the heaters to the low fifties, so we wouldn't have frozen pipes. I'd learned the hard way last year, when I hadn't turned the heater up in cabin six after being vacant most of the summer. When Sam tried to run the water, the pipes had frozen. He and Noah knew what to do, and we averted a disaster of the pipe bursting.

Once we locked up the last cabin, I said, "My treat. Dinner at Ginny's."

"It's getting cloudy out," Sam said. "Looks like we've missed the rain."

As we pulled into the parking lot, the sky opened up and as we ran for cover of the entrance, Sam said, "Looks like all hell's broke loose!"

Conversation during dinner turned towards the weather and Sam said to Noah, "Remember when the rocks on Highway 18 loosened up past Crestline and a big boulder landed on the road?" Then, to the rest of us, he said, "There was a terrible pile up. A group of motorcyclists drove right into that mess and I think two guys were killed."

"You're right. That was pretty bad, all right," Noah said.

"You know, man carved his way into this here mountain, creating unnatural places for roads. We're lucky we don't have more accidents, but that's why you have to be extra careful, especially going through the narrow part of the highway."

CHAPTER FOURTEEN
Sarah

The day we graduated from high school, my bus ticket out of town was burning a hole in my pocket. I'd considered not taking part in the ceremony at all, but Annie made me promise I would. Even though we wouldn't sit together, it would be the last time we'd see each other before I left.

Annie's mother had given me the money to rent my gown and bought us both bouquets of mixed flowers. My mother and sisters were there, and Annie's mother took photos of us with her Polaroid camera.

"Tassels on the left," Mrs. C called out to us.

My sister Jess took the one of me with Annie and her parents.

"Take two of me and Sarah," Annie told her. "That way, we can each have one."

"Why don't you take these," Mrs. C said, sorting through the photos and handing my mother the ones of me with my sisters and her.

We'd been invited to celebrate later with Annie's family, but I'd already told Annie and Mrs. C we wouldn't be there.

"Maybe you can sneak by later," Mrs. C said to me.

I thought Annie was going to cry.

I hadn't told my mother I was planning on leaving; I didn't want to deal with her theatrics, plus it added to the mystique and adventure of my journey. I was eighteen, so there was nothing she could have done to stop me, anyway. I'd never been to Las Vegas before, but I'd seen pictures in magazines of all the lights on the strip, and of scantily clad cocktail waitresses and showgirls on stage. It seemed to have the promise of adventure on every corner. Annie had gone with me to the library to look up the local college, and it had everything to offer that a local college in Long Beach would have; And it would be free once I was a resident.

The minute I got there, I'd find a place to stay and get a job.

Most of the passengers on the bus either slept or smoked the five hours it took to get to our destination, and my mind raced with the possibilities my future would bring. I was on my own, and part of me felt liberated and unrestrained. I pictured going to college, having a nice place to live, and then finally making a living. Not being successful was never an option.

I leaned my head against the window and eventually dozed. When I woke, it was dark; the desert was black and only now and then would I see a light from some building far away. My confidence seemed to have faded a little, and then I realized I could see the stars, and I tried to focus on those. As we came down that last hill on the highway, the lights of Las Vegas gleamed in the darkness, beckoning us, and I could see my future. I knew then I could be anyone, and do anything I wanted to.

The moment I got off the bus, I felt the blast of heat; even at midnight it was over a hundred degrees, and I felt like I was in an oven. I'd not given the summer desert temperature much thought when I made my plans. I took a deep breath, and it burned my throat. I obviously hadn't done my homework.

There was a makeshift bulletin board by the ticket window, so after I got my bags, I ventured over there to see if anything interesting had been posted. There were several index cards listing rooms for rent, and the one that specified "Female Only" caught my eye. It was too late to call right then, so I found a taxi driver and asked where there was somewhere safe and reasonable I could stay for the night.

I was unfamiliar with the area, and it wasn't until we drove for a while that I realized he could be taking me somewhere dangerous. My imagination got the best of me as I thought about being forced to become a sex slave, or worse.

101

"Where are we going?" I finally asked.

"I know good place for you. Is safe."

In a few minutes, we pulled into the Golden Nugget Hotel.

"Is this affordable?"

With all the bright lights, it didn't look it.

"Oh yes. You'll see. And safe. Here is my number. Call me if you need to go somewhere. I'll come if I can."

"Thanks," I said, taking his card.

I'd never stayed in a hotel, and it was heavenly. I had my own bathroom, and a full sized bed. The first thing I did after I turned the air conditioning up was unpack and then soak in the tub.

That night I slept like a log.

The next morning, I called on the room for rent and I was in luck; it was still available. I called the cab driver from the night before, and he took me to see it. Only one girl was home, but I felt comfortable with her, so we agreed I'd become the third roommate.

They worked as housekeepers, so I decided that's what I'd do too until I could find something better. I found a job at a small motel, but that lasted less than a month. The place was a dump, and the hours were unstable.

The first few weeks I was there, I'd get nervous if I saw a police car heading my way. It didn't matter that my mother had no idea where I was, or that I wasn't in any trouble; I was still worried I'd be found and returned home.

My second job was at another small hotel, but I was much more comfortable there. I still cleaned rooms, but most of the guests left tips in the room and the atmosphere was more upbeat. Cleaning rooms would not be my permanent means of income, so I started looking around for something better.

I knew enough to not quit one job until I found another, so before I gave my notice, I found a position being a hostess at a hotel restaurant where I could eventually make good money as a waitress. I knew how to defend myself, thanks to my good ol' dad, so that's the job I took. They kept trying to recruit me to become part of the entertainment, but I didn't want to go down that road, no matter how tight my budget was.

To save money on tuition, I had to claim Nevada residency, which meant I needed to have lived there for twelve months. But when six months passed, I wasn't willing to wait another six to start college. Since I still had money set aside, I went ahead and paid the higher tuition and started taking some of the general education classes at the community college on the days I had off. I knew the only way I'd make it on my own was to get a degree in something.

Between working and classes, I had little time for dating. I met Mark in my English class. He always made it a point to sit next to me, and would set a paper on my chair indicating it was taken if I happened to be late to class.

"Thanks," I'd say, as I set my notebook down.

"Absolutely," he said. "I wanted to make sure you had a seat."

"English is not my favorite subject," I one day confessed.

He swore he never studied, but I really had to focus.

"Well, I'm very good at English. If you ever need any help, all you have to do is let me know," he offered. "I can quiz you, help you where you think you need it."

He wanted to become an accountant, and he was kind of a nerd. Everyone else wore jeans and tee shirts, but he wore khaki pants and nicely pressed shirts. He had an annoying habit of pushing his glasses up on to his nose, whether or not they actually slid down, so I was glad when he finally got contacts a few months later.

Mark and I just somehow became an item. I don't remember falling madly in love with him, although he always said it was love at first sight for him. He was very kind to me, always asking if I was happy, and doing little things like bringing me flowers.

I'd never slept with anyone before him, but quickly learned he was not a very good lover. He was a fumbler; he was awkward with his hands, and groped me clumsily and unskillfully. Despite that, we moved in together before I graduated.

By this time, I knew I wanted to become a graphic designer. I learned that graphic design was in everything; advertising, magazine layout, newspaper ads, brochures and even menus. I loved the classes and ended up having a great internship at a large firm that published magazines on art and fashion.

I also learned about doing logos. I started doing them in the evenings for small companies who couldn't afford to hire big design companies and ended up building a nice side business.

Mark constantly talked about getting married, but before we did, he wanted me to quit the hotel job and find a "more suitable" place to work; I had to agree. I knew I wouldn't be working there forever, so I transitioned to one of the larger hotels and started as a hostess in the twenty-four-hour restaurant. I wasn't always happy with my shifts, but I made great tips. Sometimes I felt like all I did was work and go to school, but I'd promised myself I'd stick it out and get my degree.

I held out for over a year before I ran out of excuses why we couldn't get married, so we finally did. I found an inexpensive off-white suit that I could hopefully wear again, and Mark rented a blue tuxedo. His parents came out from Arkansas, and his mother wore a brown dress with black shoes.

We booked a thirty-minute chapel wedding with pre-recorded music and a canned ceremony. A friend of Mark's was his best man, and a gal I worked with at the hotel was my maid of honor. She wore an old green party dress so she wouldn't have to buy something new.

The entire time I stood there, I kept asking myself why I was doing this.

After the ceremony, we had a nice dinner at the hotel where I worked so we could get a discount. We spent our honeymoon at the Golden Nugget, where I'd spent my first night in Vegas, and Mark's parents booked a room there too. The next morning, we had breakfast at the buffet where Mark's dad couldn't get over how much food there was to choose from. I had an early shift at the hotel, and had to go to work, so Mark spent the day showing his parents the sights. They stayed another night, and Mark gave them a tour of the town and they got to see the dazzling lights and crowds of people. We had a late dinner at the coffee shop in the hotel, and then in the morning, they caught their plane back home. I sensed it would be the last time I saw them.

"They loved you," Mark said, as we saw them off. "I knew they would."

I'll never forget a single detail on Mark's glowing face as he sighed with satisfaction with his new life.

He loved me, and I knew he would have done anything to make me happy. On the contrary, I felt like I'd just awakened from a terrible dream; one where I'd just made the worst decision in my life. Then, a terrifying realization came over me: I was stuck.

I knew it wouldn't be long before I would break his heart, and he deserved much more than I could give him.

Mark had night classes for over a year while I worked two jobs. We hardly saw each other, and when we were together, the first thing he wanted to do was have sex. I purposely avoided intimacy and began pretending to be sleeping when he rolled over to initiate lovemaking.

I continued to work part time for the graphic design firm, learning the ins and outs of business while I also worked to develop my own business. I finally worked into a waitress position at the steak house. I could count on good tips, which meant I could start setting aside more money. I was one step closer to freedom.

I wonder now how I was able to keep up the pace. But I think first of all, it was because I could, and second, it meant I didn't have to continually dodge Mark.

I wasted the next two years figuring out ways to ease my restlessness. I had a one-night stand with a cute shoe salesman at the mall. I was older than he was, but the way he flirted with me sparked a desire in me, and he made me feel attractive.

Then I met someone at a club after work, and we went back to his place. I blamed my unfaithfulness on having too much to drink. But the most reckless of all was having an affair with a client at the graphic design firm. He was absolutely gorgeous. I'd never met a man who was so handsome that he made me act stupid. There was an irresistible magnetism between the two of us, and I didn't miss his obvious implications when he touched my hand for the first time.

"I'd love to see you," he said, slowly searching my face with his eyes.

Our eyes locked, and for a moment I couldn't speak.

"Where are you staying?" I finally asked, but it came out more like a whisper.

He was only in town for the meeting with me and a senior designer. I'd done the presentation and my senior designer planned on joining us in a few minutes, so we quickly planned to meet for dinner at his hotel.

We had wine first, and every time we took a sip, our eyes met and my heart raced. He didn't try to hide the fact he was waiting for our meal to end so he could get me into bed. My stomach was doing so many flip-flops, I had a hard time eating. I'd never been this aroused by a man. Ever.

I knew it was passion I was missing, but I'd never imagined the breadth of it. It was the way he touched me and magically explored me; and I let him in. I let him see this side of me that had remained hidden, tucked away. And I felt I'd earned this satisfaction.

And when he left, the sense of loss was overwhelming. The worst of it was I went back to being me.

Me with Mark, who thought lovemaking was the same as having sex.

About a year later, at the steakhouse, I met a very handsome and charming high roller who always asked for me when he came in. He was on the tall side, with dark hair and a mustache. His name was Nico, and his approach was respectable; he never touched me, but the way he would sometimes look at me made me extremely self-conscious. I could sense lust and desire in him, and it made me a little nervous.

He started coming in every week, and I grew curious about him, so I asked my manager.

"Stay away from that bad boy," was all she said. "I can tell he has the hots for you."

"He's so intense," was all I could think of to describe him.

She just shook her head. "Don't forget you have a sweet little husband at home," and she walked away.

Thinking about Mark made me come to my senses, but only until I saw Nico the next week. Our hostess was away from the reservation desk, so when he came in I seated him. As I walked ahead of him, I felt his eyes burning into my back. I took him to his regular table and fumbled with the menu. I knew he didn't need one, as he always ordered the New York steak medium, which he most likely would tonight as well.

"Your usual?" I asked, referring to his drink.

"Sure thing," he said, winking at me.

I went to the bar and ordered a Godfather, which was a Scotch and Amaretto.

Jack the bartender asked, "Nico?"

I nodded.

"Here you go."

When I took the drink to his table, he was still watching me, and my heart danced a little. He must have sensed it, for he touched my wrist as I set the drink down. "What time do you get off tonight?" he asked quietly.

I flashed my wedding ring at him, but he just shrugged.

"Let me think about it," I said, knowing I must have turned beet red.

This went on for a couple of weeks, and each time his touch was hot to my skin. I was looking for trouble, but I didn't care.

"Midnight," I finally said.

"Make the steak rare tonight," Nico said. "I'll need my stamina."

Was I going to take him up on his offer? My body ached for him, but I knew I was treading into dangerous territory. What would I tell Mark? Why would I need to be out all night? Nico gave me a key with his room number on it.

What was I going to do?

I had butterflies in my stomach all evening. Part of me felt alive and willing to get involved with someone like Nico. I wanted excitement. I assumed he wasn't the type of man to offer any type of stability, but that's what made him so appealing. That and the hope that he would be a wonderful lover.

When I had a break, I called home and left a message on our answering machine telling Mark that a couple of the girls and I were going to a midnight show, then have a late dinner or early breakfast.

As soon as I could finish my side work, I made a hasty retreat to the locker room and changed into street clothes. I put my uniform in a bag so I could wash it for tomorrow. I found the bank of elevators that went up to Nico's rooms. I hesitated at his door, but only for a moment as I knocked quietly, and then let myself in.

He was sitting in an armchair, legs crossed, and his grin was irresistible. He had remained dressed, which I found both odd but also respectful. If he'd been lying in his bed naked, I'd have definitely felt more awkward.

"I'd love to take a quick shower," I said.

"Sure, help yourself."

I turned towards the bathroom, but Nico called to me. "No, l want to watch you."

He remained seated while I took my top off and laid it on another chair.

"Slowly," he whispered. "Take your bra off."

His smile widened in approval.

"Just as I imagined. Now, your pants and underwear."

He came and stood so close to me I could feel the heat from his body. I don't know why, probably nervousness, but I moved away and quickly made my way to the bathroom where I closed the door and turned on the shower.

I needed to be careful to keep my hair dry, since there would be no logical reason for me to come home with it wet. Within a few minutes, Nico pulled the shower curtain back and stood there with such arousal I could hardly keep from staring.

"I love my women in the shower," he said, caressing first my face and neck and then running his fingers down my breasts. He brought me to such a high point, I thought I might actually faint. But he held me as he led me to his bed and brought us both to such an intense pleasure, I felt drugged.

I laid there for a few moments, trying to catch my breath and get my bearings again. Nico was obviously pleased with himself and his prowess.

"Are you happy?" he asked coyly.

"Oh, my God, yes," was all I could say.

And I knew it forever changed me as a woman.

I continued to see Nico for almost a year. I really struggled with myself over the mess I'd gotten myself into. With Nico, every time we were together, he made me feel beautiful, sexy, and alive. I loved looking at his firm body, the shape of his legs, and I loved the hair on his chest. The anticipation until our next moment together would sometimes distract me, and I found myself cringing every time Mark wanted to make love. I knew it wasn't his fault; he was just so...so bland.

That was it. Life with Mark was bland.

And because Nico was such an experienced lover, no matter what Mark did to try to please me, it was never enough. I knew what I was doing was hurting him. It was making everything worse. Our marriage was hopeless, but it'd been that way since the beginning.

Nico unlocked a passion in me I'd never thought possible. He fascinated me, and I was almost powerless to resist him. I also knew that I couldn't continue to live like this, being unfaithful to Mark, and thinking of only myself. But every time I told myself I needed to stop, I couldn't.

The only thing I could think of doing was leaving, so that's what I ultimately did. I quit my job at the hotel, and then I left Mark a note telling him I was sorry, and that I needed to go away for a while.

And I quit Nico too. I didn't leave a note, I just never showed up for our next rendezvous.

CHAPTER FIFTEEN
Hudson

Sitting on my desk when I arrived home late one evening was my ten-year college reunion invitation. My first response was that I wasn't interested. I'd never been a party guy, and I quickly made a mental list of people I'd kept in touch with.

None.

Plus, Deborah expressed no interest in going.

"Being in a room full of people I don't know and making small talk doesn't sound fun to me," were her exact words.

Memories of my ten-year high school reunion should have been enough to settle it; I went to it keeping a watch out for my swim teammates and the slender girls who flocked around us after a meet. Instead, what I discovered was that ten years could do a lot of damage to our waistlines, physiques and hairlines. I turned around and left.

College would be worse, depending on one's expectation level.

But, even taking all that into consideration, I still decided to risk a boring evening and attend. I sent in my money along with a brief description of all my accomplishments since graduating and marked the date on my calendar.

I'd actually forgotten about going until Deborah reminded me it was the next weekend. For a moment, I wondered why I even considered going, but being a cheapskate, I didn't want to waste the money I spent on the ticket. So when Saturday night came around, I did what most women I know would do; I went through my closet until I found the perfect outfit; a casual sport coat and pants. No tie for me.

"Dressing for success?" Deborah asked, poking her head into our bedroom.

"Nah."

I drove my Porsche 911, and like a braggart, revved the engine as I pulled up to valet parking. Several other fancy cars were parked within view of everyone pulling up, so I wasn't alone in trying to prove I'd made something of myself over the last ten years.

The room was filled with people in all modes of dress; men with Hawaiian shirts and khaki pants or Bermuda shorts, men with suits or sport coats, and lots of ties. Women wore long dresses, short dresses, shorter dresses, and pantsuits. People were heavy, slender, graying or balding, and it was obvious ninety percent of the women colored their hair.

Quickly reflecting on my shallow observation of the crowd, I located the bar across the room and headed there.

"Hey," someone who looked familiar said as I passed.

"Hey," I said back.

We chatted for a few minutes, and I couldn't recollect his name. I tried to casually look at his name tag, but his writing was illegible, so I gave up.

"Well," I said finally, "I'm off to get a drink. I need one."

"I hear ya," he said, and turned to greet another classmate.

While I was at the bar, I felt a tap on my shoulder, and when I turned, a beautiful blonde woman with a perfect tan stood there behind me. I would have known her anywhere.

"Hey, handsome," she said with an easy smile.

She was still trim, and her smile lit up her face. Immediately, I visualized images of us being together our first semester, making love, being young, meeting her father, me working, her moving back down to L.A.

She was incredibly gorgeous. Chalk one up for someone who'd actually improved with age.

"Hey back, gorgeous."

We hugged and then kissed cheeks. As I sucked in my stomach, I wondered if she was thinking back to those days as well.

"You look incredible," I said, trying to keep myself from giving her the once over. It was hard to keep my mind from visualizing her naked as I focused on her eyes.

"You're looking pretty good yourself," she said, then ordered a Perrier with a twist of lime.

"Are you by yourself?" I asked, casually glancing around to see if I recognized a husband lurking near her.

"Yes, and you?"

We made our way to a table out of the mainstream and I held a chair out for her.

"Forever the gentleman," she said.

"I try. Sometimes not hard enough."

I told her about Deborah and the boys and how she didn't want to spend the evening with people she didn't know. "I don't blame her," I added.

"I was married," she said. "No children, thank goodness, for we didn't last more than three years. It would have been a shame to drag kids through a messy divorce. And boy, was it messy."

I could imagine. And I could also imagine holding her in my arms again...

Suddenly I wasn't annoyed Deborah had decided not to come. I'm not sure what came over me, for it wasn't long before Hayley and I left to do our own partying in her hotel room.

Around midnight, I knew I needed to leave. I couldn't blame my behavior on drinking too much, or even being unhappy in my marriage. Over the years, I'd had fantasies of being with other women; what guy hadn't? But I'd never acted on any of them.

Hayley was leaving to go back home in the morning, and we made no plans to see each other again. I'd crossed over 'thinking about having an affair', to actually acting out my fantasy. And I knew from this point on, everything with Deborah would be different.

I knew I should have taken a shower before I left the hotel room. I knew the fragrance of another woman, of our sexuality, would cling to me. I'd smelled it in high school. I'd smelled it in college.

I knew my marriage was in trouble.

I was a schmuck.

Our divorce wasn't some long drawn-out affair; I think by the way she acted Deborah might have even been relieved when I told her I thought we were going in different directions. Had she been seeing someone herself? She seemed distant. But that could also have been me *feeling distanced, and a little guilty.*

I spent the next few years thinking I was a playboy. I dated a lot of younger women—more than I could reasonably handle. I juggled multiple relationships at a time, and that lifestyle eventually got tiring. I was extremely busy with my law practice, so I narrowed my relationships down to two or three women at a time.

I detected exasperation every time I asked my secretary to shop for me, so to minimize her displeasure with me—both with my lifestyle and the demeaning job of errand girl, I suggested she buy three of everything to cover a year's worth of birthdays and Christmas.

Although sometimes tempted, I had one rule I adhered to; I never dated my secretary. While she was quite attractive, she knew all my secrets, and it would have been impossible to replace her if our relationship hit the skids.

I met my new wife, Constance (not Connie, as she constantly reminded people, but Constance) at an air show. By then, I'd been doing professional aerobatic stunt flying, and I'd seen her a couple of times at various air shows around the country. She flew also, which impressed me, as there were very few female pilots in the circuit. With her blonde hair pulled back into a ponytail, tight jeans with a silver belt buckle the size of a rodeo champion, a leather jacket and plenty of jewelry, she was over the top gorgeous. She was also closer to my age than most of the other women I'd been attracted to.

I knew I'd met my match when we were first introduced by one of the other performing pilots. She arched one eyebrow slightly when we shook hands, and I wasn't certain what it was about me that caused that reaction. What I do know, though, is that it unnerved me a bit.

"Nice to meet you, Hudson," she said with that same eyebrow and a slight smile.

"Ah, likewise," I said like an idiot.

"We were just going into the VIP area if you'd like to join us," our friend said, leading the way. Of course, I followed, and I felt like a little puppy dog trailing behind his master. It gave me the advantage of watching Constance from behind, which added to her attractiveness. When she turned to glance back at me, I wondered if she'd read my mind, for I turned bright red.

"Wow, I think I've had too much sun," I said lamely, and she just grinned.

They set the VIP tent up for pilots and their guests, and inside, along the perimeter, tables were filled with food and drinks throughout the day. Fold up tables and chairs were set up along the front, and it was literally the best place to sit and watch the planes fly by. It gave pilots a chance to talk to each other between events, or it was just a place they could wind down if needed. It gave them privacy from the crowds outside, and it sheltered them from the sun.

"Can I get you anything to drink?" I asked before we sat.

"I'd love a water," Constance said.

"I'll take one too," our friend said, finding us a place to sit.

I ended up sitting across from Constance, which gave me a perfect opportunity to observe her every move. I was smitten, and later she would agree with me it had been obvious I'd fallen hard from the moment we met.

Dating Constance was incredible. We'd take turns flying each other to romantic getaways for dinner or for a weekend. She was an independent Court Recorder and had been for years. She worked primarily for the INS arbitration hearings, and traveled throughout the U.S., doing a lot of border patrol work in Yuma, San Diego, San Francisco, and Hawaii.

While she couldn't discuss names and places, it was really interesting hearing about some of her cases. Simple ones often involved disciplinary actions against employees for mistreating immigrants. In one case, a Border Patrol agent had become so frustrated he threw rocks at someone trying to cross the border illegally. Usually the punishment was getting written up and doing menial jobs, like cleaning up around the station house.

One particularly interesting case involved an agent who sneaked a woman into the U.S. from Canada because she was having a hard time getting a visa. When he was busted, the INS tried to fire him, but the union did a good job representing him, and he was able to keep his job. Constance never heard if the woman was allowed to stay in the country or not.

The best story was about a male higher up who had to fly from Washington, DC to LAX regularly, and a female INS employee would pick him up at the airport and take him to his hotel. An affair ensued, and they often had oral sex in the car before getting to their destination. After a year or so, when he wanted to end it, she reported him for sexual harassment, claiming she'd been denied a promotion. Her grievance was heard, in graphic detail according to Constance, and the judge ruled that the woman never needed to have an affair to get any promotion, and that she'd consented to having sex from the beginning.

Constance had never married, claiming she'd never met a man who didn't already have baggage, or who was smart or interesting enough. Well, I had the baggage with an ex-wife and two children, but I must have proven myself worthy of keeping her intrigue level up. She was certainly captivating enough for me.

She took my breath away. I never tired of watching her, whether it was getting ready in the morning, or flying her airplane, or just reading. And she challenged me to be a better man. I challenged her to marry me, and she did. We were married by a justice of the peace in her airplane, flying above Santa Barbara. We landed at the airport and about a hundred friends joined us on the ground for our reception.

Our first years passed quickly and were undeniably incredible. Oh, we had our petty squabbles, like if I didn't put the toilet seat back down, or if I left my wet towel on the bathroom floor. When she scolded me, I always promised to do a better job of trying to remember those little things that bothered her, but I have to admit, I always slipped back in to intolerable behavior.

When my mother grew ill, at first Constance offered to make the weekly trip with me to see her. But my mother, always being Celeste, shooed us away. She said she didn't want us to visit, often being rude and mean, but always remembering to tell us to refill her drink glass before we left. I wasn't sure when she'd started drinking again, but she was always sauced. And her personality continually changed, never for the better. When she told Constance she didn't want to see her again, we both knew it was her illness talking, but it really hurt Constance's feelings. She, of course, now regrets giving up, but how was she to know there was a reason for the drastic mood changes?

When my mother finally told me to 'Get the hell out!', even I stopped visiting. I'd been trying to be there for her, and she was pushing me away. The last thing I remember about our final visit was me telling her, "You've managed to push everyone away, haven't you? You know how to reach me if you need me."

And I've regretted those words ever since.

Her cleaning lady found her lying unconscious on the entry floor. She called 911 and then looked in Mother's address book for my number. I met the ambulance at the hospital.

Her doctor told us she was dying of brain cancer and the end was near.

"She'd wanted me to help her end her life," he said. "When I said I couldn't, she said she was going to move away and find someone else to do it."

She'd never told me or my brothers she had cancer, and now we finally understood what had been going on. She'd told us she was moving away, and now it all made sense.

Robert, Andrew Junior and I were with Mother when she died.

We tried to remember the good times we'd had, or the funny things she'd said, but those memories didn't come quickly or easily to any of us.

"I remember she'd bring something home for us when she went on a trip," Robert said.

"I remember going to the studio with her when Nanny went home to visit her family," JR said. "I was totally bored."

"I remember her telling me, 'Oh, he wouldn't have been the best role model for you, anyway. We did much better with Andrew,' when I told her I'd met my real father. Then she went on to tell me about her current movie project."

Mother had an art gallery and the young girl who ran it called me one day to ask what the plans were for it. My brothers and I admitted we hadn't thought about Mother's art, and it surprised us she'd still had enough inventory to keep it open. We all remembered growing up with canvasses leaning against each other in her studio—she actually was a pretty talented painter.

When Mother died, we agreed to auction off her paintings, so we met at the studio to see if there was anything we wanted to keep. Even though she and Mother were never close, Constance held her own with her. She shared with me that one time when she and Mother were having lunch at some posh restaurant, while Mother was reading the menu, she reached out for Constance's hand and squeezed it. Without looking up, Constance squeezed her hand in return.

Constance selected two paintings, and they hang in our home today.

Mother always claimed she never wanted a big funeral, but we all wondered if a private service was truly what would have made her happy. In the end, we decided on something small, and, as is the custom in most families, I, as the eldest, spoke first, as did a few long-time friends from her acting career.

I started with the story about Pearl Harbor. It had been a long time since I'd told it.

"As you all know, my mother was a strong woman. My father referred to her as 'a force to be reckoned with.' She knew what she wanted, and she was able to fulfill those dreams. She wasn't warm and fuzzy." I paused as the assemblage laughed. "But you always knew where you stood with her. She had an old Duesenberg from the 30s that she kept in the garage, until one day, someone approached her and asked if she wanted to sell it. She hadn't driven it for over twenty years, so to her it was only collecting dust. When one day I noticed the car wasn't in the garage, I thought she might have had it out for restoration. By then, it was worth a lot of money. But when I asked about it, she told me she'd sold it. 'What?' I asked, surprised. I knew at one time it had been her favorite car. When I asked her how much she sold it for, she said casually, 'I think two thousand dollars.' 'My God, Mother. Don't you know that car was worth ten times that?' She shrugged and said, 'Huddie, it was just an old car.'"

Everyone chuckled.

"She traveled, painted, and always brought back souvenirs from places she'd been, and my brothers and I would keep them in what we called our

own little treasure chests. But if I can be honest, I always wished for more. As it often happens when we lose someone so important to us, her death has made me think about my life, and my sons." I looked at them and smiled slightly. "And I realize it's never too late to do a better job of being a good father, or husband." I now looked at Constance, and then at Deborah, although I somehow thought that by acknowledging my first marriage, I was betraying my second. "So there's no better time than saying goodbye to someone you've loved, to make a vow to be a better person."

In the end, the estate was divided into quarters, with three of them going to us, and one being held in trust. At the attorney's office, the three of us looked at each other, and while I didn't want to appear selfish or ungrateful, I finally asked about the fourth quarter.

The attorney was forthright and said, "It appears there's another heir, a fourth child."

I remember the look on my brother's faces, as I also sat there stunned.

He continued. "There is a child that was born and given up for adoption in 1930, at the beginning of your mother's career. The fourth quarter is to be held in trust for that child, in the event he or she opts to search out his or her birth mother. The money will be held until 2011, when if by that time no one has come forward, the money will be equally divided between any birth grandchildren."

He waited a moment for this to sink in.

"I know you'll probably want a while to absorb this. There is a stipulation that if any of you three questions or contests this bequeath, then instead of receiving one fourth, you will receive one dollar." He put the paperwork down.

There was total silence as the three of us sat there. A hundred thoughts went through my mind; had my mother ever tried to contact her first child? Who was the father? And did he know? It made sense that if she was just starting her acting career, an unwanted pregnancy could have ruined her future. Not today, of course, but in the thirties, yes.

The three of us just stared at each other before I finally spoke.

"My mother's wish is what we need to respect. I'm sure I speak for my brothers that this is certainly something we never expected. But we will abide by her wishes."

Robert and Andrew nodded their heads in agreement.

The attorney said, "Then we just need you all to sign some paperwork and we can start distributing your mother's estate."

When the attorney left the room, we all spoke at once. Robert mentioned the quarter split each. Andrew and I focused on the fact there was a fourth sibling that we probably would never know.

"Hell," I said, as I rubbed my face.

"Double Hell," Andrew said.

Mother had purchased the property where the art gallery was, so since none of us wanted to become landlords, we put it up for sale. We sold her house too. My brothers and I were each left with a substantial amount of money.

CHAPTER SIXTEEN
Hudson

The year my mother died, Constance and I moved out of L.A. We no longer had the obligation to live near her, and the rat race was getting to us. I could still keep my office and staff in town, and since we both had careers that could be based out of home offices, we could literally live anywhere close enough to a local airport, so that either of us could fly to an assignment when needed.

Ocean front property wasn't on our bucket list, but lake property sounded very intriguing, so we drove up to the San Bernardino Mountains, and looked at homes in Big Bear and Lake Arrowhead.

Big Bear Lake was public, and the larger of the two towns. It had a lot of charming retail stores, skiing, a larger population, and more tourists. Lake Arrowhead, which was a private lake, didn't really have a downtown, which meant fewer crowds, but it did have a village on the lake where there was shopping and dining.

We ended up in Lake Arrowhead. We found a charming house with space for our offices, and we started packing.

Most of my law cases involved manufacturing issues, like motorcycle parts, safety and noise. Because I was considered an expert witness, I usually won technical cases for my clients, so my previous successes preceded me, both in my mind and in the courtroom. However, I had an interesting criminal *matter come up after we moved up to the mountains, where I worked for the defense. It brought me down a notch or two, for it was the first case I lost.*

It involved two young men who had been seen racing their motorcycles on the boulevard earlier in the evening. They were still on the street two hours after that sighting, when one of the motorcycles ran into a ninety-year-old gentleman who pulled his car out in front of him. The bike T-boned the man's vehicle, killing him.

It devastated both the young men, and, of course, the gentleman's family. The defense called me in to determine how fast the motorcycles had to be going in order to cause the death. I felt for certain I had enough information to prove that the older gentleman's action preemptively caused the accident, and that the speed of the motorcycle wasn't the issue.

I held my own and felt I proved, beyond a reasonable doubt, that the accident was simply a tragic event. The attorney defending the case clapped me on the back and shook my hand once we left the courtroom.

"Thanks, Hudson. We've done it."

But juries can go either way when they're deliberating a case, and they brought back an unfavorable finding of guilty for the young men. I was speechless. My friend, the defense attorney, just looked at me in shock. The two young men broke down sobbing. They were ultimately charged with vehicular manslaughter and sentenced to five years in prison with the possibility of parole after one year. For all intents and purposes, their young lives were ruined.

The other disastrous case I took involved a city of which I cannot name. The claim came from an impoverished neighborhood, and the city had on its list of improvements to make, the job of replacing sidewalks that huge old trees had uprooted. An elderly gentleman was out for his afternoon walk, and his foot caught on the uneven concrete and down he went. His outward injuries were minor, just some scrapes and bruises, but he hit his head on the pavement and never recovered.

I represented the city, and I established no intentional neglect. This, however, meant the family of the gentleman lost their original case, and were only awarded a very nominal amount of money. I'd done my job, and I'd won for the city; however, in the end, it brought me no glory for I felt like a sleazy despicable lawyer.

I believe that whether doctor or lawyer, you always remember the patient you just couldn't save, or in these cases, where justice didn't prevail. Years later, my confidence and sureness have still been somewhat tempered. I have lost no more cases since then, but I surely am reminded to remain confident but humble when I enter a courtroom. I've never taken another personal case again. The adverse sense of loss for me has never healed.

CHAPTER SEVENTEEN

Hudson

Not that we didn't love our first home up in the mountains; it was a cozy cabin which we soon realized was better suited for weekend getaways. We both agreed if we were going to continue to stay up there, then we needed something larger. I was also ready to close my office in L.A. and work solely from the mountains.

We set out looking and found the perfect home. It had been for sale by its owner, so we were able to learn a lot more about the house than a realtor would have been privy to. Through casual conversations, we also learned the homeowner was in over his head on several investments and he needed to sell the house to consolidate his assets. It was never my nature to capitalize on other's misfortunes, believing in 'do unto others', but I made use of my persuasive talents, and we got the house for a very good price.

After the previous owner moved all their furnishings out, I realized the home needed more updating than I'd thought. It appeared Constance had already figured that out, for she'd started gathering decorating ideas, and I soon discovered she'd collected several folders with things she thought she'd like to do. Being more on the conservative side, I didn't see there were that many improvements that were necessary, but by now, I'd learned that 'a happy wife is a happy life' and I wanted Constance to be happy.

Our first appointment with Annie was up at the new house, and then we went to our existing cabin so she could see what we had there.

"This is very charming," she said as she came in. "I can see why you liked it."

"I think everyone pictures living in the quintessential cabin when they think of coming up here," Constance said.

"I agree," Annie said. "When I first came up and stayed in one of the cabins, I instantly felt like I'd left another world behind. The cabin, and the mountains, provided such tranquility, it was incredible."

"And you've stayed," I said.

"Yes."

We'd kept our home in L.A. as a failsafe in case we weren't happy living in the mountains, so our second meeting was down there. We wanted her to see what we'd left behind; in other words, what wouldn't fit in to our existing cabin. It would give her an idea of the things we liked, and we were hoping we could incorporate most of it into the new house.

She took photos and measurements of some of the larger pieces, and then she went with us to our storage so she could see what we had in there.

"We may not want to use all of it," Constance offered, "but I wanted you to see what we had."

Both Constance and I had a busy week coming up, so we weren't able to meet with Annie again until the week after. She wanted to get a few more measurements at our original cabin, so we met there first.

"I keep forgetting to ask you," I asked. "Did you ever look up my mother's name in your guest books? I've been thinking about it."

"I did," Annie said. "And I totally forgot to tell you. Yes, I found your mother's name, Celeste Williams."

"Any shocking discoveries?"

"Well..."

I recognized Annie's slight hesitation; I'd seen it before in court. She was thinking. Trying to come up with the right words.

"Go on. I'm a big boy," I said, hoping to disarm her with my smile.

"Well, she stayed in one cabin with another actress for a few weeks, and then it looks like she moved into another. I found it interesting the studio kept such detailed records."

"And?"

"Hudson," Constance interjected. "You sound like you're giving her the third degree. You're pressuring her."

"No, I'm not. I'm just more curious than ever to hear..."

Annie looked at Constance before she went on.

"She moved into the cabin of John Robert Scott."

I jerked in reaction.

"The actor?"

"Of course, silly," Constance said. Then she giggled. "Well, well, well."

"Oh."

It was all I could think of to say at that moment.

"You two continue. I think I need a drink," I said as I turned towards the kitchen.

I could hear Annie and Constance in the other room as I gulped down a scotch. Eventually, they made their way back to where I was now sitting in the living room, and Constance gave me a quizzical look.

"Are you all right?" she asked.

"I think so."

"Actually, that works for me," Annie said, gathering her things. "I'll follow you to the new house if that's okay."

"I think I have it figured out," I burst out the moment we got into the car.

"Good god, Hudson. What's gotten into you?"

"I think my mother had a child with John Robert Scott. The dates work out, and I can see why he wouldn't have wanted it. He might have been married."

At the new house, while Annie sketched, and I helped measure all the rooms, I had a difficult time focusing on what they talked about. I had a million thoughts, and all of them were about the mystery of the fourth sibling.

"I see mostly cosmetic work," Annie said. "That's easy. We just need to decide on paint colors."

I was so pre-occupied with my sensational revelation, I wasn't listening. And then the double whammy came.

"How do you feel about updating the kitchen and bathrooms?" Annie asked. She directed this question to Constance, who glanced at me sideways.

I think I reacted like a deer caught in a headlight, for Annie quickly added, "I'm not suggesting it..." Then she paused. "It would just be easier to do any remodeling before you moved in."

"Now that you mention it, I like that idea..." Constance said.

"Cha-ching." I said, rolling my eyes. I realized any further comments I might have had would be pointless.

"What do I say to my brothers?" I asked once we were back in the car.

"Just tell them what you think to be the truth. That's always the best."

"But what if they want to find him? Or her?"

Constance turned towards me and frowned.

"Hudson, what's the problem?"

I hated it when Constance always sounded so pragmatic.

"Just tell them, and then the three of you can decide what to do. I'm not sure how you'd go about it, but see what they want to do."

I don't know which would have been more disappointing. If Robert and Andrew Jr. wanted to find our sibling? Or if they didn't.

It turned out, for the time being at least, they were both ambivalent. So we decided to do nothing, and see what the future brought.

We met Annie again in the store and looked at flooring and fabrics. I should say, I sat and watched as the girls looked at everything. We started bringing home samples of everything, and I could see the dollar signs adding up quickly.

CHAPTER EIGHTEEN

Noah's cabin had a very charming one bedroom guest house above the garages and workshop. It had a good-sized bedroom, a small dressing area and bathroom, a compact but complete kitchen with an eating bar and bar stools, pine-paneled walls, an open-beamed ceiling in the living room, and a large stone fireplace that would definitely put out the heat in the winter. It still had the previous owner's furniture in it which worked for the few nights Noah stayed there while they refinished the hardwood flooring in his cabin, and now he and Josh were talking about fixing it up and making it Josh's place.

They spent a couple of weekends doing some minor repairs; they'd taken out a built-in captain's bed in the living room to make more floor space and replaced missing pine paneling to match what was already on the walls. We ordered pine wood blinds to match the walls, and then once the new carpet was installed, it would be finished.

Noah put his old iron bed, wood dresser and night stands up in the bedroom for Josh, and we found a larger log bed with an antique dresser and night stands that Sarah said she could paint with pine branches and pine cones for Noah in the cabin.

Josh's things were in the garage, so he, Noah and one of the other guys they worked with brought everything up and Sarah and I supervised where it would all go. The under counter refrigerator was too small for full-time use, so Noah found a used, full-sized one and put it down in the workshop with a washer and dryer.

Josh moved out of the main house and into his new digs. It was a win-win for everyone: it would give Noah his house back, along with his privacy, and it would bring in some additional income, which would come in handy. It would also give Josh an affordable place to live.

For the time being, Sarah kept her cabin, but ended up spending a lot of time at Josh's.

"Before I make it official, I need to talk to Mark," she said one day at lunch. "I just can't imagine going back to him, and we need to get everything sorted out."

We'd never talked more about what had happened between the two of them, and I was comfortable with that. I didn't need the gory details; she was obviously unhappy with her marriage and needed to get away.

"Do you need to make a trip back home?"

"Probably. There's nothing I want to keep; I brought everything I wanted..."

"We can start saving boxes at the store..."

"I don't know. I suppose I'm being a coward if I don't go back, but I really don't want to. Can't I just have a lawyer here start divorce paperwork?"

"Yes," I said. "I remember bringing Noah with me when I made my last trip down to pick up what I wanted, and David was such a jerk. He called Noah my cowboy."

I watched as Sarah picked at her salad.

"No one says you have to go back. If you don't want to, don't. And you're not a coward. You were obviously unhappy," I said, then thought about David...he had been unhappy too.

"I feel like a shit."

"That's because you're not angry with him. If you hated him, it wouldn't even be an issue. My opinion, even though you didn't ask, is to have an attorney take care of it. If there's nothing else you want to bring up, call Mark and tell him what you're doing, so he's not blindsided. *That* would be cowardly. Tell him, and then just do it."

I gave Sarah the number of the attorney in town that helped Sam and me with the sale of the cabins. That next weekend, she moved in with Josh, and that's when Noah reminded me we'd talked about me moving from my cabin.

My heart said yes. My brain said, 'you've made a lot of serious decisions this last year and a half, and one wasn't a good one.' We only had two more weeks before Christmas, and I wanted to spend time at At The Cabin. I'd have to pack up all my things and clear out my storage. If I waited until after the holidays, I could use any leftover boxes from packing up the unsold holiday inventory.

A hundred thoughts went through my mind, and not all involved logistics.

What would I tell my parents? "I'm moving in with Noah?" I was thirty-two and not a teenager, but I worried about how my father would feel.

What would I tell Sam? Would he be all right here by himself? I'd still be around when he needed me. I still liked to check guests in, but he could do that.

I loved Noah, and while I could see no reason why we should live separately, I was suddenly anxious. A warning voice in my head asked, 'What if it doesn't work out?'

I knew if I didn't make the move, it would most likely end our relationship and we were finally at a really good spot. I knew I wanted to be with Noah, but I wanted to be certain this was the time to take the next step.

One thought barely crossed my mind before another one followed. Was there ever any guarantee of anything? Was any relationship going to be perfect? Would Noah grow tired of me and my constant adventures? Or was he growing more tolerant of my personality?

Then I thought, why not? Why don't we do this?

What was the worst thing that could happen?

The thought that it might not work out sent me into a slight panic. How would I tell him it wasn't working?

Then I realized, if it didn't work out, I'd have the cabins to fall back on.

Could I live with these consequences?

I could.

In the end, I told him yes.

I left the store early the next afternoon, and before I headed for my cabin, I stopped in to tell Sam I was planning on making the move.

"I'm not surprised," he said. "You two make a good couple."

"I feel like I'm abandoning you," I said.

"You're not. I know you're around, and I can always call if I need you."

I gave him a quick hug.

With Noah's help, we finished packing my cabin that night. We filled his truck and my Jeep with most of the boxes, and as I closed the door to my cabin, I was excited but already a little homesick. We made sure the cats and their belongings were in the office, then after I told them to behave, I gave them kisses and gave Sam another hug. We grabbed a bite at Ginny's and then unloaded everything into the sunroom at Noah's cabin. There wasn't anything I needed right away, so I planned to unpack during the next few weeks.

Just as Sarah had learned to feel comfortable in the design store, Lily, who'd worked there for several years, mastered the cash register at At The Cabin. The three of us worked the two weeks before Christmas, alternating stores. Customers who shopped at At The Cabin ended up browsing the flooring and design store, and we met a lot of new people. Our mailing list sign-up sheet was filling quickly, and after the first of the year, I'd have Sarah help me send something out about spring merchandise and decorating, and include something about the cabins.

Somehow we found time to decorate a tree at Noah's, and I felt a little guilty bringing out the fishing poles, creels and miscellaneous fishing gear again to decorate it with; but it was going to be that or nothing. By Christmas Eve, I was exhausted and ravenous. My feet were so sore,

I thought they were going to ache permanently. We decided to spend a quiet evening, just the two of us, and I'd brought home sandwiches from Ginny's.

I longed for a soak in the tub, and afterwards, Noah massaged my feet.

"I owe you one," I said, moaning.

"I'll take you up on that."

"I need to call my parents," I said. I'd been so busy I hadn't had time to think much about them or my sister. "I'll do it in the morning."

We poured some wine and sat in front of a warm fire, the dogs at our feet.

"There must be something wrong with me," I finally said.

Noah's brows furrowed.

"You don't feel well?" he asked.

"No, I'm fine. I was just thinking about Loni. I was actually *thinking* about how little I *think* of her, and sometimes that makes me feel selfish. It's like she was more of a friend from school I'd lost touch with than a sister."

"Just because you're blood doesn't mean you're obligated or guaranteed a close relationship. Obviously, I never had a sibling, but I know plenty of people who were never close with their family. Some people actually move away and only see each other on holidays."

"I know you're right, but I'm still angry with her for hurting my parents."

Noah pulled me towards him and kissed me on the cheek.

"You'll be fine. Just let time take care of things. It has a way of doing that, doesn't it?"

"Yes, you're right, as usual." I pouted, then said, "I miss the kitties."

"I know you do. Maybe we can get one for here."

"But Jezebel and Socks would be jealous."

"They'd never have to know."

"Hmmm." I said, laying my head back on the sofa.

That night, I slept like a rock. And when I woke in the morning, there was a small wrapped package on my pillow.

"For me?" I asked, sitting up in bed.

"For you," Noah said.

"Well, go get yours then," I said.

The minute he got back in bed, I unwrapped Noah's gift and it was a diamond eternity ring. It fit perfectly and I put it on my left ring finger.

"It's beautiful, Noah. How did you know the size?" I asked, admiring my outspread hand.

"I borrowed one of your rings," he said with a proud grin.

"It's beautiful," I said again. "Now open yours."

I'd bought Noah a dress watch. I thought when we went out, it would be nice if he wore something other than the scratched up watch he wore for work.

"It's great, Annie. I really like it."

Noah reached over and kissed me.

"I had another Christmas present for you but you were too tired last night...how do you feel about this?" he asked, kissing me more firmly.

Noah's love had unlocked my heart, and I sometimes still found myself so emotional after making love, that I couldn't believe my feelings for him intensified even more. I couldn't envision our intimacy becoming complacent.

Josh, Sarah and Shep walked over from the guest house and joined us for Christmas breakfast. Shep pranced with excitement to see us and licked everyone's hands. We gave the three dogs treats, and then he, Coco, and Rufus finally snuggled up against each other and slept.

We drew straws to see who would cook. Noah was in charge of the pancakes, Sarah cooked bacon and ham, Josh cooked the eggs, and I made hot chocolate and made sure everything was on the table. I also volunteered to do clean up since they all did the hard work.

It was cold enough for snow, and we'd all wished we'd have a real white Christmas, but the weather didn't cooperate. Snow wasn't predicted again until mid-January. I tied the new scarf Sarah had given me around my neck, and after breakfast, we all put our coats and mittens on and sat out on the deck and enjoyed some quiet time together. Rufus and

Coco begged us for treats again, while Shep behaved like the gentleman he was, and stood back waiting.

"Here you go, boy," Noah said.

The temperature kept dropping until it got too cold to sit outside any longer, so Sarah and I went inside. Sam and Ginny were joining us for dinner, and I wanted to finish cleaning up.

"I've almost forgotten what it's like to have a day off," Ginny said as she came through the front door.

Christmas and Thanksgiving were the only days Ginny closed the restaurant. All the other holidays, when the mountain welcomed visitors and part-timers, were usually busy. Even though we all swore we'd never eat again after that large breakfast, Ginny had brought over sliced turkey, pastrami and bread for sandwiches and assorted desserts for afterwards. I set out chips and nuts, and somehow we managed to eat again.

We had two bookings for the Christmas week and three for New Year's. Sam said he could handle those while I was at the store. I told Sam I'd come over and help give the cabins a thorough cleaning after the New Year.

For our after Christmas sale at the store, I brought in a vintage Bingo spinner and marked the balls with the numbers forty, fifty, and sixty. Between Christmas and New Year's, customers got to spin for their discount and it created a lot of excitement. We sold off most of our stock, which meant we had less to inventory and pack up.

Noah and Josh went back to work on a big project they needed to stay on schedule with. It turned out a family from down the hill came up over Thanksgiving and discovered someone had been staying in their cabin, and had damaged the walls, flooring and doors. Noah was hoping to have it all restored by Christmas, but they needed a few more days. He promised them he'd have it ready for New Year's.

CHAPTER NINETEEN

As predicted, our first real snowfall was in mid-January. I would have loved it if I could have sat with Noah and our fur babies, snuggled in front of the fireplace all day, but it turned out to be just a dusting of a few inches. I loved to watch the white flakes falling, and even though the snow would quickly melt, it was nature's way of replenishing the earth.

Snow, no matter how light, made breathing in the cool clean air invigorating, and was necessary to fill our reservoirs and the lake. A good snow season also relieved concern about fires.

On one of my visits to Timberline, I'd seen an old green canoe hanging from the ceiling above the cash register, and it gave me the idea of hanging one in Noah's cabin. The ceiling in front of his stone fireplace was the perfect height, and when I mentioned it to him, he liked the idea. We started looking for one, and then Noah remembered a customer he'd done work for having an old one in their garage. He said he'd call them and see if they wanted to sell it.

A week later, he and Josh were hanging a vintage red canoe off heavy rope and pulleys from the ceiling beams. They tilted it just enough to show off the wood slat interior and the wooden oars. It made quite a statement, as it was the first thing you saw when you came into the room.

I found an old chopping block island that worked perfectly in the kitchen. We painted the legs black to go with the black granite countertops and black and white diamond painted wood flooring. We wouldn't use it for food preparation, but I still cleaned it with soap and water and vinegar.

I'd had my eye on an antique grandfather clock I'd found in a clock shop, and I knew it would be perfect for the office. It was out of my budget, but I asked the clock smith if he could call the owner and ask if they had any wiggle room on the price. When he called back and told me his customer was interested in reducing the price, I bought it. However, when he asked where I'd like it delivered, I'd changed my mind.

There was an ideal spot in Noah's living room, and while I waited for the clock to be delivered and set up, I went to the hall closet and brought out boxes of treasures I'd collected from garage sales and estate sales. Pine shelves lined the upper portion of two walls in the living room, and Noah had already set up an old oak library ladder I'd found. It took me about two hours, but when I was finished, I stepped back and admired my handiwork. I filled the shelves with old encyclopedias, dozens of vintage leather books, old lanterns, several fishing creels, copper pots, a taxidermied fish, an old striped canteen, and some old painted oars.

A potential new decorating client took up the rest of my morning, and by the time I met Noah for a late lunch, I thought I was going to burst. I wanted to tell him about the clock and shelves, but I also wanted him to be surprised.

All I said was, "I've had a great day so far."

We sat in our usual booth, and one of the girls took our order. Before our meals came, Ginny went to the news flash on the television mounted above the counter and turned the volume up.

A female newscaster said, "They have arrested a Lake Arrowhead man by the name of Jeffry Coombs in the case of the two young girls recently assaulted while camping with their families."

"There's no way. I know that guy!" Noah blurted out.

I raised my eyebrows. "You do?"

The color had drained from his face.

"Are you okay?" I reached for his hand across the booth.

He looked at me like he'd seen a ghost.

135

"Sheriff Randy Holmes, of San Bernardino County Sherriff's Department, can bring us up to date."

Cameras flashed continually as the Sheriff came to the podium.

"At this time, Jeffry Coombs is in custody for assault and murder of last year's victim, six-year-old Sophia Rodriguez, who was taken from her family's campground. She was later found unresponsive and face down in the lake. He's also admitted being responsible for the abduction and molestation of five-year-old Jasmine Benson, who was taken from her family's campsite but reunited with her family earlier in the summer."

"Good *god!*" Noah pinched his forehead and shook his head.

"That'll be all for now," the Sheriff said, and the original newscaster returned to the screen.

"How the hell do you know him?" I asked.

"He's been up here awhile, and everyone thought he was just a loner. Shit. I've had him help me haul off debris a couple of times. I had no idea he was capable of doing anything like that...Oh my god."

Noah sat back in the booth and sighed audibly.

"I've just lost my appetite. He's been walking among us like nothing ever happened. I can't believe this," Noah said again. He leaned forward and covered his mouth with his hand.

"Want to take that to go?" our waitress asked.

"Yes. I should get back to work," Noah said, leaving his money to pay our bill. "I'll bring this back for one of the guys. I don't know if we'll hear any more details later, but if I hear something, I'll let you know."

I got up with him, and we kissed goodbye. He was still shaking his head as he walked out.

Everyone who came in to both stores that day talked about Jeffry Coombs and the two little girls. One woman said she'd had him do some handyman work around her cabin and was horrified.

"I never would have suspected him," she said, just as Noah had.

Another customer only said, "Thank God they found him."

That afternoon, we received a large shipment of spring merchandise, and Sarah and Lily started unpacking and pricing it. It'd been several days since we finished taking down what was left of the holiday décor, and the store needed an update. It was lightly snowing again, and the combination of the snow covered ground and the change of merchandise really brightened up everyone's mood.

I'd been so preoccupied during the day, I'd forgotten about the work I'd done on the book cases until I pulled into our driveway. Noah hadn't come home yet, so I went inside and rummaged through the refrigerator to see if there was anything worth eating. Just as I was concluding I needed to make a trip to the grocery store, I heard Noah come through the front door, and he was covered in dirt.

"I had to climb under a house," he offered as he went directly into the laundry room. "But we got their problem fixed."

"You must be freezing. I'll put your clothes in to wash," I offered, grabbing his clothes before he dropped them to the clean floor.

"Thanks. I'll just take a quick, hot shower. Want to meet Josh and Sarah for dinner?"

"Sounds good," I called. I was dying to show him the shelves, and the minute he came back out, I dragged him back into the living room.

"What?"

"Just look," I said.

"Where'd you get all this stuff?" His mood had lifted. "This looks great!"

"I've been collecting while you weren't looking."

"You're incredible. Have I told you that?"

He stood there with his hands in his pants pockets, looking like a young boy. Then he took me in his arms and kissed me.

"Several times, but I love hearing it," I said, kissing him back and grabbing his butt.

"Now that's an invitation if I ever felt one."

"Tonight," I promised.

A few days later, Noah went to the Twin Peaks Sheriff's Department and found out more details about Jeffry Coombs, and then stopped by the flooring store. He sat, anxiously waiting for a customer to leave.

"A family rented a cabin for the weekend, hoping for more snow. Their two children were playing outside, trying to find enough snow to make a snowman, and one of the girls went inside the house to get her mittens. The younger girl stayed outside and went looking for something to use for the snowman's eyes and nose.

"Jeffry Coombs had obviously been watching them and saw the opportunity to make his move. But the little girl screamed, and when her father heard her, he came running out of the cabin. He saw his daughter being dragged into the forest behind the cabin.

"He yelled at his wife to call the Sheriff! And then told his other daughter to get the rope out of the Jeep and to follow him. He beat Coombs silly, then rolled Coombs over on his stomach and tied his hands behind his back. He sat on him until the Sheriff arrived about thirty minutes later," Noah said, scratching his beard.

"Turns out, Coombs confessed to the abductions. It was his cigarettes at each site." Noah said, finally taking a breath.

CHAPTER TWENTY
Sarah

"Move in with me," Josh said again.

We'd been seeing each other for only several months when Josh first asked me to move in with him. We spent most nights together, either at his place or my cabin, and I knew this was heading toward a serious relationship. I knew he truly cared about me and he seemed genuine in his expression of feelings. I hadn't expected to see such a mature and reliable side to him after hearing about him and Bunny.

He was a caring and gentle lover, concerned I was happy with him, and I think if I had to find one word to describe my time with him, it would be contented. I felt I'd come the closest to belonging here than ever. While it tempted me to take the next step with him, I had also started thinking about my marriage to Mark. I knew I'd have to confront him eventually, and I also knew I needed closure on that part of my life.

"I need to call Mark," I said one morning as we were eating breakfast at his kitchen counter. Josh had made a tasty omelet with feta cheese and spinach. When we were at his place, he cooked, and when we stayed at mine, we went out to eat since I didn't have a kitchen.

Even though he continued eating, his face tightened. I hadn't meant to just spring it on him like I did, and I couldn't tell if he was stressed thinking I was actually thinking about Mark, or realizing I had a situation I needed to address.

When he said nothing, I continued. "I've decided I need to start our divorce. I've talked with Annie about it, and she thinks I can just have someone up here take care of it. But I keep thinking I need to go back."

Josh set his toast down and looked at me. "What does that mean?" he asked. I saw a flash of apprehension cross his face.

"It means I need to see him. To bring the paperwork to him. To begin the process?" I ended the sentence with a question. "I mean, if you and I are going to move forward with our relationship, I need to cut the ties to my marriage. I can't be married."

"Far be it from me to tell you this, but I agree—just take care of it up here is the easiest way to deal with it."

"Don't worry," I said, reaching for his hand.

I hadn't realized he'd been holding his breath as he tried to stifle a sigh. I never thought Josh was the least bit insecure in our relationship, but I supposed I'd feel something similar if he told me he had to talk to Bunny again about something from their past.

"I'll call him and find out when I can drive out. There's not much I want or need, but I also don't want him to throw anything away." I collected our plates and took them to the sink to wash them. I turned to look at Josh. "He may have done that already."

"Want me to go with you?" he finally asked.

"No," I said, maybe a bit too quickly. "I don't have much and I think if I came with you in tow, it would just make him feel worse. He's really sensitive." I dried my hands and set the dish towel down. "I'll be fine."

"I know you will...I just want to be there for you."

"You're the best, Josh," I said, coming to stand by him. I gave him a kiss, and then said, "I should get into the store. Annie has an appointment and is going to be late this morning."

"Let me know what you decide to do," Josh said, grabbing his own jacket and pushing the counter stool in. "Dinner tonight?"

"Of course," I said, and left.

I called Mark later in the morning, and I could tell my call rattled him. "Are you coming back?"

"No, Mark. I'm not. We need to figure out what we're going to do, and I need to get the rest of my things."

I thought I heard him begin to cry. I might have been able to kick some-one's ass, but I wasn't so heartless I couldn't feel his pain.

"I was hoping the time away would make you realize how much I loved you," he said.

"I know you do, Mark. I just feel I need to start over. I wasn't happy." There, I'd finally said it.

I told Annie I was heading out in the morning, and she gave me a sympathetic hug. I'd already taken her advice and had the attorney draw up the paperwork, but I'd put it in a drawer, still trying to summon up the courage to decide what to do.

The drive out seemed interminable. I stopped twice for a pit stop and a soda, just to stop my brain from overworking. I knew I'd made the right decision, so why did I feel so rotten? It might have been that I'd pushed all thoughts of being with him from my mind while I was up in the mountains. I'd been trying to find a place that felt right.

I'd wasted so much of his life. It didn't bother me I'd wasted mine too. I tried to look at it as a way to transition from my life in Long Beach into what I was ready for now. It had been my landing place. My interim life, my stepping stones to happiness.

During the drive, I thought the brown desert would never end, and it mirrored the bleakness of my mood. As I started the final descent into Vegas, I recalled how bright the lights had been on the bus that night, beckoning me to a new life.

I'd brought some plastic bags and boxes, and I tried to make a mental note of what I even wanted to bring back. I had little extra space either at my cabin or at Josh's, so I'd have to keep it to a minimum.

As I got closer to our apartment, my stomach fluttered and realized I was nervous. When I pulled into the parking lot, I seriously considered just turning around and telling Mark to throw everything of mine out. My heart raced as I rang the doorbell. And when he answered the door, he looked so forlorn and lost, it broke my heart.

"Oh, Mark," I said as I hugged him.

He stepped aside and let me in.

"I've sort of been collecting some of your things since you called, but I figured you wanted to go through them," he said, showing me a pile of things on the sofa and coffee table.

"Do you want to talk first?" I asked, setting the boxes and bags down.

"No, I know we're getting a divorce, so there's not much to talk about," he said. He inched his way to one chair by the sofa.

"Well," I said, not knowing where to start. I thought we could still talk while I packed. "I talked with an attorney and he said if we were both in agreement with everything, he could just handle the process for the both of us, which will save us a lot of money."

"What about the checking and savings accounts?" Mark's voice broke.

"You can have what's in there," I said, assuming he hadn't already taken all the money out. "I don't need anything. I'll keep my car and continue to make the payments."

I was finishing up the second bag of clothing when Mark asked, "Was it something I did?" He gave a choked laugh and looked as if I'd struck him in the face.

I ached inside for him and I could hardly look at him. I'd never tell him I knew before I did it that marrying him was a mistake; knowing that now would only hurt him more. I felt like such a bitch for everything I'd done, but I also knew that by being there now, it confirmed I was not in love with him. I tried to swallow the lump in my throat and said, "No, it was nothing you did. I just didn't know what I wanted."

I went to where he was sitting and knelt down to look him in the eyes. "I made a terrible mistake and have hurt you while I was figuring it all out. Will you ever forgive me?"

I felt selfish even asking.

A look of tired sadness passed over him.

"Yes."

There was no reason for me to stay, and even though I knew it was going to be a grueling drive, I got back on the highway and headed home. I must have cried on and off all the way back. Once I got to the bottom of the hill, though, I immediately began to think of the new life I'd started up in the mountains. While there was no way I could know for certain how everything would end up working out for me, I, for once, saw a future that could have a happy ending.

And as I pulled into the parking area of the cabins, I noticed a single daffodil had broken through the ground. I hadn't seen it there earlier, and I took it to be a sign of a new season...both in time and in my life.

CHAPTER TWENTY ONE

My friend and former boss Susan called me one afternoon in early spring. She and her husband John had been friends of David's before we were married, and John had handled our divorce.

"I've missed you," she started.

My heart skipped a beat. "I've missed you too. I'm in another world up here, and I haven't had to come back down much." Then I felt guilty I hadn't called her. She'd been a good friend to me when David and I were married, and I'd learned a lot working for her in her real estate office, but they stayed his friends once we divorced. I never held that against them, and now I wondered how they were doing.

"I heard you bought some cabins," she said.

"I did." Obviously, David had told her about them.

"Well, a girlfriend and I wanted to have a girl's weekend one of these times and I'd love to see you."

"That's a great idea," I said, genuinely. "I've missed you. Just let me know when you want to come up." Then, before I gave it another thought, I said, "My treat on the cabins, your treat for dinner. I can't thank you enough for all you did for me back then."

"You were a delight. Watching you grow was really special for me. And your deal sounds great. When do you have a cabin available?"

"When do you want to come up? Spring up here is a lot different from down there. It's still really chilly at night, but during the day it's clear and comfortable. Summer is usually pleasant, but when it gets hot, it gets hot."

We planned for her to come up at the end of March and I penciled her in on the calendar. I knew I'd be nervous to see her, not that she ever made me feel that way, but I was inviting my past into my present, and I wasn't sure exactly what to expect.

"You and John are still okay?"

"Of course. He knows a good thing when he's got it," she said cheerfully. Then we hung up.

I wasn't sure how Noah would react to my newest guest, but I had to tell him.

"That should be interesting," was all he said. I looked at him a little funny, and then he said, "I didn't mean it that way."

"What way did you mean, then?"

"Can I start over? You caught me by surprise. How do you feel about that? You haven't really had much contact with friends from down the hill. It should be interesting, and I hope you'll enjoy seeing her."

I raised my eyebrow.

"Was that better?"

"You're not worried, are you?"

He wrinkled his face. "No. I'm not. I was just surprised."

"She was a good friend to me. She took me under her wing and got me started. I've missed her." Then I realized...she was the one who told me she'd seen David with another woman. Shit.

When I told Sarah about it, she asked if I wanted her along for moral support, but I didn't think I'd have any issues I couldn't deal with. I decided to just enjoy the visit with an old friend.

I put Susan and her girlfriend Christine up in the larger one bedroom cabin that used to be mine. They opted to not bring in a cot but to share the bed. They wanted to drive around and check out the area before we had dinner, so I made sure the fireplace was filled with wood and showed them how to light it before they left.

We agreed to meet at the Cowboy Bar for steaks and music. Of course, the food was great, and the music got the two girls up and dancing. Even though they encouraged me to dance, I didn't feel comfortable joining them. As much as I tried to enjoy the evening, I couldn't help but have flashbacks to David and what my life was all about back then.

It was too noisy to talk about much, which was fine with me, so we agreed to meet for breakfast at Ginny's before they took a road trip to Big Bear Lake.

When I got home that night, Noah said, "Hey," as I walked in.

"I had a good time," I offered. "I'm in a different place now, up here, not in that old social world. I hadn't thought about that, but I don't miss it."

"That's good," he said, hugging me. "I'm glad you went."

"We're having breakfast at Ginny's in the morning if you want to join us."

"Nah, I need to get an early start."

It was almost midnight before I could fall asleep. I thought back to the day I met David and how I knew I'd marry him. And how I thought I was happy enough until I realized how big a jerk he'd been. Had he ever truly loved me?

I reached out for Noah and kept my hand on his arm all night.

I found a booth up front so the girls wouldn't have a hard time finding me, and once they were seated, Ginny came out and gave me a big hug and asked who my friends were. I introduced them, leaving out the part that I knew Susan from being married before. I think Susan was eager to know more about my new life, so once we ordered, she jumped right in and started asking questions.

"So, are you happy up here?"

"How is the cabin rental business going?"

"Are you seeing someone?"

Knowing Susan, I felt she was more curious about what I'd been doing rather than acting like a spy. While I thought about embellishing my successes, I answered her questions basically and honestly. I didn't know what she'd end up sharing with David.

"I bought a flooring store up here so I can now showcase my interior design," I finally said.

"You *did?* Don't you ever stop?"

"Opportunities just seem to keep falling in my lap. I'll take you by there before you hit the road. I don't think you ever met my friend from school, Sarah, but she's up here now with her graphic design business. It seems like a perfect place to start your life over."

"I *do* have to tell you, Annie, I don't see David much anymore. I made it clear to John I didn't want to be a third party if they see each other. And that's not all that often anymore."

I knew she'd bring him up eventually, and I thought I'd prepared myself. But I must have given way to the surprise of her frankness, for Susan put her hand on my arm.

"I think he made a terrible mistake by being unfaithful to you, Annie," Susan whispered. "He's lost his verve; his drive. Oh, did I just say that out loud?" She said, startled at her own voice. "I didn't mean to drop that on you like that. But I just can't get over how good you look, and how awful David looks."

Susan's voice drifted off as I felt a twinge of the same anger I had when she told me she'd seen David with another woman. And then satisfaction I'd experienced when I ripped his clothes from the hangers and let them fall to the ground. After I tore our wedding album apart, I left everything on the floor. I'd been so angry with him in the past, I wasn't sure how to react to her comments now, but suddenly I found myself feeling a little sorry for him.

"I've hated him," I said.

"I'm sure you have. And I wouldn't blame you. If John did to me what David did to you, I'd kill him. Or at least cut his you know what off."

This made me smile.

"I'm with someone," I finally said, and I could feel my face flush.

And as if on cue, Noah walked up to our table, his tool belt keeping time to his footsteps. I almost jumped out of our booth. I could tell he'd made sure his hair was pulled back perfectly, and he gently stroked his beard.

"Hey babe," he said casually.

I was speechless.

"I saw your car. Hey ladies," he then said, acknowledging Susan and Christine. "I'm starting a new job today and I might be late getting home. Can you stop and pick up dog food? I gave the kids the last of it this morning."

Oh, my god. He was making sure they knew I was with him! I was shocked, and then I burst into laughter. I didn't think Noah had that in him!

When he left, Susan turned to me and said, "Well, he wants us to know he's staked his territory," and we laughed. "Plus he's gorgeous! Well done," she said, giving me a high five.

I showed Susan and Christine the stores and I could tell she was genuinely in awe.

"I'm in awe of how you manage all this," Susan remarked.

"I don't know if I would have had the courage to do what I'm doing if you wouldn't have given me the opportunities. I'm very thankful you came into my life."

We met at Ginny's for dinner that night, and Noah, Josh and Sarah joined us.

"So Annie tells me you two go way back," Noah said to Susan.

"I thought for sure she'd end up in real estate, but she brought her design talents to the company, and I see she's had no problem continuing up here. Great for her," she said, toasting me with her iced tea.

"I don't know if I told you I have a couple of realtors up here that I've been doing some staging for."

"She never sits still, does she?" Susan said to Noah.

"Not since I've known her," he said, winking at me. "And now I know who to blame for all this."

"And the cabins are marvelous. I'm really proud of you. I know John will be pleased. And Sarah," she said, turning to her, "I hear you're

Annie's friend from school. How wonderful you two are together again! I don't really have anyone I knew from high school."

"I've become a transplant too," Sarah said. "I love it. And Annie has helped me jump start my business up here. I also work with some of the realtors doing their brochures and marketing."

When we finished dinner Susan said, "Well, I'm pooped. We're thinking about getting up early and heading back down. You won't think we're party poopers, will you, Annie?"

"Not in the least. We're going to hang out for a bit, so if I don't see you, be sure to give John my best. He was a very good friend to me."

"I will. You keep up the good work."

"And you drive down carefully. Take your time with all the curves."

When a slow song came on, Noah took my hand and led me to the dance floor.

"I love it when we dance," I said.

"I love *you*," Noah said.

"I know you do."

"Do you ever think of him?"

I would have been lying if I said I didn't, so I said, "sometimes, I do. But I also know that if things hadn't gone the way they did for us, I wouldn't be here with you. So when I think of it that way, it had to happen."

CHAPTER FIFTEEN

Spring was always my favorite time of the year. Dew still covered the hoods, windshields and tops of everyone's cars, and the trees that lost their leaves and looked so bare in fall were starting to bloom. Plants that I thought for certain had died came back to life. In the mornings, the sun barely came up over the horizon when it flooded through the window. If I wanted to wake naturally, I only had to wait until it hit my eyes.

There was still a briskness in the air, generally a warm sun during the day and just enough chill at night to keep the fireplace going; I still kept my neck scarf and mittens handy in a coat pocket. I've caught myself after a springtime rain, sitting in the car, mesmerized by the windshield wipers clicking back and forth. When the glass was dry and the wipers vibrated across it, the spell would be broken and I'd have to move along. I couldn't help but marvel at how beautiful it was up here.

Usually in April and May, the dogwoods bloomed. We had quite a few of them on the property and they made a spectacular sight as they lined the highways and filled the gullies with millions of white flowers. Sam once told me his wife Trudy would tell him stories about them.

One was that the Cherokee believed little people lived surrounded by dogwoods, and they were sent here to teach people to live in harmony with the woods.

Another was from biblical times; they were Adam's favorite tree in the Garden of Eden, so the devil sneaked in to try to knock all the blossoms off the tree. But the blossoms were shaped like a cross, and so he failed.

The third one was that Jesus loved dogwood trees, which during that time, grew to the size of oak trees. This was the tree that was chosen for his cross. Once Christ was crucified, God decreed that from that day forward, the dogwood would never grow large enough to be used for a crucifix again. Therefore, it's remained a small tree with leaf-like flower petals flower that signify the shape of the cross. The cluster of fruit in the center represents the blood of Christ, and the center flower resembles the crown of thorns.

When everything else turned green, some trees remained brown, and it became clear some they were dying. Sam showed me an article in the newspaper regarding our progress in the constant fight with the bark beetles, which were the culprits.

"Reminds me of a story about John Muir," he said. "Born in Scotland, John Muir actually visited Lake Arrowhead. He was a well-known naturalist who came up in the late 1800s with the U.S. Forest Reserve Commission to document all the trees that had been lost by logging. He was very disheartened to discover that a lot of the mature trees were gone, but noticed there were quite a few new growths of ce-dars, dogwoods, sugar pine and oaks. I heard tell they named the John Muir Road up here after him."

I could always count on Sam for a story.

CHAPTER TWENTY TWO

Hudson

We stayed in our first mountain home while we worked on the new house. Once we got underway, I found I enjoyed the remodeling process. Constance and Annie would meet and make some tentative selections, then they'd lay them out for me to look at. I liked everything and decided the girls had pretty good taste. My only request was that the home be comfortable, a little rustic, but sophisticated. No cutesy cabin signs and décor.

The house was a three-story monster; the entry level top floor comprised an immense living room, large dining room and large kitchen with a massive island, along with an office overlooking the lake for Constance, a guest bedroom and bathroom and the elevator. The second floor, going down, had a large master bedroom and bath, another guest bedroom, a media room, a family room with a full bar and a niche for my office, plus an additional office, if needed. On that floor, there were another two guest bedrooms and bathrooms. The third floor down was smaller and had two more guest bedrooms and bathrooms.

We certainly didn't need that much space, but we could definitely use the bottom two floors for storage, and they'd be the last rooms to be worked on.

Literally at the top of the hill behind the lake, the house gave us three hundred sixty-five degree views of not only the entire lake, but the valleys and desert behind us. The views were incredible, and the house was large enough to merge all the furniture we'd had in storage when we got married and combined households.

Before we put Mother's house on the market, I'd rented a large storage space and hired a couple of guys to help us take the furniture and artwork Susan and I wanted. Now, I saw the current remodeling as a perfect opportunity to eliminate the space and the extra expense. I had everything brought up to the mountains and put into the garage until I could figure out where it would go in the new house.

"Why did you choose to do this now?" I'd exasperated Constance again. "We're still in the middle of painting and putting in new flooring...and we've already decided what pieces we're keeping."

"I guess I'm a guy and didn't think it through?"

"Hudson," she said, annoyed. "Let me have Annie come look at it again and see where she thinks it'll work. Then we can move the rest down into storage."

"See," I said, trying to shrug it off. "I knew you'd figure out what to do with it. Sorry," I said sheepishly.

I knew Constance would eventually forgive me, but I also figured taking her to a nice restaurant for dinner would help. I called Annie.

"I'm in the doghouse," I said, "And I need to wine and dine Constance."

"She already called me. We'll figure out what to do, and in the meantime, if you haven't already been to the Saddleback Grill, take her there. She'll love it."

"You're a lifesaver. I'm sure it won't be the last time I'll need you to bail me out."

"Not to worry," she said, and laughed. "And one day I might need you. I hope not, but you never know."

With a new kitchen and master bathroom, we were finally ready to move in. We brought in our office furniture and equipment first so we could get everything set up without interruptions.

Then we spent a full day with the moving company loading up the L.A. house, which had just gone on the market. By the time we got to the bottom of the hill, it was too late to make the drive up and do any unloading, so *we came up by ourselves, and the truck and men stayed in a local motel. The next morning, I went back down, bought the men breakfast, and they followed me back up.*

Voluminous gray clouds threatened us throughout the day, but there had been no prediction for either rain or snow, and thankfully we got completely unloaded with boxes in place before the truck headed back down.

The next day, the gray clouds were now the darkest I'd ever seen, and the sky opened up. There was something peaceful about listening to the heavy rainfall on our roof. Constance and I kept taking breaks from unpacking and would just stand at our floor to ceiling windows looking out over the lake, which was now covered with a layer of fog.

"Look at the trees," she said, hugging herself as if she were cold. "The green is wonderful against such dark gray."

The water in the lake mirrored the dark color of the sky.

"This is cool," I said.

Annie referred us to her friend Sarah, who helped us update our business cards, letterhead and envelopes. She arranged for all the printing and when I asked her about helping me with advertising and printing for the air shows I was flying in, I sensed her readiness to take on another project.

"I'd love to," she said.

CHAPTER TWENTY THREE

In April, we all gathered around the large table in the back of Ginny's and celebrated spring birthdays; Noah's and Sam's were at the end of March, and Ginny and I were just a few days apart in April. Sarah was in charge of decorations, so she covered the tables with red and white check tablecloths and set out matching napkins. She made a fabulous centerpiece with red tulips, yellow irises, purple hyacinth and white asters. And in its center was a clay pot of pink roses. At each place setting, she set small pots with mixed tulips.

"Oh my god, Sarah. This is incredible," I exclaimed. "These are just beautiful."

"Why, thanks," she answered. "I'm just full of surprises."

"Indeed, you are. A woman of many talents!"

Ginny outdid herself for dinner. She'd cooked a beef roast with broasted potatoes, plenty of gravy and au jus, creamed corn, a green bean casserole and garlic bread.

"Well, I'm in heaven," Josh proclaimed.

We brought two bottles of wine and poured everyone a glass.

"If you leave hungry, it's not my fault," Ginny said once everyone had their plates full.

Midway through the meal, Sam stood to make a toast.

"Hear, hear," he said. "I'm not real good with this kind of thing, but I wanted to wish everybody a happy birthday, and I especially wanted to say how much I've loved having you all up here. Annie, you brought a spark of light into my old life. Noah, you've been like a son to me, and Ginny, well, what can I say about Ginny…she was there for me when I needed her most and she has a place in my heart. When my wife died, she even fended off all the crazy women who came calling, wearing sensible shoes and bringing me casseroles."

"Why thanks, Sam," Ginny said. "You have a place in my heart, too. You've always been there for me, through thick and thin," and then she patted her stomach. Everyone laughed. "Seriously, you've supported me in ways you'll never know."

"Sounds like wedding toasts to me," Josh joked.

"Well, now, if it was, you'd all be the first to know, right Ginny?" Sam said.

"Absolutely," she said.

"No-ah. No-ah," Josh chanted.

"I guess that means I need to say something too? Well, first to Sam, you've been like a dad to me, and I love ya for it. To Ginny, you've been there for me, too. Plus, you make the best food around. To Annie, what can I say? I love ya, babe."

"My turn?" I asked. "Well, to Sam and Ginny, you've been such a big part of my new life up here, and I can't thank you enough for everything you've enabled me to do. And to Noah, you've been there for me since the first day I met you. You took me under your wing, told me to get boots if I was going to be up here for long, and have helped make me love the mountains. I love you too."

Josh was right. The way Sam and Ginny toasted each other, it surprised me they weren't announcing an upcoming wedding. When I asked Sam, he said, "Ah, no. We've talked about it, but we're happy the way we are. It's not like we're planning on a family," then he chuckled.

About a week later, Sam fell off one of the cabin porches and ended up with a badly sprained ankle.

"Dad gummed old age," he said when he called me at the store.

"I'll be right there," I said. I popped in to tell Ginny what happened and then rushed to the drugstore behind the restaurant to get an Ace Bandage. By the time I got back to Ginny's, she had a bucket of ice ready for me.

"What happened?" I asked when I saw him.

He'd managed to hobble to the office where he sat in one of the chairs and elevated his swollen foot up on the coffee table.

"Well, one minute I was on the porch and the next I was on the ground. Obviously I wasn't watching where I was goin'."

He winced as he moved his foot.

"I made it to one of the Adirondack chairs and rested for a few minutes before I limped back to the office to call you."

I wrapped his ankle in a towel loaded with ice, then found a large plastic trash bag I could put his foot in so ice wouldn't melt all over the table.

"Always thinking practical," he said, wincing as he laid back down.

"Try to take it easy and either Ginny or I will come check on you."

"Thanks. Hurts like a son of a gun."

"I'm sure it does. Try to rest."

Ginny stayed with Sam in the cabins while he recuperated. She got him some crutches so he could at least get around. We had one booking, so I worked from the cabin office, and between me, Lily and Sarah, we made sure the cabin got cleaned after our guest left.

There were weekends we were now completely booked at the cabins, and we had one permanent renter, so we were finally showing a profit! We were getting ready to plant flowers again and spread more gravel where for the last year, the old rocks had been crushed into the ground. Another project on the spring list was to replace the old window screens on the cabins, and a fellow from town was coming out to do that next week.

After Memorial Weekend, Noah started a new job that would keep him busy throughout summer and into fall. It was a home previously owned by Brian Wilson of the Beach Boys, and I had to admit I was impressed

157

with its celebrity history. I met with his client a few times, and they hired me to design the project. For someone "famous", the house was unassuming yet inviting; it was more of a New England style Cape Cod than a mountain lodge. It had four bedrooms, three and a half baths, all in a charming setting with roses in the garden, and a cobblestone walkway. They wanted to make quite a few cosmetic changes, and I shared how I loved to see the older homes up here keep their character while undergoing any updates.

The home was in an older part of Arrowhead, in the Tavern Bay area on the north side of the lake near the UCLA Conference Center. A few rooms had been updated, meaning old wallpaper had been removed, and the walls had been painted in somewhat current colors, but almost every other room had wallpaper and window treatments from the thirties. Even with Lily and Sarah's help, I had my work cut out for me, but I was up for the challenge.

Hudson and Constance were thrilled with the progress on their new home, and the remodeling made a huge difference. They'd moved in after we finished remodeling the master bedroom and offices, and once we hung all the artwork, we started working on smaller projects throughout the house.

In June, I had Noah help me pack up the rest of my boxes and I closed down my storage. My plan was to bring everything to the cabin and unpack a few boxes at a time so the task wouldn't be so overwhelming. Some of the accessories and books I'd kept looked good on the bookshelves, and even though my sideboard, mirror and samovar urn from Long Beach were on the traditional side, the mix with the cabin decor worked well along one wall in the sunroom.

The last box was filled with scrapbooks and photos. I thought about finding a place in one of the closets to store it, but the storage space was limited. I remembered the small wooden chest I'd set next to a chair in the reading alcove. I brought the cardboard box over and cut the tape holding the lid flaps open. I'd randomly tossed everything in it when I was packing up the house in Long Beach and sat for a moment to look at what I'd saved.

Right on top were some photos of Loni and me as children. One was of me on the swing my father built up at the Lake House, and several others were of my mother driving the boat. There was one of Mrs. Richmond's garden next door, and one of Loni and me building our first snowman.

I was hot and tired and I hadn't intended to spend a lot of time going through the photos, but I got swept up in them. There Sarah and I were on graduation day, me knowing she was leaving that afternoon, and then there was Loni and I again in our Easter Sunday dresses, and festive hats. My heart fluttered a bit, seeing how innocent we both were at those young ages; I placed us at about five and eight. We curtsied in front of the camera, and I did recall on the rare times we sported new dresses and shoes, I was always so proud. We attended a non-denominational church down the street from our house, and even after the service, I wore my outfit until my mother harped on me to take it off before I got it dirty. Loni, on the other hand, could hardly wait for the photos to be taken so she could remove her hat and shoes and run around.

There were photos of me as a baby sitting next to Loni, who even then seemed to frown. I tilted my head in thought and wondered if I just imagined it, or had she frowned and tolerated me our whole lives? I remembered the story about her cutting my hair off once, and my mother was furious. Of course, the rest of it then needed to be cut so it would look like I had short hair intentionally. And once I was so frightened of her when she pushed me down in the backyard and told me she was going to bury me in the flower bed. It didn't matter that all she had was her plastic beach bucket and shovel; it was so real and terrifying.

"You'll be with Tabby Cat," she'd said.

At that, I'd run away from her, letting the screen door slam behind me as I ran into the kitchen.

"Don't slam the door!" my mother called too late.

I wondered when it was I started giving up on Loni and me; I think it was when we bought the Lake House. I *know* it was after my thirteenth birthday. I sat for a few minutes just thinking, and then my mind went blank. I hadn't thought of her lately, and emotion eluded me. I didn't miss her, and that fact made me feel sad.

I suddenly wasn't in the mood for further reminiscence, so I started grabbing photos by the handful and putting them in the cabinet. I stopped when I came across one of me with David. I thought I'd left all our photos in Long Beach, and my heart skipped a beat as I saw his image from almost ten years ago when we first met. We looked so happy. In my mind, I had become a woman when we married, although there would be so much more I'd need to learn. It seemed like each day brought with it a new challenge to finally make something of my life.

The world we'd shared seemed so long ago and blurred...it was nothing like the world I lived in now. I should have taken the time to finish going through the rest of the stack right then, but instead, I pulled out all the photos I'd already put into the chest and rearranged them so that the ones of my life with David would be on the bottom. I no longer consciously thought of him, but for some reason, I wasn't ready to dispose of them.

Was I betraying Noah by doing so?

The end of June, one of our local realtors who was involved in dog and cat rescues, wanted to do a pet adoption day at the store, and I thought it was a great idea. It would help find homes for the animals, and it would be a great event for us to sponsor. We put an ad in the local newspaper and set up a tent with tables and chairs on one side of the building. I couldn't believe there were twenty cages with signs on them describing the dog or cat; their name, approximate age, their disposition, and spaying and neutering details.

It surprised me how many people came to check the animals out, and since Noah had such a big heart, I was hoping he would be too busy that day to stop by. As luck would have it, he and Josh came by, and he took one look at a mutt named Max and fell in love.

"Pleeease?"

"Oh, my god, Noah. You sound like a whiny child," I said.

"But he'll fit right in. And if we don't take him, what will become of him?"

"Noah, we don't need another dog..."

The first night we had Max, there was a lot of growling and barking going on in the house. When it was time to go to bed, I lay there with Max on one side of me, and Coco and Rufus on the other. The next night, the three dogs did their circling routine until they could figure out how the three of them could peacefully snuggle next to the fireplace as we sat and watched TV.

For a few nights, bedtime was a challenge for us, but it wasn't too long until they found their places in bed, and we were finally able to sleep without being awakened by intermittent growling.

July fourth was a big deal up in the mountains, and that year, it fell on a Saturday. We'd watched all the fireworks from land the year before, so this year, we decided to take the boat out, have a light dinner and sit up close and front. Noah and Josh filled a cooler with soda and beer, and Sarah and I stopped at Ginny's to pick up sandwiches, potato salad and cookies.

We'd invited Hudson and Constance to join us, but Constance was hosting about a hundred people at their house while Hudson did a fly-over in his plane. Noah found what looked like the perfect spot for us, until other boaters with the same idea started milling around us.

"Hey," I wanted to call out to a boat that parked in front of us.

"There's plenty of room for all of us," Josh pointed out. "And it's not as though we won't be able to see the fireworks."

"You're right, but people can really be annoying," I answered.

The lake's patrol boat made several cruises around us and reminded everyone to be careful and watch their drinking. Noah never had more than a couple of beers if he took the boat out, so I wasn't worried about us.

During the fireworks presentation, the patrol boat circled around again, but this time, they stopped at the boat in front of us. It had become obvious from the noise they were making they were doing their fair share of partying. An officer took over the boat, and once the occupants were loaded onto the patrol boat, they were escorted back to shore.

"What happens in a case like that?" I asked.

"Never having been in that situation, I'm not sure," Noah answered. "I assume they'll be ticketed, and maybe even arrested for being drunk."

"Their boat might even be impounded," Josh added.

"Serves them right for parking in front of us!" I laughed.

Summer time up in the mountains could be unpredictable, as I'd learned, and it had been cool enough that some trees started losing their leaves. Piles of them covered our garden areas and collected along the roads. Since it was July, no one had predicted the freak thunder and lightning storm two weeks later. The skies turned gray—then it seemed everything lost its color. First came the clap of thunder, then the sky lit up. I'd gone to the store early to unpack some boxes, and it was just before ten when the phone rang. I considered not answering it, but I moved the boxes and carefully stepped over the wrapping to grab the phone.

Sam's voice pierced through the phone.

"We're on fire! I've called 911, but cabin six is in flames!"

"Sam?"

"Lightning struck us."

"Good god!" I yelled back. "I'll be right there."

"The fire truck will be here by then, so you might not be able to get in. The highway will be a mess. I gotta go!"

I climbed back over the mess I'd made on the floor and rushed to the front door. I didn't have my keys, so I had to backtrack to grab my purse. My heart was pounding as I got in my car, and I tried to calm myself down.

I'd obviously seen the lightning and heard the thunder roar, but I hadn't realized it'd hit any trees. All I could think of was that we needed to get the cats out, and then I hoped rainfall would follow to help put out the fire.

As I pulled up near the cabins, two firemen were redirecting traffic, turning vehicles back to where they came from. I got out of my car anyway and ran to them.

"It's my place that's on fire," I cried out, and they let me through the bushes.

"Stay out of the way!"

I made it to the office and quickly closed the door behind me. The cats were wild with all the smoke and noise, and at first they wouldn't let me touch them. Then Jezebel meowed and came out from under the bed, with Socks not too far behind her.

"Good girls," I cooed. "You'll be fine."

I locked them in Sam's rooms, and once I knew they were safe inside, I went back out and watched as black smoke filled the air in front of us. The fire crackled and sparks exploded almost artistically, then they quickly disappeared into the air. The smell of smoke burned my nostrils, and I put my jacket up to my nose.

"Is there anyone else here?" a fireman asked.

"No, just us," Sam answered. "And we got the cats inside."

I looked at Sam. "Did you call Noah?"

"No, I figured he was out workin'."

"You're right, we probably won't be able to reach him. I'll call and leave him a message anyway," I said, going in to use the desk phone.

Within another half hour, the fire was reduced to white smoke. One fire truck left, leaving two firemen left. While one raked, the other doused any remaining smoldering ashes with water. I could tell the complete roof was gone, and one wall was down.

"Oh, Sam," I cried. "All our hard work..."

"It's just a cabin, Annie. It doesn't seem like it now, but it'll all be fine. We'll call the insurance company and they'll take care of everything." He said, gently patting my back. "There, there."

I needed his comforting arms, right then, and couldn't help but think back to when I was a child, and I sought the comfort of my mother's arms. When she held me, my worries suddenly vanished.

There was nothing we could do, so we went back up to the office and tried to reassure the cats they were going to be all right. My hands were shaking as I flipped through our Rolodex to our insurance agent's number. When he finally came on the line, he took all our information and reassured me the damage would be covered. He said he'd turn it in the minute we hung up.

Even though everything could be replaced, it still broke my heart to see how fast fire could destroy the cabin, and how quickly everything could change.

"I need to open the store," I suddenly realized. "Are you all right if I go?"

There wasn't anything more I could do there.

"You go ahead. We'll be fine. I'll let the girls out after everyone's left. If they don't hide under my bed, I'll give them some treats."

It was impossible for me to focus on much other than the fire for the rest of the day. Noah came by to see how I was doing, and I found myself crying in his arms like I'd done with Sam.

"It'll all be fine," he said. "Can you reorder what burned?"

"Yes. I'll try to do that now, even though I know it'll be a while before the cabin's ready. I'm sure the other cabins have smoke damage too." I sighed heavily.

While everything in number six would need to be replaced, thankfully, only the cabins on either side of five smelled of smoke. Once the insurance adjuster came out, we took down the draperies, packed up the bedding and linens, and took everything to the dry cleaners to be cleaned and deodorized. Noah's guys cleaned the walls and floors, and Lily from the store came in to clean the windows and wipe down the bathrooms and kitchenettes. The artwork wasn't damaged, nor was the furniture.

We had one guest coming in, and while I hated to have them see the damage to cabin six, there was no way to avoid it.

I urged Noah to make a bid to do the fire restoration, and when he heard he got the job, he made his material list and ordered everything from the lumber company up in the mountains. We had the logs custom milled to match the rest of the cabins, although there was no way we'd be able to match the old wood exactly.

They started demolition right away, and once all the debris was hauled off, they could make a final assessment of the pine flooring. It turned out it was so badly damaged it had to be completely replaced.

"We should probably take the closet out when we tear out the floor," he suggested. "It'll be easier than working around it."

"Can we make the bathroom and kitchenette look original?" I asked.

"Yup," he said.

I was at the store when Noah called a week later with his progress.

"Babe," he said. "You've got to come see this."

"Can it wait? I'm in the middle of something."

"No, it can't," he said breathlessly. "You need to see this."

"Can you cover for me?" I asked Sarah. "Noah wants me to go to the cabins."

"Sure," she said. "We'll be fine."

I grabbed my purse and headed back. When I got there, everyone was standing around Noah and an old black leather bag. "Inland Empire Bank" was imprinted on the side, and inside, it was filled with banded twenty-dollar bills.

"Where did this come from?" I asked, my eyes wide.

"We found it while tearing up the floor in the closet. The wood was loose," Josh said.

"This is crazy," Noah said.

"It's unbelievable, is what it is." I frowned. "What do we do with it? Is the bank still in business?"

"I've never heard of it," Noah said, "but that doesn't mean anything."

"I'm going to the library on the way back to the store. I'll see if there were any old bank robberies. Wow, this is really crazy," I said.

I made it just before the library closed and asked the librarian to help me with the microfiche. It took me a while, but I found it.

Public Help Sought
in Inland Empire Bank Robbery

"On June 23, 1930, notorious bank robber John Francis Johnson and his gang robbed the Inland Empire Bank of $65,000.00. Police said at around nine that morning, a passerby heard the alarm coming from the bank and called it in. They're still looking for Johnson, and although no one witnessed the kidnapping, bank president Frank L. Bellamy is missing. His wife told police she hasn't received any ransom call or note."

I searched a few months ahead, and there were no follow-up stories that I could see. However, I might have missed something, for I hated using the process itself. The first thing I did when I returned to the cabins was to pull out the old guest registers and see if I could find anyone who stayed there around that time.

Sure enough, on June 23, an F. Bell checked in, and he was given cabin number six for his stay. Like the other stories the cabins had to tell, there was no way of knowing what ultimately happened to Mr. Bellamy; obviously he never made it back to pick up his bag of loot.

Even though Noah worked on it constantly, the restoration seemed to drag on forever. Noah found a color stain that closely matched the other logs and that helped, but I was disappointed the old patina wasn't there. Fortunately, it was on the side of the cabin and not the front where it would be obvious.

I had everything I needed to redecorate the interior, and I was impatiently waiting to get it put back together. Any new guests could now not even tell there had been work going on, and since the exterior looked finished, I could re-do the landscaping. When the day finally arrived, I had one of Noah's guys, Kirk, help me get everything out of storage and bring it to the cabins. He put the bed together and then Sarah, Lily, and I finished it up.

"Ta-da," Sarah said, said wiping her hands together. "We did it!"

"Thanks to you," I said. "We're back in business. I'm buying lunch. You too, Kirk. Join us."

Ending Are New Beginnings

Sarah and Josh have moved in together, which seems like a natural thing
to do. They're very much into each other, and Sarah thinks she may have
found Mr. Right. We've never had that conversation, except in snippets...
the one about what happened to our marriages.

"I should have never married him," she'd said. "I really hurt him."

"You were trying to figure out what you wanted to do," I said in
her defense.

I hadn't told her about my involvement with Grayson Underwood,
and I decided to keep my indiscretion to myself. Truthfully, I hadn't
wanted to relive the experience. In the end, neither of us needed to know
any of the details. For both of us, it was all in the past.

"For the first time, I think I've found what I've been looking for,"
she said. "And I've been thinking about putting up a Christmas tree this
year. I've never had one, you know."

"Wow. You really *are* serious," I said.

She's kept in touch with her sisters, although mostly through answering machine messages. Her mother's still in Barstow, and still with
Charlie. Sarah hasn't been back down to see them, but she calls her mom
now and then.

Constance Fisher came into the design store one afternoon in early July.
She wanted to add some area rugs to the living room and entry.

"If you don't mind me asking," I said, "I've been curious if Hudson
has ever tried to find the mysterious fourth child."

"I don't mind you asking at all. There's not a lot he can do. He
doesn't know the name of the hospital, and I'm sure the records are
sealed. He does regret not knowing about it all before his father died; he
could have asked him if he knew anything about it. I honestly think he
and the brothers have no choice but to see if someone looks for Celeste.
It's quite interesting, isn't it?"

"Yes, it is."

"Well, let's see if Hudson likes any of these," she said, taking the bag
of samples I handed her. "Even if he doesn't, we'll decide and tell him
his choice was back ordered!" she said, laughing. "I'll give you a call."

One day at the end of September, out of the blue, Noah said, "I've made a new path that winds around the property. I'd like you to see it. Let's go for a walk with the dogs."

I'd never really walked his land because it was more like a forest, with a thick layer of leaves and pine needles that stuck to your boots. And the last time I'd ventured out, I wasn't watching where I was headed and a low-lying branch scratched my forehead, exactly like it happened when I was ten and at our Pinecone Lake House. The path he'd made was just like the ones at the cabins and matched what he already had out in front: lined with smaller tree trunks and medium-sized rocks.

"This is like an adventure," I said as the dogs ran ahead of us.

"Now that we have a family, what do you think about doing the right thing?"

"The *right* thing?" I asked.

"Yeah, make an honest woman out of you."

"Make an honest woman out of me?"

"Yeah."

"Hmm..." I scrunched my face as if in contemplation.

I thought back to the first morning we spent together, when I'd stood and watched Noah combing his hair, shirtless, and I couldn't help but love everything about him; his muscled arms, his lean chest. And an involuntary smile came to my face as I remembered the first time I'd seen him waiting for me in Las Vegas, with his shirt unbuttoned, and that sexy line of dark hair leading down just below his waist. But mostly, it was the heart inside him I remembered the most; the one that loved only me.

Before I'd fallen in love with Noah, I often wondered if I'd be able to let another man into my life. How would I truly let him see my weaknesses? But he'd seen them, as I'd seen his. I knew there would be things I'd never share with him, so that neither one of us could get hurt again. One thing I knew for sure was that life with him would be different than it was for me with David. I wouldn't just be playing house.

For the first time in a long time, I thought about David's children. I'd only been given them for a short period, but then again, it was one of the most important times in a young person's life; their teenage years. I hoped the time we spent together as a family, especially with David's parents, helped them find some balance.

I now knew the difference between being a naïve twenty-year-old and finally learning about the complexities of life. I'd wished for happily ever after with David, but with Noah, I knew he was someone I would share a lifetime with.

The sun was setting, its warmth quickly fading, and the frogs and crickets from the stream that ran through the property seemed to sing together. Noah spotted the largest and most interesting spider web I'd ever seen, with a rainbow on its threads, and thankfully with no spider in sight. We'd just completed the last turn when the fog, notorious as it is up here, suddenly began rolling in, and we called to the dogs.

When we got back inside, we called my parents and made plans to spend a week with them at the end of October. We'd tell them then. I planned on visiting Loni's grave, which would have been a given for my parents, but it was my decision to bring her flowers and try to make amends for our past. I wasn't sure yet, just what I'd actually say, but I knew I'd think of something.

I knew I needed to officially say goodbye.

CELESTE

1910–1980

My father, Johan, was a physician, and he wanted only the best for his family, which included me, my mother Margaret, and my older sister Ruth. We lived in the Gold Coast neighborhood in Chicago, in one of the more modest mansions. We had the requisite cook, Nita the housekeeper, and several maids. A man came in weekly to care for my father's car. Ruth and I were never allowed to answer the phone or go to the door.

"Nita can greet anyone who rings our doorbell, and obviously, none of the phone calls would be for you two girls, so it would just be a waste of time for the caller," Mother would remind us.

Both my parents were for women's suffrage, and even though my father preferred she was less so, my mother was active in campaigning for it. I was too young to understand the importance of it all back then, and when I was ten, they granted women the right to vote. While the vote didn't immediately affect Ruth or me, Mother stayed active in her endeavors, now focusing on better public health and education. And this meant raising her expectation of our achievements.

One of those was to marry a man who was wealthy enough that we could continue to make a social difference. That suited my sister Ruth, who dreamed about marrying someone rich and handsome. Because my parents were not members of an elite club, there would be no coming-out parties for *her to meet someone, so once she was old enough, she made sure she was on the guest lists for all the fashionable parties around town. All she read was fashion magazines. My mother encouraged her and was hoping I would become just as interested when I grew older, but I was more fascinated by movie stars and reading about how glamorous their lives were.*

Mother would take us to the movies where we saw Marlene Dietrich, Mary Pickford, and Gloria Swanson. For days after, I would daydream about having the exciting life I imagined they did. I could picture myself in either a scarf tied around my head to avoid messing up my hair, or wearing one of the latest new hats as my driver drove me about. Of course, I was always glamorous. I saw it now; Celeste Williamson, the glamorous film star...

My sister and I were both strongly encouraged to go to college after graduating, which was getting to be very popular. It delighted Ruth when she ended up finding a husband before she had to go away. I was not interested in college or a husband, and I made it perfectly clear to both my parents. Whenever I talked about it, my father would harrumph and sulk for a while, until he broke down went back to reading his newspaper. He was never really home during the day, and depending on how busy the hospital was, sometimes he wouldn't come home until long after we'd had our dinner. When that happened, Mother had Cook wrap up his meal and leave it in the oven.

Mother didn't approve of a lot of the new women's clothing coming out during that time, but wanting to keep up with the times, she gradually dressed a little more casually; she actually cut her hair and had it styled in one of the new popular short hairdos.

"That looks wonderful, darling," I could hear my father say as she paraded in front of him in a new outfit and hairdo.

However, under no circumstances were either Ruth or I allowed to cut our hair. Mine was long and curly and I hated it. I also had a tender head, so brushing my hair was a major ordeal. Mother never learned to hold on to a section of my hair before she combed it, and I always cried out that she was hurting me. Ruth did her own hair, and had mastered pulling it back and tying it in to a complicated bun.

Both sets of my grandparents came to America when they were young. My father's family was Swedish, hence the name Williamson. And my mother's family was German.

Chicago in the 1920s and 1930s was home to some of the most notorious gangsters, like Al Capone, Bugs Moran, John Dillinger and Dion O'Banion, and I recall my parents being exceptionally cautious and careful when we went out.

One place we frequented, The Blackstone Hotel, was architecturally designed to help keep out Chicago's sooty air. The wealthiest guests had special elevators that took them to exclusive events. The premier restaurant had a window with the largest pane of glass in America, and from there you could see a panoramic view of Lake Michigan. Mother never admitted it, but when we went there, I could always tell she was looking around to see if there was anyone she knew. Being seen in prominent places was important to her.

It became known as the Hotel of Presidents because it later housed twelve consecutive U.S. presidents. Unknown to us at the time, Al Capone held meetings in the windowless barber shop there. In the early thirties, after I'd left for Hollywood, "Lucky" Luciano hosted a gathering in the Crystal Ballroom.

We also went to The Art Institute, and for hours we were made to gaze at hundreds of paintings and sculptures. I think Mother was hoping we'd learn to appreciate art by osmosis. She also loved going to the Garfield Park Conservatory, where inside was the world's largest plant collection under a glass roof. All those plants made my sinuses ache.

My favorite place to go was Marshall Field & Company. Ruth liked it too. It was Chicago's most famous department store, and the world's largest at the time. I looked it up once at the library and it had 76 elevators, 31 square miles of carpeting and 125,000 feet of pneumatic tubes that processed payments from store departments to accounting. I thought this was quite fascinating.

Marshall Field was where Mother allowed Ruth and me to shop on our own, while she was off in other departments. When she would come back to get us, we'd show her everything we'd selected, and she usually approved of it all. I think because she loved shopping so much, my mother encouraged us to enjoy it as well.

I knew I'd never become an actress if I stayed in Chicago. I didn't want to work at the Majestic Theater and get into vaudeville, so I set my sights on Los Angeles and Hollywood.

By 1928, I'd already planned my escape, although I wasn't sure if I was going to tell my parents ahead of time, or wait until the day I actually left. My father's mother died the year before, leaving me a thousand dollars, a gold necklace with a locket and a diamond watch, so I knew I had the money to support myself for a while.

The stock market crashed in 1929 and while we somehow were sheltered from the worst, the newspapers were filled with terrible stories about people losing everything and committing suicide. My father never really said where he had invested his money, but I was assuming he had been wise, for we never went without. I do recall that during that time, he had a lot of patients that didn't have the money to pay him for his services, so he'd come home with all kinds of things people gave him. Sometimes it was jewelry, or original edition books. A patient who was a cobbler made shoes for him, and we had free coal delivered several times during the winter. If I remember correctly, the iceman who delivered for our ice box had three or four children who were always getting sick from something or another, so we always had ice.

I chose springtime to leave. Although there was still snow on the ground, you could go outside without wearing heavy clothing, and I knew the weather would get warmer as I headed west. I was leaving all my winter clothes behind.

I'd decided not to tell my parents ahead of time, so I waited until the day before I left to break the news to them. My father wasn't home, so I told my mother first. I thought she was going to faint the way she put her hand up to her forehead; she could have become an actress herself as she dramatically plunked herself down onto the drawing room settee.

"You can't go!" she cried out, appalled. "A young woman would never go out on her own and do such a thing!"

Her hands were shaking, and I truly felt awful breaking the news to her that way, but I knew if I tried to talk her into it, she and my father would never agree.

"I knew something was up when I saw all those magazines in your room," she said, gathering her composure. "I should have figured something was going on."

My eyes narrowed, for I never suspected she'd go into my room and find them.

She blurted out, "The maid showed them to me when she was cleaning your room."

"Mother, they were under my mattress. What was she doing looking there?"

I shot her an awful look that I would remember and regret much later in my life. That saying, "If looks could kill," was what I felt, and I know she saw it in my eyes.

"Oh Celeste, this is the most awful thing you could do. You have a future here. You can go to college, and then you can find a husband. You could have a career...and you're willing to throw all that away? To be what? A wanna be actress?"

She took a deep breath and I could see she was trying to calm down. "Oh dear, what will I tell your father?" She put both hands to her temples and rubbed. "Why could you never be like Ruth? You've always been so strong willed."

I hated it when my parents compared me to my sister. We were so opposite in what we liked and what we wanted out of life. Ruth was going to be content being married and having children...and fitting into society. I never wanted that. I wanted adventure and challenges. Even if it turned out I ended up failing.

I knew I needed to at least say I was sorry, for I wasn't made of stone and I could see how distressed she was.

So I said, "I'll be fine, Mother. You and Father have taught me the difference between right and wrong, and I know I'll be successful. This is something I've always wanted to do, and I would regret it if I didn't try." I thought I should tell her I already had my train ticket, so I said, "I leave on the noon train for California tomorrow."

She started crying then. I'd never seen my mother in such a state, and it was beginning to wear me down, so unable to think of anything else to do, I left her there and went up to my room to finish packing.

175

When my father came home, I gave Mother enough time to break the news; and since I didn't want to see him angry with me, I waited until he knocked on my door.

"Button?" my father called as he stood at my door. He hadn't used that nickname in ages. He used to call me that because he thought I had a button nose as a baby.

"Come in," I called to him as I pretended to be packing.

"Well, Mother has told me the news..."

"I'm sorry, Father. I didn't mean to just drop it on her, but I couldn't figure out how else to tell you both."

"Your mother will be all right. She's just being a mother and worried about her little bird leaving the nest." He moved a few things off the chair to my desk and sat. "Would you be surprised if I told you I wanted to leave home when I was your age?"

I was shocked. "You did?"

"Well, yes, and no. My father wanted me to go into his hardware business. I'd had to work there all my young life, but I hated that place. I knew I'd be so miserable if I stayed there, so I told my father I wanted to be a doctor. Of course, he was shattered; flabbergasted that I would even consider giving up the opportunity to carry on the family business. And he'd made it clear he'd always planned on me taking over. I ended up convincing him my sister Josephine could run the business just as well as he could. And that's what she ended up doing. Her initials were J.J. Williamson, the same as my father, so no one ever suspected it was actually run by a woman. Of course she had her hurdles to jump," he said. "But she made it. In fact, she's been very successful."

He then sat next to me and took my hands in his, and said, "I want you to be happy. I know what you want to do is unconventional, but if it's what you want to do in your heart, you'll do it. I've never regretted stepping up and pursuing my own dreams."

He smiled, and it was the first time I think I thought of him as the kind man he was, and not just my father.

I arrived in Los Angeles via a somewhat eventful train ride. First, I met several men who, upon hearing I was going to Hollywood, said they knew *someone who could help me if I wanted them to. Would I be interested in having a drink? Of course, my answer was no. Even though it's every starlet's dream to be discovered in ordinary surroundings, I let my somewhat cynical nature take over, and decided I'd rather take my chances of finding my own way once I reached my destination.*

I'd traveled once by train with my mother and sister, but we'd stayed in a sleeper. I had an idea of what I'd be dealing with, but this trip wasn't first class. The meals were decent, but I detested the sleeping berths. They were very uncomfortable for me. I hated sleeping above someone I did not know, yet I didn't want to be on the bottom berth, for I was afraid someone would come by and rob me.

On the first day, I sat next to a young woman with a well-behaved child, and I surprised myself when I offered to watch him a few times when she had to get up to use the bathroom. We colored in one of his books, and I read to him from his storybooks. I wasn't particularly fond of children, especially when they misbehaved. But this young man proved that not all children were mischievous.

On the second day of the trip, I met two young women, Maude and Lila, who were a little older than I. It turned out they were also on their way to Hollywood. Their hair was coiffed, and they were quite made up. They flirted with just about every gentleman who passed by them. While I felt they were not as sophisticated as I was, they appeared to be experienced performers. I learned they'd been in several traveling vaudeville shows, mostly singing and dancing. At that time, the typical acts in a show included musicians, comedians, magicians and even some celebrities. If you weren't well known, your act was toward the end, so that they could start closing down the show and get customers to leave.

They usually held vaudeville shows in palace-like theaters, which made them even more attractive to patrons, especially if there were acts that included opera singers and classical musicians. Now, in the late 1920s, these grand theaters were replacing vaudeville with talking pictures.

"We're tired of constantly being on the road," Maude said.

"We know we're going to make it big once we get to Los Angeles," said Lila. "I can picture it now, as we step off the train..." With this, she held her arms out wide, as if greeting her audience.

"Once we get our luggage, the first thing we're going to do is find a motel near the studios so we can be where the action is," Maude said.

Since I had no idea where that would be, I asked if I could tag along with them once we reached our destination. And they both said, "Sure. Three can stay anywhere cheaper than two."

We found a small run-down motel and planned on staying for only a short time until we could get the lay of the land. It was a small dark room with bold wallpaper and terrible smelling carpet. It had one dresser and a full size bed that Maude and Lila would share; I offered to sleep on a folding cot that was brought in. I figured it would not be much worse than trying to sleep on the train berths.

The first thing we did was draw numbers for the bathtub. We hadn't bathed in days, and when my turn came, I think I stayed in there for about an hour, just soaking and dreaming about what our first day in Hollywood would be like.

"Hurry up," Lila called through the door. "We're starving."

The second thing we did was find a diner.

"I've eaten so much, I don't think I'll ever eat again," I said once we were finished. "But let's take the bread and butter back to our room in case we want a midnight snack."

"I'm stuffed, but I'm bringing my leftovers home, too," Maude said, leaning back in the booth and stretching.

The next morning, after a big breakfast, we found a newsstand on the way to a beauty parlor we'd seen, and bought all the latest film fan magazines they had. Reading them in Los Angeles, where the agents and studios were actually located, was going to differ greatly from reading them in Chicago, where they were just ads for places only in our imaginations.

My hair was still long, so I had it cut a little and combed it off my forehead with soft ringlets. Maude and Lila both had shorter hair, and they had theirs done in wavy curls. While we waited for each other, we circled all the ads, and Maude said she'd make the first call from the phone booth around the corner. We all looked very glamorous, and I just felt there was no way we wouldn't find work.

One agent agreed to see the three of us, but at our appointment he made it clear it was almost impossible to get anywhere in this business, unless you "slept around" and, of course, it would start with him. He said if we told him where we were staying, he'd get back to us if something came up. For a few minutes I thought Maude and Lila were considering it, but we hightailed it out of there and we all agreed we'd be better off looking for someone else.

After that, I decided to pursue my career on my own. I couldn't see how three girls could all find jobs, so I dressed with gloves and a hat, bold red lipstick and pencil thin brows, when I met with the second agent I contacted. His name was Artie Bell. He was handsome and looked to be around forty. With a full head of dark hair and a matching mustache, he looked as though he himself could have been an actor once.

There were no insinuations about any type of relationship with him, which was an immense relief.

"It's tough to get an honest break in Hollywood," Artie said. "There are hundreds of young girls all wanting to become movie stars, and there are only so many who make it."

It encouraged me when he suggested I have professional photographs taken so he could get a better feeling about how I came across in various poses. I would have to pay for the photography though, and I assured him I was willing to invest in my future.

He recommended someone, and I made an appointment for a photo shoot the next afternoon. The photographer's name was Ross Baker.

Because I wanted to give it my best shot, I had my hair done that morning at the same beauty parlor we first went to, and I wore a new dress I'd purchased the day before. Glancing at myself in the shop windows I passed, I felt on top of the world.

I found the photography studio in a small storefront. I'd only had professional family photographs taken, either in our home, or in a somewhat glamorous studio setting, so when I walked into Mr. Baker's place, I was instantly dismayed.

The room was in a shambles, with all sorts of photographic equipment strewn about; tripods leaned against each other, table tops filled with lenses, spent light bulbs and fabrics. I was almost ready to turn and leave when an extremely handsome man with disheveled light brown hair came out of what must have been his dark room to greet me. His dark brown eyes and long lashes mesmerized me. He ran his hand through his hair as if to tidy up.

"Miss Williamson?"

"Yes."

He finished tucking his shirt in before saying, "I'm Ross Baker. Pleased to meet you. Give me a minute to get set up."

He must have seen the surprised look on my face as I looked around the room again, for he said, "Sorry about the mess. I'd lie to you and tell you it's never like this, but it always is. Thank goodness, I'm busy."

He motioned for me to sit and then realized the chair he was pointing to was covered with papers and another camera. He quickly gathered up the mess and again indicated for me to sit.

"I understand you're looking for some head shots...to get into the movies?"

"Yes. Mr. Bell said you're the best."

"Well, he does refer a lot of actors to me. Plus," he said, "he's my uncle."

I sighed.

"Don't worry. I do great work. And it looks like you have a lot to work with, so this should be fairly quick."

I wasn't exactly sure what he meant by that, but I said, "Great. Where do you want to start?"

"You can start by getting comfortable, and if you sit here, I'll set up around you. We can take a few photos with you with your gloves and hat, and then we'll get a little more relaxed."

The moment I heard the camera clicking, the more exposed I felt; like the camera could look deep into my soul, and I felt uncomfortable.

"Relax," he said, waiting for me to let out my breath.

I tried to recall the poses of famous stars, how they tilted their heads or looked over their shoulders, and Mr. Ross seemed to know how to pose me for the shots he thought were the best.

Several times, when he set the camera down and came over to me to adjust my head, the way he looked at me sent a shiver down my spine. He took a few moments longer to look at my face before he looked straight into my eyes and moved a tendril of my hair. He let his fingers lag, and then he ran them down my cheek.

I'd never been touched by a man, and I wanted to close my eyes and imagine even more! I know my face colored, and then he smiled.

"You're beautiful," he breathed as he pulled his hand away. "You'd make an extraordinary model for me if you're interested."

I wasn't sure exactly what that meant.

"While most of my business comes from doing what I'm doing for you, I have a friend who has a magazine that publishes beautiful women."

I was taken aback. I'd never think of doing such a thing, and all I could think about was what my father would think if he ever saw me. Then I realized he wasn't the type of man who'd look at that type of magazine, since he saw more than his share of women as a physician.

I was fully dressed, but my instinct was to cover myself with my arms and I became indignant.

"Mr. Baker, I'm not interested in any such thing." I was so furious I could hardly speak.

He quickly came to stand by me, totally flustered himself. "I didn't mean to suggest you do something unsavory, Miss Williamson. This is a legitimate publication, and I've submitted several photographs and drawings to them."

"Who on earth reads this type of thing?" I asked.

"Well, mostly men, but I've heard some women read them, too." He took my both my arms gently and said, "I only meant you would be a perfect subject. And I could use someone as beautiful as you..."

"I don't think so," I said defiantly, but I was suddenly not as angry. He seemed genuine in his pursuit of me.

"Ok, then, let's just continue with your photographs?" he asked hopefully. I took a deep breath and said, "Yes."

We were somehow able to start over and he filled the remainder of the shoot with positive comments like "great," "that's perfect," and his last comment before I left was, "You truly are a beautiful woman; you'll love all of these."

While I was still upset, I suddenly felt more confident about myself and my dream of becoming an actress.

When I came back to pick up my photographs, I had to wait for Mr. Baker to finish a shoot, and I peeked through the curtain that separated the entrance of his building from his studio. He was working with another young woman, probably there for the same reason I'd come to him, and while he was very positive with her, commenting on the shots he got, he never touched her, or told her she was beautiful.

"These will be great," he told her as their session came to an end. "They'll be ready in a week."

I quickly made my way to a chair in the front and picked up a magazine, not wanting him to know I'd stood there and watched. He opened the curtain and said, "Oh, hey. Just a minute." And then he let the other woman out.

"Hey there," he said again as he found my photos. I thought he fumbled slightly with nervousness as he pulled the images out of a folder.

He'd obviously been thinking of his prior proposal, for he put his hand over mine as it sat on the counter, and said, "I'm really sorry if I offended you last week."

I'd thought a lot about him and his comments about me being beautiful. I'd also thought about the modeling proposition, and I was planning on reminding him how reprehensible the whole matter was, but now that I saw him again, I didn't feel he'd meant to be vulgar.

"As I made you aware, your suggestion originally took me aback, but after thinking about it, while I'm still not interested, I do see it as a viable medium. However, I don't believe it's for me." I meant what I said, but I felt like I sounded like my mother.

His eyes met mine like they had when he was photographing me, and I felt that shiver again. There was something about the way he looked at me.

He came to stand near me as he laid out the photos, and I was truly amazed at how he'd turned me into someone lovely and sensual. I could feel my face color again and he saw it.

"Don't be embarrassed. I told you, you were beautiful."

He was so close to me, I took in his masculine smell, and it was intoxicating.

Ross Baker became my first lover.

I had always been the romantic; daydreaming about what it would be like to make love to a man. Or, more secretly, what it would be like to have a man make love to me. And that's what Ross was able to do; he fulfilled that fantasy.

He adored me. Almost worshipped me, and he constantly told me how beautiful I was as we joined together. He started doing sketches of me in just about any imaginable pose, but never drawing my face so no one could recognize me. Enough time had passed, and I knew he cared about me, so when he asked me if he could show them to the magazine he'd told me about, I trusted him. He began selling his work, and we were both making a little more money. I felt like a queen.

Artie had my photos and had been trying to get me some studio interviews, but when he would find something, he'd tell me whether I'd be expected to perform personal services if I applied for a role. I immediately turned those down, for I was going to be no one's trollop.

Maude, Lila, and I had found a one-bedroom apartment several months earlier, and they'd taken the path of sleeping with industry moguls to get noticed. They began getting bit parts in low budget movies, often working together on a film. I wasn't jealous or resentful of them, but I didn't want that lifestyle, so when I told Ross about it, he asked if I wanted to move in with him for a while.

"This could work out for both of us," he'd said. "You wouldn't have to pay rent, and I'd have more time to photograph and draw you."

There were several other artists gaining recognition for the pin-up girl and etching look, so we were doing quite well.

One day I asked Ross if I could show some of his work to Artie, who could in turn show it to some of the studios, and it worked. I got a call for an interview. I ended up doing a screen test and got a part working on a movie being shot in the San Bernardino Mountains, with John Robert Scott. I'd have to be on location for about thirty days.

When I came home to tell Ross the news, the curtain to his studio was closed and I could hear him with a client. When that happened, I'd take the side steps up to his apartment and wait for him there. That day, I noticed the other voice was that of a man. I was curious who it was, so I peeked through the curtain as I'd done so many times before. Ross was telling the client to turn again to the right, then he set his camera down and went to the young man and posed his shoulders so they were facing another direction. Ross then tilted the man's head, and as he'd done with me so many months ago, he gently touched the full head of blonde hair, and then his cheek.

As I audibly gasped, Ross turned in my direction and knew that I'd seen the exchange between the two of them. I pulled the curtain closed and ran up the stairs.

A hundred thoughts went through my mind. I'd never, ever, thought about two men being attracted to each other, but the young man Ross was photographing was terribly handsome, and I could see how Ross might be attracted to him.

Was he planning on having an affair? And if so, had he done so in the past? I was almost dizzy thinking about it all, and then I realized I wasn't actually angry with him, but found it curious and interesting. I didn't even feel that I was being betrayed. What was wrong with me?

Ross eventually made his way upstairs and I could tell he was distraught. He stood there forlornly, and I couldn't help but feel sorry for him. I took the humiliated man that I'd come to care about into my arms, and comforted him.

All I could say was, "I came to tell you I got a part. I'll be going to Lake Arrowhead to film with John Robert Scott."

I held him at arm's length and said, "You poor dear. I did not know."

A look of despair spread over his face.

I stayed with Ross, in his bed, until I left for the filming. We never shared intimacy again, not because I didn't care for him, or him for me, but because what we had together had been destroyed. I knew when I returned, I'd find a place of my own.

Almost a month later, several small buses drove the cast up the narrow winding road to where we were going to stay while filming. The director, producer and the more well-known actors were in one bus, and the rest of us were in the other. Mr. Scott followed us up in his own car.

We were staying in a series of cabins built by the studio in the late 1920s, which made it very convenient for everyone. It was the middle of summer and especially hot. The two major stars, and the director and producer, each got their own cabins, and the rest of us doubled up for the remaining three. They were very rustic, but charming. I'd seen nothing like them in Chicago, so they intrigued me. They were built out of logs and had separate gardens and paths leading up to their doors. Inside were twin beds, paintings of bear and deer, a small bathroom and kitchenette and ample closet space.

I shared with another starlet, and we flipped a coin to see who would sleep in which bed; she got closest to the bathroom, but I got nearer to the window. Once we put all our things away, we went outside to see what the others were doing. They'd pulled the large red wooden chairs around a fire pit and were chit-chatting.

Hoping someone would stop and hear me, I said to no one in particular. "I'm starving."

"Me too," someone said, so we made our way into town and had lunch.

I ended up sitting across from the film's producer and you know how you can tell if someone is attracted to you? Well, I could tell he was. His name was Joseph Keller, and he was in his mid-thirties, medium height, with curly dark hair. Even though we were in a diner, his manners were impeccable, and he constantly wiped his mouth to make sure there were no traces of food left on his face.

He was from Brooklyn, New York, but had come to California with his family when he was about ten. He was raised in Los Angeles, and when he became interested in films, he started meeting people in the industry. Instead of coming out and asking them for help, he instead became interested in them. That, in return, made them interested in him. That was a lesson he tried to share with me and with anyone else who would listen.

"Make people want to know you," he said.

185

The man sitting next to him was our director, Cecil B. Demille. Mr. Demille, as he preferred to be addressed, was short on words unless, as I later learned, he was directing you; then he let you know what he really thought about you and the job you were doing. It was a wonder any actors who worked under him had any confidence left to do their job once he'd finished with them.

Another man sitting at our table was John Robert Scott. He was tall and lanky, and I loved his voice. I could tell he was watching me as I ate, and even though he was at the end of the table, I'd look up and meet his eye. This was one man I needed to worry about! He was irresistible.

After lunch, most of us went back to the cabins to practice our lines. Mr. Scott caught me as I was going into my cabin and asked if I'd like to sit outside with him while we read our scripts. Of course, I was elated, but also very nervous. I'd never actually talked with any stars yet, just admired them from afar.

"Don't worry," he said in his long, drawn-out voice. "I won't bite."

How could I resist?

He was in Cabin 7, so once I came back outside with my script, I joined him in his little garden area. As I stood there, I saw a squirrel climb up the tree next to me, and it watched me for a moment until I sat down.

"What would you feed the squirrel?" I asked.

"Nothing, unless you want him to continually pester you," Mr. Scott said coolly.

I thought his comment was borderline rude, and uncompassionate for the good of an animal. I almost had second thoughts about sitting with him, and then I realized I'd be making a huge mistake if I angered him. I planned on finding something I could feed the squirrel anyway the next time we went into town.

"Where are you in here?" he asked.

"I'm in there somewhere," I said, trying to make light of the fact that I only had a few lines here and there. He looked at me, and then he smiled. He was so handsome, and his eyes glistened with amusement.

"Well, we'll find you. And if there isn't enough of you in here, I'll see what I can do," he said, going back to his script.

How did he even know I'd be good enough to add more of me? Then I realized, since he was the star, he could probably do whatever he wanted to do. I pretended to be reading my script and in a few minutes, I looked up at him, and he was looking at me. I thought I was going to die!

"Shall we have dinner tonight?" he asked quietly.

Oh dear, I thought, as my hand involuntarily went to my neck. I could feel myself change color, and I was angry with myself.

"Of course," I managed to eke out.

"Good, then. That's settled," he said, going back to reading.

I tried to focus on what I was doing, but found I couldn't concentrate, so I just pretended to read the pages.

That night, although I did not know what types of restaurants there were in town, I dressed up. I wore a black skirt, a white blouse and a white sweater with glass buttons. The shoes I'd brought weren't optimal for walking in the gravel and pine needles of our courtyard, but they were all I'd brought. I made a mental note that when we were in town again, not only did I need to find squirrel food, I'd find a pair of flat shoes so I wouldn't end up killing myself.

We drove in style in Mr. Scott's 1928 Stutz BB Blackhawk Boattail Speedster, with its racy look, and we took up two parking spaces when we finally found a charming little restaurant.

It wasn't fancy, but it was definitely not as casual as the diner we ate lunch in. I was a little overdressed, but I didn't feel conspicuous. I noticed that when we walked in, people turned to look at us, undoubtedly recognizing Mr. Scott. He smiled and tilted his head in acknowledgement, and kept his hand on my back, guiding me to our booth.

"Are you John Robert Scott?" our waitress asked?

"Do you think I am?" he replied.

"Well...yes," she said shyly.

"Then I guess I am," he said, winking at her.

He squeezed my hand as I looked at the menu. It caught me by surprise, but through his touch, I could feel the sexual magnetism that gave him his confidence. I didn't return his stare.

We ended up having Salisbury steak with mashed potatoes. I'd never had that before, and it was delicious. We made small talk, and when I called him 'Mr. Scott' he took my hand again and said, "Mr. Scott sounds so old. And formal. Call me John."

He asked where I was born, and what made me want to come west.

I told him I always wanted to be an actress.

I asked him the same.

"I grew up in the Bronx, and when I was in high school, on a dare, I joined the theater class and ended up liking it. Once my drama teacher told me I was pretty good, I decided to give it a try in Hollywood. I didn't find an agent right away," he said.

"I'm surprised. You're so handsome." I couldn't believe I'd said it aloud.

"Well, I was pretty gawky when I first came out here, and when I finally got an agent, he told me I needed to eat more and gain weight if I wanted to make it." He laughed then, and that same sparkle glinted in his eyes again. I had a tingling in the pit of my stomach. I tried to turn away from him as his eyes seem to study my face, then settle on my eyes.

My second lover was John Robert Scott.

It was very obvious to the other cast members that John and I had become an item. I stayed with him in his cabin throughout the production of the movie, and we were inseparable. He was a magnificent lover, which meant he'd had a lot of experience. I was certain women fell for him wherever he went. He was kind and caring, and although a little rough with his sexual appetite, he never hurt me.

He did as he'd promised, but not at my request...he had the director add more lines for me. I saw the raised eyebrow the next time I was scheduled to film, but since he was the star of the movie, they did as he asked. I tried very hard not to be self-conscious about it, but it was difficult for me. I found, though, that the extra exposure gave me more confidence in my acting, and I knew after this, I would be ready to take on more parts.

However, when we returned home, my next part was more than I bargained for.

I was pregnant.

I really didn't want a child; not that I wouldn't one day, but this was definitely going to put a damper on my career. I obviously told John, and the first thing he asked was, "Is it mine?"

Even though our affair had become public, I was insulted. I'd never gone into our relationship with any misgivings that John was in love with me, but it had become obvious I was just another plaything for him. When I assured him I'd not slept with any other man, he said, "You'll just have to get rid of it. I know of a doctor."

I didn't want to risk an abortion, so I told him I'd step out of the lime-light and once I had the baby, I'd give it up for adoption. I could tell this wasn't ideal for him, but he was relieved, and I suddenly detested him. He never contacted me again. I assumed he felt he should keep his distance. A child out of wedlock would damage both our careers, and neither one of us wanted marriage.

A few weeks after we returned to Los Angeles, Joseph Keller, the movie's pro-ducer, called me. We met for lunch and I told him about my predicament. He was well aware I'd had the affair with John, and confessed he'd been interested in getting to know me, but he'd kept his distance once he saw the two of us together.

"From the moment I first saw you, I knew I was in love with you," he said quietly. He reached across the table and took my hands in his.

I struggled to hide my surprise. First, I'd had no idea he'd been inter-ested in me, and second, I couldn't understand how he could profess such feelings for me after what I'd just told him.

"I would marry you," he said, "and everyone would think the child was mine."

His offer startled me. I tried weighing my options, and my mind was spinning.

"Celeste, I could make you a good husband."

"Joseph, I can't ask you to do this for me. I'm the one who got me into this...this mess."

"But," he insisted, "I would have no problem raising this child, if you'd let me."

While I could be attracted to someone like him, I wasn't looking for a husband or a child right now. I couldn't just go from one relationship to another, at least not without getting to know him. I knew this wasn't what I wanted to do.

"I'd like to go somewhere and have the baby. Then, I'd like to find it a home," I said, already coming to terms with the harsh reality of what I was willing to do for my career. I was determined to do whatever it took to become a star.

"Then I will help you," Joseph said as he came to sit by me.

We made arrangements for me to stay with his sister, Emilia, at her home on a ranch in Northern California. There was plenty of room for me, and I'd have lots to do, helping her with her catering business and taking care of the animals. So, within the month, Joseph drove me to my new home.

When we got there, he stayed for dinner, and that night, he slept in one of the other guest bedrooms. When he left in the morning, I gave him a hug and said, "I can't tell you how much I appreciate everything you're doing for me."

"I'd like to come see you," he said, "if you wouldn't mind."

"I'd really like that, Joseph. I'll write to you and let you know how I'm doing."

I was certain this wasn't what he'd hoped for, but it was all I could give him.

"I'll look forward to hearing from you."

I could tell he didn't want to leave, but he needed to get back to his current project. A new movie, he'd said, and not starring John Robert Scott!

Emilia and I got along terrifically. She never pressured me for details, but I eventually told her about my affair with John. She let it escape that she was aware of how Joseph felt about me, and it surprised me she wasn't resentful. I told her I hadn't known he was interested in me when I started seeing John.

"I think you made the right decision to not get rid of the baby," she said to me one morning as we had breakfast. "Together, we'll find someone who will give it a good home."

Joseph visited regularly, and I genuinely enjoyed spending time with him. He brought me up to date on his latest project, and he even told me that once I had the baby and felt up to it, he had another project I could have a part in. It seemed the timing would be perfect.

I learned a lot about catering in those months I spent with Emilia. She had a small business on the side, but regularly worked for a hotel. When they had a large function, she managed their kitchen, making sure the food was prepared as ordered, and then oversaw the execution of the serving. Pregnant women weren't out and about in those days, so I was confined to working behind the scenes in the kitchen, which was fine with me.

I also learned more than I wanted to about caring for horses, cows and chickens. Emilia's husband George had me doing light chores, and once I got used to all the smells, I actually enjoyed being outdoors.

When my delivery time grew closer, Joseph came to visit again, this time planning on staying with me until the baby arrived. At first, I didn't want him to see me, for I felt bloated and ugly and I was suddenly ashamed of my situation.

"Celeste, to me, you're beautiful and I want to be there for you," he'd said.

I never saw my baby. I never knew if it was a boy or a girl. I wanted it that way so I wouldn't change my mind. The hospital assured me a loving family was waiting for my child, and I felt in my heart this wasn't the right time for me to be a mother.

Even though I felt that way, Joseph held me as I sobbed. He told me that he loved me and that he wanted to marry me. I didn't feel I could love him that way; even half as much as he loved me, but when he brought me back to his home in Los Angeles, I realized I could be comfortable with a man like him. He had an even temperament and was pleasant to look at. I don't know why I was surprised, but he was a gentle and tender lover. I grew to care for him because he loved me so much.

Unlike John Robert Scott, who only thought of himself..

I made my second movie, opposite Clark Gable. It was critically acclaimed, and when he was nominated for an Academy Award and I wasn't, I was extremely disappointed.

"Celeste," Joseph reasoned with me. "Don't show your emotions to your public; instead, be outwardly grateful that Mr. Gable was nominated. Ride on his shirttails. Bask in his success."

At first, I couldn't set aside my unhappiness. But as I've learned in life, time heals a lot of wounds, and eventually I came around. Joseph had a new film for me and rearranging the living room furniture did the trick.

In 1936, I purchased a 1931 butterscotch color Duesenberg with tan leather interior and a convertible top. It was my fashion statement, and I felt absolutely glamorous in it. I drove it mostly, but I'd let Joseph drive if we were taking a long trip. I loved that car!

In 1939, just after my newest movie, Britain and France declared war on Germany after it invaded Poland. Americans entering another World War seemed so frightening, yet hopefully unlikely.

I was just wrapping up a movie when I discovered I was pregnant. Joseph was beside himself with joy and begged me to stop my career and raise our child. I hadn't planned the pregnancy, so I naturally hadn't planned on putting my acting career on hold.

"I'll think about it," I told him, but I knew I wasn't going to change anything.

In November 1941, I had our son, Hudson, and when he was a month old, we went to Hawaii so Joseph could scout some properties for his next movie. We stayed in a complex of cottages, complete with small kitchens, and I'd decided against bringing a nanny, for I thought being in Hawaii would be an automatic vacation of sorts. It turned out, having a small baby in tow was no vacation, and I soon regretted my decision.

I asked Joseph if we could fly Hudson's nanny over, and instead, he recommended we contact the manager of the cottages to see if he could find someone to care for Hudson so I could at least enjoy my evenings out. I found a woman, whose name was Malie, who would come and watch Hudson during the day. That way, weather permitting, I could lie on the beach or just go shopping. She was a lovely woman in her sixties; a perfect grandmother type. Unlike when he was with me all day, Hudson was very calm with her.

Joseph was gone throughout the day and well into the evenings with meetings. I grew anxious and annoyed that he wasn't spending more time with us, but, being 'devil-may-care' as he sometimes referred to me, I soon found some wonderful restaurants with cocktail lounges and live music. Malie didn't mind staying the night, so soon, I had no shortage of new friends.

It was the first of December, and because Joseph was Jewish, we'd never celebrated Christmas. On a whim, I had this crazy idea of getting an artificial tree and decorating it. But stores there didn't have them, so I eventually gave that idea up and found a green tree. I found a small store with tons of old glass ornaments and hung those with clip on candles. I bought and wrapped clothing and toys for Hudson, and when I stepped back and admired my work, I couldn't help but feel proud of myself for adding a little hominess to the cottage.

My Christmas spirit was shattered only a few days later, when, on December 7, 1941, the Japanese bombed Pearl Harbor. Joseph was not home as usual, and the nanny wasn't coming that day, so I had to quickly think of what to do to protect Hudson! The only thing I could think of was to put him in the icebox. I emptied it of ice and food and then laid blankets in a box that fit perfectly inside it. I left the door slightly ajar so he could breathe and then crawled behind it to protect myself. Somehow, Hudson slept through the entire bombing.

Eventually, when the sirens stopped and there were no more bombs, I brought him out and held him tightly as I cried. I just sat on the floor rocking him and wishing we were at home in L.A. We could have been killed. Then it dawned on me Joseph had never come home, and I worried he was out there somewhere, possibly injured or dead.

Eventually Joseph burst through the front door panic stricken and pale as a ghost. He rushed to us and cried out, "Are you okay? Are you okay?"

Once I told him yes, we were fine, just shaken, he picked Hudson up and kissed his forehead. He then helped me up, and we three stood there in a hug.

"Thank God," he said over and over.

A week later, the police came for Joseph and took him away. He continued to profess innocence to whatever they were arresting him for, and I was beyond myself. I'd never witnessed him doing anything illegal, and with Hudson in my arms, I reached for Joseph, but I was pushed away.

Joseph was gone.

And I was stranded in Hawaii.

I eventually made it back to Los Angeles, and once I made arrangements for Hudson's nanny to come back to work, I began trying to find out what happened to Joseph. No one wanted to talk to me, and on several occasions I worried I myself might be taken into custody, if I didn't stop asking questions. But apparently there was no evidence I'd done anything wrong. The problem was, I couldn't figure out what Joseph had done wrong, either.

One afternoon, when I was at the studio, I noticed most of the production company was avoiding me. I hadn't thought so when I first got there, but I began to see that people were doing everything they could to stay clear of me.

Finally, I saw the director, Mr. Demille, and I asked if I could speak to him.

"What is going on?" I asked.

Reluctantly, he said, "Joseph was arrested."

"Well, I know that," I said, agitated. "What is going on? And what do you know?"

He turned to walk away from me, and I reached out for his arm to stop him. He gave me the dirtiest look ever.

I pleaded with him. "Please, Mr. Demille. Please tell me what's happening."

In a cold and exact voice, he said, "It's believed your husband was sympathetic to the Nazis."

His bold, cool manner irked me.

"This is impossible," I stammered.

"Impossible that you did not know?"

"Impossible for Joseph. He never shared that with me." He waited, and I boldly met his eyes. "Tell me what you know," I pleaded.

"Joseph's been suspected of having been part of a plan to infiltrate Los Angeles. At one time, he and his group were planning to carry out acts of anti-Semitic violence, and unfortunately, we here in Hollywood were a target. They planned on destroying our theaters and executing Jewish producers *and directors." With that said, he just stood there, tightening his lips as if he could not, or would not, say another word.*

I couldn't rally against him quick enough and I stared at him in astonishment.

How could this be true? Joseph was such a kind man. And how could I not know anything about this?

"Dear God," was all I could get out. I turned away from Mr. Demille, and he walked away.

"Why would he do that when this was his livelihood?" I called out. "And mine." No one heard my last words, "But Joseph is Jewish."

I had to make some harsh decisions, and quickly. Once the word got out, my career would be over. People would think I knew what Joseph was doing. I would be plagued by the media and my public could turn on me as quickly as they've done to others in the past. The only thing I could think of that made sense, was getting a divorce.

I did not know where Joseph was, or when he'd be freed—if at all. I talked to my lawyer about starting the proceedings, which gave me a pro-active response that would hopefully work in my favor.

I closed all our bank accounts, and opened new ones in my name only. I also went to the gas station and the stores I frequented and had them take Joseph's name off their credit ledgers. I'd shortened my last name to Williams, ages ago, and I was grateful I never took on Joseph's name when we married.

I laid low for the next few months, and employed my nanny full time, so I'd have a chance to relax and not get up at all hours of the night if Hudson cried and needed to be fed. My publicist found a strict diet for me to follow so I could lose my baby fat, and eventually I began feeling like myself again.

I hadn't seen my parents in a couple of years, so Hudson and I made the train trip back to Chicago and we spent a couple of weeks with them. As we passed through all the different towns and the varieties of landscapes, I couldn't help but remember that first train trip to Los Angeles in 1928, and thought how amazing it was that time had flown by so quickly. I remembered Maude and Lila and wondered how they were doing. I'd never heard from them once we went our separate ways. I wondered too if they'd seen me in my movies.

My father was still active in his practice, and my mother had a full plate with her social activities and wanted to take me to every function she had while I was there. Of course, she wanted to show off Hudson, and I loved watching all her friends make over him.

I'd long since been forgiven for leaving like I had. Once my parents saw me on the big screen, they were very proud of me. Ruth had two children by then, and seemed content in her married life, although I couldn't imagine how boring it was to stay at home with no one around but little ones.

When I returned to Los Angeles, I tried to settle into a routine with Hudson. To keep me busy, I remodeled the Pacific Palisades home I'd purchased before I married Joseph. I knew I couldn't be satisfied until I had a new film to work on, so I continued to read scripts my agent recommended. Joseph's incarceration didn't seem to affect my career, which was what I had hoped for. I hadn't heard from him, so I still did not know what was happening. My attorney was handling all my legal issues.

In 1944, I attended the Academy Awards gala at Grauman's Chinese Theatre and afterwards made it to the parties at Ciro's, Romanoffs, Mocambo and ended up at Chasen's. I'd become more socially reclusive, but I understood the importance of making an appearance and I wanted the industry, and my fans, to understand I was not involved in Joseph's troubles.

It was at Chasen's that I met a very handsome General named Andrew Fisher. He was on a quick leave, and would soon have to go back to Italy. Once we had a chance to sit and talk, I was naturally curious about what he'd done and seen, but quickly realized my blunder in military etiquette. He was both unable to talk about what he was doing, and he was visibly uncomfortable with the subject.

"I'm terribly sorry, General Fisher," I said softly once I realized my faux pas. "I was only curious and just meant to start a conversation...but I never thought about what you've been through. I'm terribly sorry," I said again, looking away and wishing I could disappear.

He turned to look at me and said, "You're fine, Miss Williams."

He then took a sip of his scotch and water.

"How long will you be home?" I asked.

"A week. Just long enough to catch my breath, but not nearly long enough to decompress."

I wanted to change the subject, so said, "Shall we dance?" I was hoping to lift his spirits.

"I'm afraid I have two left feet."

"That's okay. The dance floor is crowded enough so that no one but me would know and if you step on my feet, I won't cry out."

I stood and held my hand out to him, and once he smiled, I knew I hadn't ruined everything. We danced several slow dances and as he drew me to him, I took in his aftershave and hair cream. He smelled fresh, and I closed my eyes to drink him in more. We moved together like we'd been dancing like this forever...our steps were fluid and smooth.

"You're quite stunning," he whispered in my ear, and his warm breath sent a shiver down my spine.

"You're not bad yourself," I said, pushing myself away from him so I could see his face. When his eyes found my lips, I knew Andrew Fisher was going to become my third lover.

I told my nanny that I needed to be away for a week, and I booked us a room at the Chateau Marmont Hotel overlooking Sunset Boulevard. It was unexpectedly warm for March, and we spent the afternoons down at the pool basking in the sun. But other than that, we never left our room. Between making love and Andrew taking much needed naps, we ordered room service for breakfast, lunch and dinner. And a lot of scotch.

We also got to know each other. I shared my experiences coming out on the train, and how I really hadn't missed Chicago's weather. I answered his questions about being an actress, and I told him about Joseph.

Andrew was from a farming community in Iowa. Even before Black Tuesday in 1929, farmers struggled with low prices on their crops. At least they could grow their own food and provide for their families, but when the depression was officially over in 1939, there were still so many people struggling, and his family had been among those who feared bankruptcy.

Andrew joined the Army as soon as he turned eighteen. His father had told him, "With so many young men joining up, our families will have fewer mouths to feed."

There's something about getting to know a person that's intoxicating. You watch their every move; their funny mannerisms, their eyes taking you in, or just sleeping. Andrew was very handsome, about six feet tall, broad shoulders, brown crew cut hair and matching brown eyes.

He'd never been married, although he'd met someone once, also while on leave; it turned out she had a thing for men in uniform, and he'd stopped by unexpectedly to see her one evening, and found her in bed with another soldier.

When Andrew's week was up, neither of us actually came out and said it, but I think we both felt something special between us. He said he'd write, and I hoped he would. Wherever he was, he told me his mail would get to him, and he even asked me for an autographed photo of myself so he could keep it with this gear.

I told him I'd send him one.

I tried not to, but I cried the morning he had to leave. He held me tightly and wiped away my tears with his fingertips.

'Please come back,' I said to him with my eyes. I didn't dare want to say it aloud. The war wasn't over yet, and I had no idea where he was going.

I received my first letter from Andrew about two weeks after he left. It surprised me it came so quickly, but it eased any doubts I'd had that he felt about me the way I felt about him. I missed him.

I was due to start filming about six weeks later. I'd done as I'd promised and sent him a large autographed photo of me, along with a letter telling him how I felt our short time together had been wonderful, and how I thought about him every day.

He wrote me right back, and I knew then we had something special.

However, about eight weeks after he left, I knew I'd have to figure out how to share what I was certain would change everything. I'd seen the signs before. I was going to have a baby.

I was on pins and needles waiting to hear back from him, letting me know either way how he felt about our predicament. And about two weeks later, when I hadn't received any letters from him, I felt for certain I was going to be left figuring out what to do about having another child. I would have to make arrangements to terminate the pregnancy.

My current filming was going well, and thank goodness I had only a little morning sickness. I was certain I could hide my secret until I knew what I was going to do. At some point, though, I was going to have to act.

I finally heard from Andrew.

My dearest Celeste,

It took me a day to get over the shock of your news, but I was never anything but delighted to hear I'm going to be a father. I'm still in shock!

There is so much devastation here; human lives on all sides are being lost, beautiful buildings have been bombed and destroyed, and yet here you've brought me the best news I could have ever have expected! You are my love, and as soon as I have any information about my return, I will be there in a heartbeat!

You've given me all the more reason to make sure I come home safely.

Yours,
Andrew

I met with my costume designer, but before I could finish telling her about my pregnancy, she looked at me with that 'I know...' look. So I spared her the details. When I could no longer hide it, I told my director so that filming could be modified to show me from perspectives that didn't accentuate my new curves.

I started clearing out one of the extra bedrooms at my home; in my mind, I wasn't ready to decorate, but I wanted to begin thinking about my new addition. Hudson was only three and would probably love a brother or sister. As long as I had my nanny, I'd be able to continue with my career.

When I picked Andrew up in my Duesenberg at the airport, he later admitted he'd felt like royalty. He'd never been to my home and was genuinely impressed with the area and the house itself.

"You look like you're exhausted," I said, helping him with his coat. He still had his uniform on since he'd left directly from the base.

"I am, and I can hardly wait to get into something comfortable. Actually, I'd love a shower."

"Come this way," I said, leading him down a long hallway to what would now be our bathroom.

He carefully folded his uniform, setting it on a chair. "I'll deal with getting that cleaned later," he said, going into the bathroom. I turned the shower on for him and set out a towel. He climbed in and I left him, but only for a moment. In the other room, I undressed and then joined him.

He took one look at me and pulled me towards him, and then he touched my rounded baby stomach.

"I'm going to be a dad," he said, madly kissing me. "Will you marry me?"

"Shall I have Nanny make something for us to eat?" I asked after we made love.

"I'm exhausted…that would be great," he said, drifting off to sleep.

Andrew did look wiped out. As I watched him sleep, I felt as though I was looking at a man who had aged tremendously in a short time. I knew it was because of what he'd gone through in the war. Even years later, he would never share details of what he'd seen in battle. He said he never wanted me to know.

My divorce had become final by the time Andrew returned home. I'd contacted my parents as soon as we started making plans for our wedding, and my mother was clearly annoyed. She said things like 'How wonderful you're having another baby' and 'Isn't this a little short notice?' Andrew's parents were ecstatic.

"I think they thought I'd never marry and settle down," Andrew said after he hung up. He got up to make himself a drink then asked me if I wanted something.

I had a wedding gown made to suit my motherly figure, and we were married in a private ceremony in Iowa, with only our parents. Hudson stayed at home with his nanny. We had a wonderful dinner at a charming hotel where we all stayed. There were no photographers, and no stories about the wedding ran until we returned home.

I had wondered how Andrew would take to instant fatherhood, both with Hudson and the new baby, and when I asked him how he felt about Hudson calling him Daddy, he thought it was a great idea.

"That's what the baby's going to call me anyway," he said.

Andrew had a few details to wrap up, but when he was finished with some debriefing, he officially retired. He was wonderful with Hudson, and I couldn't have been happier. When Robert was born, Andrew got up to help our nanny until she convinced him she was fine and he could go back to bed. He loved having a baby around, and he'd take the two boys out to the park and sit with baby Robert in his stroller while he watched Hudson play on the swings.

By the time we had a second son, Andrew Jr., two years later I noticed Andrew constantly had a drink in his hand. I understood the pressures he was under; the after effects of war, being married to an actress with her own means, and having the responsibility of three young boys. He was also having a hard time figuring out what he wanted to do with his life after retiring from the service.

He still suffered periodic nightmares, and when he would cry out, I'd gently wake him and tell him everything was all right. He'd go back to sleep and not remember anything in the morning.

I'd thought about retiring from the film industry so we could travel, but as much as I loved our sons, I just couldn't think of being home and doing nothing all day. When we traveled between filming, we brought Nanny, which satisfied Andrew, for it meant we weren't leaving them at home.

One year, between films, we took a trip to Europe. We flew to New York, then London, and cruised the Atlantic Ocean through to the Mediterranean Sea. I hadn't been to Europe and was very excited.

Nanny and the children had a cabin next to ours, and the trip turned out to be just what we needed. It was romantic and restful, and Andrew only had a couple of nightmares while we were gone. Andrew taught me to play blackjack, which I thoroughly enjoyed, and in fact became addicted to. Each night, we had cocktails before dinner, and I noticed Andrew was drinking more than usual. We were invited to sit at the Captain's table a couple of evenings and thankfully, Andrew never drank to where he made a fool of himself...or me. I reminded myself to talk to him about this if it continued.

For the most part, other guests respected my privacy, and only a few young girls came up to me and asked for my autograph. The children stayed occupied and one warm day when we were out at sea, I went down to the pool to watch them play in the water. I couldn't help but notice how they'd grown so quickly. It was almost as if I saw them so infrequently I didn't really know them. I was always so busy with what was going on in my life I was missing out on their childhood.

When we returned home, I'd ask Nanny what she thought I should do.

I supposed I could have also asked Andrew what he thought; I would have to work on including him in my thought process.

It was in the early fifties when I sold my Duesenberg. You know how cars depreciate so rapidly; when my mechanic told me someone was interested in purchasing it, I told him to get a couple thousand dollars for it and be done. In its place, I bought a 1954 Biscay Green Cadillac Fleetwood as our new family car. That dark blue/green color with leather interior called to me when I pulled into the car lot. I also bought a Mercury station wagon for the boys and Nanny. When Andrew pouted, I bought him a 1954 Chevrolet Corvette.

I was almost forty-five, and there weren't as many parts for 'mature women' in those days unless you were willing to play someone's mother or grandmother. I'd made it clear that wasn't a role I wanted to play, so there were even fewer options for me. I had made plenty of money, and I didn't really need to work.

I began thinking about becoming an artist. I'd always admired people who could paint, so I bought some supplies and started taking painting lessons. I wasn't interested in painting people, but places appealed to me. I started with my own backyard, which was very picturesque, then went to parks and other local areas of interest.

My instructor, Giovanni, was a rather handsome young painter from Italy, here on a student visa. Teaching private lessons was his way of generating income to afford to live in wonderful Southern California. After a few months with him, he shared he was nearing the end of his time here and would need to go back to Italy. I, who never seem to lack serendipitous questions, wondered if I could accompany him back and he could continue teaching me in his hometown. Of course, I'd include Andrew in this plan, for even though I wasn't interested in Giovanni intimately, I was fully aware it wouldn't look right for me to travel alone with such a handsome younger man!

Surprisingly, Andrew was interested in going along, so we planned another trip. The boys would stay home, so I wouldn't feel the constraints of time. I wanted to be able to focus on my painting. I figured Andrew could find things to keep him occupied while I worked, then we'd have the evenings to spend together.

We left for Italy at the beginning of summer, although I knew it would be warm. I brought plenty of sundresses and capris with sleeveless blouses. This trip could help accomplish several things; one was to paint to my heart's delight, and the other was to try to rekindle my relationship with Andrew. Marriage and children, and of course my ever demanding schedule, had created a gap in our romance, and it would be ideal if we could fix that.

After less than a month, Andrew became restless, and his drinking had gotten worse. I had to admit that sitting around while I painted wasn't the most exciting thing he could do. And if I were in his shoes, I'd feel the same way. So, he flew home and spent the rest of the summer with the boys.

I spent another month by myself; then I had all my art work removed from the stretcher bars and shipped home, which was no small feat. I had no idea what I was going to do with all those paintings, but I couldn't just leave them behind.

When I returned, I met with my agent, good old Artie Bell, who was still active in Hollywood but aging in dog years. He had a new script for me to read; one that would be for someone my age; it was about starting over. Since I wasn't playing someone's grandmother, I thought I'd give it a try.

While I was gone, Andrew had been busy. He'd been drinking, of course, and ran a red light. He narrowly missed hitting another car, but crashed his Corvette into a light pole. The car was totaled, and he'd been arrested for driving under the influence and spent a night in a jail cell.

My better judgment niggled at me and said 'don't do it' but after Andrew promised me, for the umpteenth time he'd slow down his drinking and driving, I bought him another car, a red 1958 Porsche 356. He loved it. And I hoped he would live long enough to enjoy it!

In 1959, Hudson graduated from high school and was accepted to Oregon State University. While we didn't need the financial help, he was an expert swimmer and got a full scholarship. He wanted to leave early in the summer, so we flew up and found him an apartment for a few months before he went into the dorms. I could tell he was like me, anxiously waiting for the time when he could go out on his own.

We had a pool house, or cabana, where I painted every day. I was eager to travel again, but this time, Andrew wanted to stay home with Robert and Andrew Jr. I was, in all honestly, relieved in a way, not only because he didn't mind keeping them busy, but I found I had more freedom if I traveled alone. I was still in touch with Giovanni and wrote and asked if he knew someone who could travel with me and teach me more.

He wrote back that he was available if I wanted to continue with him. He asked if his girlfriend could join us, at their expense, of course. This time we could travel to Spain. I made all the travel arrangements, and within the month, we met at the airport in Madrid. He had filled out some, no longer the lanky young man I remembered. His brown hair was now down to his shoulders, and he wore his sunglasses so that they pushed his hair off his forehead. Sofia, his girlfriend, was quite lovely. Tall and slender, and in a lightweight sundress and sandals, she was the epitome of a lovely European young woman. Ah, to be young again!

We painted by day; Sofia found plenty to do on her own, and in the evenings we drank wine and had lovely dinners. Sometimes when they had the room next to mine, I could hear them making love and it made me feel ancient. Even though I was only forty-nine, I was old. Those days of lust and intrigue were gone for me, and I mourned them. Listening to them through the paper-thin walls, I'd lie there trying to ignore the passion I so missed.

One evening, while I was sitting at the hotel bar waiting for Giovanni and Sofia, a man quietly approached me and asked if I was with anyone. He was Spanish and had a wonderful, heavy accent. I told him I was waiting for my two young friends and that we were going to have dinner. He sat, and then asked if I'd like another glass of wine. I looked at his tanned face, his dark full eyebrows and wonderfully thick hair with just a touch of graying at the temples. He looked like he would make a wonderful lover, but I knew that was not a direction I intended to head in. His name was Santiago Diaz.

Once Giovanni and Sofia arrived at the bar, Giovanni gave me a slight tilt of his head and raised an eyebrow, as if to ask, 'Are you okay?' I smiled and nodded.

I introduced everyone, and our visitor stood as if to leave.

"Would you like to join us?" I asked.

He looked at me first, then at Giovanni for approval, and said, "I'd love to, signora."

Dinner was especially good, but possibly that was because I was hungry not only for food but for what the evening might bring. We all shared our stories; I learned Santiago was from Seville and a widower with three grown children. By the time the evening was over, we'd had two bottles of wine, and I knew I was going to do something I might later regret.

We waited until Giovanni and Sofia went upstairs to their room before Santiago followed me up to mine. I had a tendency to leave my things lying around, so I was glad that housekeeping had folded and neatly stacked my clothing onto a chair. I asked Santiago to give me a minute, then to join me in the shower, which he did.

I'd always wondered if European men made better lovers than American men, and Santiago proved to be a passionate Spanish Don Juan. Since the next day was Sunday, and Giovanni and Sofia were free to do their own thing, we slept in and then had breakfast on the terrazzo. It was such a beautiful day we decided to walk down by the water and afterwards found a small sidewalk café and had a late lunch.

I could tell Santiago wanted to go back to my room again before he left, and I had to think twice about being with him one more time, but this time I used my better judgment and told him I was meeting someone for dinner and wanted to take a quick nap.

He took my left hand in his, and after twisting my wedding rings in his fingers, his lips gently touched my hand. I kissed both his cheeks, and then he walked away, and didn't look back. Once back at my hotel, I took a quick shower and washed my hair before I laid down to take a nap.

That night, Giovanni, Sofia and I would decide where we wanted to stay next.

I called the house when I got back in my room, even though I knew it was a long shot anyone would be up; it was one o'clock here, so it would be eight in the morning at home. I'd been gone two months, and I had to admit I missed the boys. I got a chance to talk with them, and Andrew, and when the boys asked when I'd be home, I said, soon.

"I still have some places I want to see and paint," I said.

I promised to bring them all something special.

If I was honest with myself, I wasn't a particularly good mother. I thought I would have been, especially since I was given three more chances to have children. I loved them dearly, but my tolerance for the noise and constant care just wasn't there for me. I wondered how so many other women did it... how they let their lives revolve around their children.

Sometimes I wondered what my first child was doing. Had he or she found a family who adored them? And what would they be doing? Studying in college? I never felt a need to tell Andrew about giving my baby away. There just wasn't a time that a conversation like that would have fit in. And in truth, I think he would have been disappointed in me. It was so long ago; I knew I'd never bring it up at this point.

I'd also wondered if Joseph had kept in touch with the hospital where I'd had the baby. Would he have tried to find out who adopted it? It would be like him to do something like that. I hadn't seen or heard from him since I asked him to stay away from Hudson, and he'd obliged.

When I returned at the end of that summer, Andrew had been a dear and gone school clothes shopping with the boys. Like all other young men, all they needed were shirts, pants, socks, underwear, and shoes, and everything was still sitting in their rooms in bags.

We were still living in my home in Pacific Palisades, when I turned fifty-five. My father died that year, so I made the trip back to Chicago for his funeral. My mother was lean and pale, but she held herself in the same grand style and dignity I recalled from my youth. Thankfully, my sister Ruth had prevailed when they made the decision not to have the body brought home to rest in the parlor, but to just have the reception in the house. That was difficult enough. I hadn't brought Andrew or my boys, and both Ruth and Mother admonished me for that. But the boys were all in different stages of their lives, and truthfully, they hadn't known either of my parents well.

Even though the circumstances were somber, it was good to see some of my parent's friends, and even some of my school friends came to call. I was shocked at how much our neighborhood had changed since I was a child. Most of the old mansions had been torn down to make way for apartments and condominiums, and I wondered if in the years to come, the city would regret allowing that to happen.

While I was there, I learned that a number of years ago, my father had developed some sort of vaccine that was being used in Central America that helped children with eye bacteria. Apparently, he'd sold the patent to a large pharmaceutical company, so in his will, my sister Ruth and I each received a hundred thousand dollars.

When I returned home, I purchased an apartment building which would bring me quite a comfortable return on my investment. That build-ing, along with my other property investments made over the years, paid for my retirement.

Not too long after my father's death, Andrew developed cirrhosis of the liver and was growing weaker and weaker by the month. He finally got into his last car accident in his 1965 Shelby GT350 and lost his life when he drove it into a bridge.

Despite his drinking, Andrew had been a good husband and father. He made up for the time I never spent with our boys, including Hudson. And now that he was gone, there definitely would be a void in my life. But I also felt some relief knowing I wouldn't have to see him continue to suffer with his liver, nor would I have to tolerate his alcohol abuse. In reflection, I wondered if he took his own life.

A few months after Andrew's funeral, I turned fifty-six. I was definitely over the prime acting age, or over the hill as they said, and I hadn't done a film in five years. Since my agent Artie died some time back, if a new script ever came my way by my new agent, I still refused to play the role of someone's grandmother. I knew I needed to get over that hang-up if I wanted to act again.

That next summer, I took another extended trip to Europe. I'd stayed in touch with Giovanni, but he had married Sofia and settled down, so for him, accompanying me was not an option. He told me he had a friend named Demetrios, who was also a painter, and who lived in Greece. I contacted him, and he said he could be my companion and teacher. I was delighted.

My sons were off doing whatever they wanted and I told them they could come stay at the house if they desired. They were young men now, and I didn't worry about them taking care of themselves. My only request was that if they came home, they would call the housekeeper to come in and clean up any messes they made.

Demetrios met me at the Athens airport, and I was pleasantly surprised to discover he was what I'd envisioned a Greek God to look like. He was only about ten years younger than me, had very thick dark hair, a bold mustache, and gorgeous dark eyes. He spoke very good English, and his accent only added to his handsomeness. Unless he had a wife he was madly in love with, I thought this could prove to be a very fruitful trip.

As it turned out, there was no wife and when he kissed my hand, I knew for sure we were going to have a wonderful trip. I ended up staying in Greece for three months, and together we explored and painted, and of course made love under the hot Greek sun. We were both tanned, and often we sunbathed nude.

I hated to return home, but I needed to, so I made myself. I shipped my artwork and decided since I had enough finished work to open a gallery, that's exactly what I did. Even if it was temporary, it was somewhere I could display and sell my work. I found a building in a trendy area and set up shop. It took me a couple of months to get everything framed and ready to go, and then I advertised the gallery opening.

I had to admit I was nervous; putting yourself out there on canvas was almost as bad as being on the screen. But I figured if I could do one, I could do the other. And, I was pleasantly surprised to see there was interest in my work. At the grand opening, I sold a number of pieces, and once they were taken down and wrapped, we hung more. I had a friend of the boys come help me and she did a wonderful job.

She suggested I reproduce and frame some of my old film posters, which I thought was a terrific idea. I autographed them, and then we hung those as well. Amazingly, they all sold, and we had to run a second printing.

I also did something I swore I'd never do...my agent showed me a script where I could star with three other well-known actresses, and we'd be grandmothers! We'd be childhood friends, and the story was about us and our children. I had to admit the story piqued my interest, and I agreed to do the film.

One evening, while I was reading the script again, I developed a terrible headache, and took several aspirin and laid down. I'd been in the sun that day, and I wondered if I might have a slight case of sun poisoning.

When the headache came back a few days later, I called and made an appointment with my doctor.

It took some time to figure out exactly what was wrong with me, but figure it out they did. After a multitude of scans and tests, the consensus was that I didn't have long to live. Someone my age was not a candidate for any aggressive treatments, and I didn't want any. I'd always thought about what I would do if I had a life-threatening disease. Would I treat it? Or would I go somewhere and die?

My last performance was going to be dying of brain cancer.

I refused to break down. I could have. I was angry, but also sad that my life had come to an end. I decided to handle this in the same manner in which I dealt with everything else in my life; with distance and objectivity. I met with my attorney and got my affairs in order; I wanted everything to be distributed equally among my children.

Would anyone miss me? I hadn't exactly been Mother of the Year, had I?

I'd asked my doctor to help me die. I did not want to suffer; I did not want the pain, and I certainly did not want my family to see me wither away. When he said he couldn't help me, moving away seemed the only thing I could do. I'd find someone to prescribe pills. I'd leave Hudson's contact information as he was the executor of my estate.

The most difficult decision I had to make was choosing the painting I would take with me. It had to be small enough to take on a plane. Once I decided, I took it down from the wall and set it against the glass and metal entry table. I would only need a few clothes, so I packed underwear, an extra bra, nylons, and a few outfits. I was shocked that my entire life could fit into one suitcase.

I then went to my jewelry box. In the top drawer, I took out my wedding rings; the first from Joseph, and the second from Andrew. I hadn't worn either in years. In the second drawer, I had some of the costume jewelry I'd worn in my movies. I couldn't recall which pieces I'd worn in which movie, but it didn't really matter. And in the third drawer, I found what I wanted. Under one of my mother's embroidered handkerchiefs, I found the gold necklace with the locket and the diamond watch my grandmother left me so many years ago when she died.

I wrapped them in the handkerchief and put them in my purse. I carried my suitcase downstairs and set it next to the small painting in the entry. I'd forgotten I needed to wrap it to pack it safely in between my clothing. I would do it after I called my travel agent to book me a flight.

But first, I had to remember; where was it I wanted to go?

Suddenly, I had an excruciating pain in my head, and I thought it would pass. But I didn't. I turned to look at myself in the mirror and the movement made me suddenly dizzy. And then my knees buckled beneath me, and I fell to the floor. If only I could sleep, I knew the pain would go away.

The Cabins

Hudson & Constance's Living Room

Hudson & Constance's Family Room

Celeste's Duesenberg

AUTHOR'S NOTES

As with the first two books of the Trilogy, I need to thank my husband **Larry Braun**, who still is, as Bette Midler sings, the wind beneath my wings. Throughout our marriage, he's been the most encouraging and positive influence in my life. When he'd ask, "Are you going to work on your book today?" it was never with question or criticism, but with encouragement. Whenever I doubted myself, which was often, he'd say, "Just write it. Write what you want to." And eventually I came to believe him.

Most importantly, he supported me when I was diagnosed with ovarian cancer while still working on book two. I never shared with him the times I wondered if it was all worth it while I was undergoing chemotherapy. But he continued with his undying support, taking me to what seemed like a hundred doctor's appointments, and always checking to see how my writing and editing were going.

I had a hysterectomy and lost my wonderful curly hair. And the wonderful news is that my cancer was confined to just one ovary, and I've been given a clean bill of health! I finished three more rounds of chemo and am now impatiently waiting for my hair to grow back. I tell my "no hair" dresser (who works in the cancer center) that I look like Bruce Willis, and she constantly says I don't look a bit like him! I had a sign made for her work room that says "Hello Beautiful...You've Got This" with the hopes it will brighten someone else's day.

This is where I want to stand on my soapbox and tell all the women out there that if you still have your "lady parts" ask your doctor for an ultrasound; that's how my cancer was discovered. Without that, I never would have known until it was possibly too late to treat!

In all three books, **Gary Marsh** sketched the cabins and the rooms Annie worked in so you'll get a glimpse of decorated mountain life. Just when I needed a kick in the pants with my first book, my friend and Graphic Designer **Susan Newman Harrison** painted a cabin in the woods and made it look like a book cover with my name and book title on it. It was the first time I could actually imagine my work in print, and I'll be forever indebted to her for doing that. Graphic Designer **Susan Leinen** formatted the images in the books and helped me visualize my book covers before I sent them to my publisher. She does all my website updates and reads my mind when she lays out my emails.

Again, I also want to thank my best IT friend, **Tim Novak**, for still not picking on me when I had dumb questions about downloading or saving my work. I think I've finally got it figured out! My editor, **Pam Sheppard**, is the best; her critiques have always been kind yet true, and I've appreciated having her as my sounding board. And I want to thank my early readers, **Myrt Perisho**, **Susan Denley** and **Pat Aldridge**. I came to them first, a little nervous, but when I left with what I needed to know, I have since totally appreciated their suggestions and comments. And my proofreader, **Sue Jorgenson**, did her best to find all my typos and grammatical errors. Hopefully, there won't be many. (If there are, blame her, haha). And let me know.

And last but not least, I'd like to thank *you* for reading my book. If you enjoyed it, visit my website at www.chrysteenbraun.com, and sign up for my newsletter. You'll be the first to know when my next books are ready. And speaking of books, I wanted to write a prequel about the cabins before Annie bought them, and what started out as a novella has turned into a full-blown book! It's about the woman who owns the cabins and sells them to Sam, who ultimately sells them to Annie. It'll be called **The Maidservant in Cabin Number One.**

PLUS, I'm working on the sequel, **Dear Noah,** which is about Annie from the time she was in the mountains, until she's in her eighties when she wrote the books. My trilogy has turned into five books!

If you ever want to chat, please email me a chrysteenbraun@gmail.com

Like most authors, I always wanted to write, but for years, life, teenagers and being self employed took all my creative juices. For several years, I wrote decorating articles for our local newspaper; my husband and I were remodeling contractors, and for many of those years we had a design store filled with furniture and accessories, much like Timberline mentioned in my stories. Our philosophy was that everyone deserved a beautiful home, and no matter what your budget was, our interior designers did their best to make that happen.

We'd always wanted a second home, and found a wonderful old cabin in Lake Arrowhead, (which turns out to be Noah's cabin) and then I couldn't resist opening a store selling mountain décor called At The Cabin. We eventually bought another home, with tall built-in bookcases filled with almost a thousand books, and twenty foot tall windows in the living room that looked out to a forest of trees. That house in Cedar Ridge was the model for Bunny's house in book two.

You can find photos of both homes at *www.chrysteenbraun.com*.

When we retired, I decided I still had enough "good summers" left to write the trilogy, if I set my mind to it. I believe I was sixty-eight. I came up with the idea of a series of restored cabins that had their own stories to tell.

Set in 1980, I had to remember my characters couldn't use the internet, Mr. Google, computers, color copies or cell phones and instead had to use landlines, pay phones and the library to research one of the Hollywood guests.

Hopefully, I did a good job covering my bases. If I've made any errors or omissions, I take full responsibility.

All three books in the trilogy take place in Lake Arrowhead, California, and I've taken the liberty of changing a few names and dates to make them suit my story.

A friend of ours purchased a home formerly owned by Beach Boys' Brian Wilson near Tavern Bay, and I thought it would be fun to include it in the story as one of Annie's design/remodel projects. Another friend has a wonderful home at the very top of a hill overlooking the lake. So with their permission, I've made this the last home Hudson and Constance purchase and remodel. The dates are inaccurate, and I've taken creative liberties to make it work for the timeline of the book.

We never bought the flooring store near "Ginny's" in Blue Jay, but the idea of it fit perfectly into the story.

A friend who used to live in Lake Arrowhead (and who read my book) couldn't recall a place called the Cowboy Bar, and there wasn't one. It was a product of my imagination.

When Annie adopts a black store cat from the store next door, I named her Black Dahlia, after our old store cat, Dahlia. In 1947, Elizabeth Short, posthumously known as the Black Dahlia, was murdered and mutilated in Los Angeles. The media highly publicized her case due to the gruesome nature of the crime and it has never been solved.

While Celeste and the filming in my story are fictional, many movies have been filmed in Lake Arrowhead, including:

"Giant" (1956) with Elizabeth Taylor, Rock Hudson & James Dean

"The American President" (1995) starring Michael Douglas, Annette Bening, Martin Sheen & Michael J. Fox

"It's a Mad Mad Mad Mad World" (1963) with Spencer Tracy, Milton Berle, Ethel Merman and Mickey Rooney.

"The Parent Trap" (1961) with Hayley Mills, Maureen O'Hara and Brian Keith

"The Great Race" (1965), "Heidi" (1937), and most recently "The Terminal List" with Chris Pratt (2021)

While my character Joseph Keller is fictional, there was a period in the late 1930s when the German consul in Los Angeles did everything in his power to ensure that the Jewish-dominated studios followed a production code that regulated movies that attacked Hitler and the government. Movie studios were "encouraged" (threatened) to delete scenes from movies the German government found offensive, and there have been many stories told about a Nazi infiltration of Hollywood, complete with plans to murder film producers Louis B. Mayer and Samuel Goldwyn, and star Charlie Chaplin.

If you ever visit Lake Arrowhead, don't forget to stop in to see some of my favorite places:

Wildhaven Ranch is real, established in 1994, by Diane Dragatto Williams. It's a wildlife sanctuary for animals that cannot be released back into the wild. All their animals, such as their raccoons, bobcat, bears, and birds of prey, were rescued with the hope of rehabilitation, but were un-releasable.

Wildhaven depends solely on public donations. (I'm a Wildlife Patron.) If you love animals, please look them up and help support them. www.wildhavenranch.org

Timberline in the Glen, Cedar Glen, is one of my favorite stops. It always has the most wonderfully displayed décor and collections, both vintage and new. They totally transform the store for the Christmas holidays and create a truly winter wonderland. They even sell my books!

Cedar Glen Inn, Cedar Glen, is a favorite family-owned restaurant and serves portions large enough to share.

Cedar Glen Trading Post is next door to the Inn and is a family run hardware store where locals and contractors can pick up just about anything from fishing licenses to materials necessary to work on a project.

Bill's Villager, in Blue Jay, was also a family-owned restaurant. Spoiler alert; it was my inspiration for Ginny's. At the time of publication, I understand they will be retiring and the mountain will be sorry to see them go.

I've mentioned Diet Coke in this book, and technically, it hadn't been introduced until 1982. As an interesting side note, Diet Coke quickly overtook Tab in sales, although it wouldn't be until 2020 and the Covid-19 pandemic that Coca-Cola discontinued Tab along with other slower-selling drinks.

The Guest Book Trilogy continues...

Book One, The Man in Cabin Number Five, begins when Annie first comes to Lake Arrowhead, where she buys and restores a series of cabins. Looking towards her future, her life parallels with Alyce Murphy, who wants to find closure when she discovers her father committed suicide and didn't die of a heart attack as she'd always believed.

Book Two, The Girls in Cabin Number Three, is about Annie and a woman named Carrie, who inherits her mother's beloved lake house. She and her mother have both stayed in Annie's cabins, one of them in 1930 and one of them in the present. Carrie eventually learns more about the secrets her mother kept, and about The Tudor House speakeasy.

Coming Soon

Book Four, The Maidservant in Cabin Number One
Book Five, Dear Noah

If you liked The Starlet in Cabin Number Seven, I'd love it if you let your friends know so they can enjoy it too.

One of the best things a reader can do to help an author be successful is to give a review of their books. Here's all you need to do:

- Log in to your Amazon account.
- Go to the product page for the book you want to review, then select the book format.
- Scroll down to the Customer Reviews section and click on "Write a Customer Review"
- Rate the book (hopefully with 4 to 5 stars)
- Write your review, and then press "Submit"
- You'll see a message: "Thanks for your review."

Email me at chrysteenbraun@gmail.com

Chrysteen Braun

Check out my website!

Turn the page to read

Chapter One of the Prequel,

The Maidservant in Cabin Number One

Part One

Ruth Ann Landry

CHAPTER ONE

My father died when I was young, leaving me and my mother alone in a one-bedroom apartment, that even with my mother's meager wages, they'd barely afforded. Mostly, her earnings helped pay for our heat, and now, with my father gone, we were often so cold, we sometimes wore three or four layers of clothing. Weather in Seattle, Washington, was always unpredictable; even during the dead of winter, it could be foggy and raining in the mornings and clear and sunny in the afternoons. I remember the skies were mostly gray.

We originally came from rural Nashville, Tennessee, way before it became famous for country music. I was five, and I don't recall much about our home there; what I remember was that my father was a drinker. When he was sober, he was my idol. He'd read to me at bedtime, and then when it was time for me to go to sleep, he'd tuck me in so snugly, he'd say "you're snug as a bug."

During the day, he worked for the railway, and at the end of his long shift, he spent his nights drinking at the local saloon. My mother worked for the gunpowder plant.

After the 1918 train wreck, they laid my father off while the tracks could be repaired, and he took this as a premonition he would permanently lose his job. For months he hung around the house until one day, my mother pointed out that we needed his wages to survive and she suggested he look for a job at the powder plant where she worked.

"I ain't gonna work at some woman's job," he said.

That's the first time he hauled off and hit her.

Eventually, they called him back to the railway, but by this time he'd been drinking so much, he reeked of alcohol, and they fired him.

My mother never said a word, but my father took that as a silent accusation of his failure, and he raised his arm to strike her. That was the second time he did it. Over the next few weeks, it got worse. One day, thinking I could stop him, I gallantly stood in front of my mother and acted as her shield.

"Get outta my way," he yelled.

He backhanded me and knocked me down. I fell flat on my back and it knocked the wind out of me. I couldn't breathe and I thought for sure I was going to die. My mother kneeled beside me and then he kicked her. When she tried to get up, he kicked her again.

He was gone for two days, and when he returned, I stood in our doorway and said, "If you touch me or my mother again, I swear I'll kill you in your sleep."

"Shut up," he said, pushing me down. "We're going to where I can find a better job."

In 1919, we made it west to Seattle, and to my father's credit, he found a job at the Spokane, Portland & Seattle Railway. By the end of that year, my mother answered an ad for a maid's position for a wealthy financier who owned a hilltop mansion in the Harvard-Belmont Historic Landmark district.

While I had no plan to actually kill my father, for a while, I thought he took my death-threat seriously. He still drank, but my mother and I made it a point to stay out of his way if he was riled. My mother sometimes worked until all hours of the evening, so I learned to make our meals. The first few times my father didn't come home, I thought maybe he too had to stay until his boss let him leave. But then I started smelling liquor on his breath when he came through the door; even prohibition had no impact on him finding something to drink. After about a week of this, I quit making his dinner. This infuriated him, but I was wasting the little money we had on food that had to be dumped into the garbage.

That Christmas of 1920, like so many in the past, we had no tree, and there were no packages to open. My mother brought home some leftovers Cook had prepared for the servants, and she and I sat and ate them. When my father finally came home, he'd been drinking, and wanted to know where his dinner was.

"There was just enough for me and Ruthie," my mother calmly said.

My father reached for her plate and threw it, food and all, on to the floor. My mother jumped from her chair and pulled me to her, I know thinking she'd be able to protect me from his rage. As he'd done before, he shoved me to the side and grabbed my mother's arm, twisting it until she winced in pain.

He finally released her, but not before he threw my plate on the floor, too.

Then he stomped out of the apartment and didn't come home until the next evening.

On New Year's Eve, my mother worked late to help with the party at the mansion. I made myself a simple dinner of bread and cheese, and then I went to play Parcheesi with the girl who lived next door. At midnight, we watched the fireworks from her apartment window, and then I came back home. I lit the kerosene lamp that sat on the kitchen table and fully intended to read *The Swiss Family Robinson* book my neighbor lent me, but I fell asleep.

It was still dark out when the door to our apartment burst open, crashing against the wall, jolting me awake. Even in the dim light of the streetlamp outside our window, I could tell it was my father. I jumped to my feet and there in the threshold he stood, drunker than a skunk. His eyes squinted as he tried to determine who it was that had been sitting at our table, and then when he figured out it was me, he looked around for my mother, who hadn't returned from work yet.

"Where the hell is she?" he bellowed.

I didn't give him the satisfaction of an answer, which made him furious. He staggered to the table and picked up my book and began ripping pages from it.

"*Stop!*" I yelled.

But he kept on tearing pages and watching them fall to the floor. He came around the right-hand side of the table as I backed closer to the sink. I hoped to give myself space enough to run from the apartment, but even though he was drunk, he was quicker than I was. He grabbed my left arm as I grabbed onto the sink. I kicked him in the shin and he momentarily released me, giving me just enough time to turn and pick up our cast iron pan.

When he looked up at me, I swung the pan with all my might. He fell to the ground, out cold. Suddenly, my mother was there, standing in the doorway, and she looked in horror, first at me, and then at my father.

"Dear god," she said, dropping her bag on the table. "Help me get him up. He's bleeding."

I'd broken his nose, and his face was black and blue for two weeks.

Made in the USA
Las Vegas, NV
12 October 2023

78982734R00143